The Wr

By the same author

The Wrong Sort of Girl

VALERIE-ANNE BAGLIETTO

The Wrong Mr Right

CORONET BOOKS
Hodder & Stoughton

Copyright © 2002 by Valerie-Anne Baglietto

First published in Great Britain in 2002 by Hodder and Stoughton
A division of Hodder Headline

The right of Valerie-Anne Baglietto to be identified as the Author
of the Work has been asserted by her in accordance with the
Copyright, Designs and Patents Act 1988.

1 3 5 7 9 10 8 6 4 2

A CIP catalogue record for this title is available from the British Library.

ISBN 0 340 76802 9

Typeset in Plantin Light by Phoenix Typesetting, Ilkley, West Yorkshire

Printed and bound in Great Britain by
Mackays of Chatham plc, Chatham, Kent

Hodder and Stoughton
A division of Hodder Headline
338 Euston Road
London NW1 3BH

To my perfect romantic hero

ACKNOWLEDGEMENTS

I would like to give special thanks to Dinah Wiener and Carolyn Caughey for their patience and understanding.

I am grateful, too, to all the team at Hodder who put in so much effort. Especially Lucy Dixon, who also 'suffered' back in February 2001 . . .

It is never too late to be what you might have been

George Eliot

I

Six-year-old Emmeline Finlay peered around the kitchen door from the hall, but it wasn't a good time to ask for leftover spaghetti hoops for breakfast. A moment ago Mummy had forgotten to let a Pop Tart cool and had dropped it on the floor with a squeal, and now she was balancing on one foot as she peeled a label off the sole of one of her new shoes while still wearing it. The big hand of the kitchen clock was almost on the twelve, the little hand on the eight.

Uh-oh. Emmeline turned and hurried up the two flights of stairs to the attic bedroom where her nanny slept.

Paloma, the nanny, was still lying in bed with a pillow over her face. The duvet was half on the bed and half off. Maybe Paloma's alarm clock was broken again, thought Emmeline, who had already dressed herself for school in a white shirt and grey pinafore, regulation socks pulled symmetrically up to her knees.

Suddenly, as if sensing someone was there, Paloma sat up in bed with a start, the pillow tumbling into her lap. She blinked at Emmeline. 'What time is it?'

'Eight o'clock in the morning. Nearly.'

'Oh sh—' Paloma bit her lip.

'Mummy dropped her Pop Tart. I think she's going to be late—'

She was interrupted by a voice calling urgently up the stairs, 'Paloma, is Emmi ready yet? Are you going to give her her breakfast?'

'Er . . .' Paloma rolled off the bed and pulled a fleece top over her nightshirt. 'We'll be down in a minute!' she yelled, running a hand through the mass of black curls spiralling around her face.

'You look like that gypsy in the book we were reading last night,' said Emmeline. 'Are you going to put on socks?' she added as an afterthought.

'No time.' Paloma led the way downstairs.

'You're always saying I'll catch cold if I don't wear socks when it's chilly.'

'That's because you will.'

'But why won't you?'

'Won't I what?'

'Catch a cold,' stressed Emmeline, running into her bedroom on the first floor to fetch her school bag.

'Colds don't like me,' said Paloma, as Emmeline ran out again. 'I wasn't very nice to one once.'

'You made that up. Didn't she make that up, Mummy?'

Her mother was at the foot of the stairs, slipping into a coat. 'What?'

'Colds. They haven't got feelings, have they?' insisted Emmeline. 'Paloma says they have.'

Her mother frowned. 'Of course they haven't.' She picked up her handbag and paused to plant a kiss on Emmeline's head. 'I've got to run or I'll miss the eight-twenty. Have a nice day, darling, and be good. Bye Paloma.'

Emmeline waited until the door slammed shut before turning to her nanny. 'Can I have spaghetti hoops for breakfast?'

'No,' grinned Paloma. 'You can have ice cream, just like me. So long as you promise not to tell a living soul.'

'Ice cream!' Emmeline's eyes widened.

'We're celebrating,' explained Paloma, rummaging about in the freezer. 'I've been looking after you for exactly a month. Which means, little munchkin, that my trial period is O-V-E-R!' She gleefully held up a tub of Häagen-Dazs. 'In other words, it looks as though I've cracked it this time. I'm actually here to stay!'

Emmeline hurriedly fetched two spoons and two bowls and sat down at the big pine table. She had seen *The Wizard of Oz* three times from beginning to end, but now was not the moment to mention that munchkins were already little.

The short, stout man on her left had fallen asleep against her shoulder. Kate could have shrugged him off, but she'd been reading his John Grisham out of the corner of her eye, so she felt it was only what she deserved. She glanced out of the window. They would be in Liverpool Street in a moment anyway; let him doze for a while longer. She just hoped he didn't have dandruff.

The train pulled into the station, passing what seemed to be miles of empty platform until at last it came to a juddering halt. The man woke with a start, and as he stood up to collect his briefcase from the overhead rack,

Kate sighed and discreetly brushed the shoulder of her wool and cashmere coat. She ought to be accustomed to the hazards of commuting by now. But there were other hazards she hadn't got used to, she mused dolefully. Such as being a working mum with a full-time job, desperately seeking the perfect nanny.

Climbing off the train, she dodged the lethal tip of a furled-up golfing umbrella and joined the stampede of commuters heading towards the automatic ticket barrier. Her shoes were already beginning to pinch as she made her way hurriedly towards the Underground.

Of course, she would settle for a decent nanny, really. She wasn't as fussy as some mothers she knew of. But if she set high standards for herself in her chosen profession, why couldn't she find someone willing to do the same in their own?

Take Paloma, for instance. Five weeks ago, after Kate had interviewed the pitiful supply of nannies sent by the agency her sister had recommended, Paloma had seemed the best of the bunch. But it just hadn't worked out. The agency would have to try harder to find someone suitable.

If only the need for a nanny hadn't arisen, thought Kate, with a sigh. And if only Paloma wasn't such an annoying bundle of contradictions. It was obvious that she took good care of Emmi – which was, admittedly, the most important thing – but around the house she was totally disorganised, even though she had hours to herself while Emmi was at school.

Kate couldn't bear to come home of an evening to find everything in a worse state than when she had left, a pile of ironing resembling the Leaning Tower of Pisa in the lounge, and fishfinger crumbs scattered around the kitchen like confetti. She needed someone who could do all the chores she didn't have time to take care of herself. And she'd stipulated the need for such flexibility to the agency, accepting that her choice would be limited. An old-school nanny with years of experience would never lower herself to tackle housework. Kate would have to make do with someone younger, perhaps newly qualified. But now she wondered if expecting a bit of help around the house was too much to ask.

By the time she hurried across the lobby of the office building which Anthony & Gray Corporate Design shared with four other companies, and by the time she'd skidded gracelessly up to the open lift doors, she had decided it wasn't. Paloma received bed and board, after all, and she had an ample salary for someone who didn't have to worry about electricity, gas and water bills, not to mention—

'If it isn't Kate Finlay.'

Bugger. The lift was already occupied. Kate drew herself up to her full height of five-foot-two. 'Oh . . . hello.'

'What a coincidence, I'm late myself this morning.'

Kate shifted from one foot to the other. The new shoes were massacring her toes. She looked up and tried to smile. Dick Anthony was tall, lithe, lean and loaded. He pushed back a lock of straight, dark hair and adjusted his tie. The lift climbed steadily upward, whirring hypnotically.

'I was delayed,' said Kate after a pause, trying to think of a suitable excuse rather than just the fact that she'd overslept. 'It's my nanny, you see.'

'Ah.' Dick's gaze held hers. 'What's the problem?'

'She's an absolute nightmare—' Kate stopped, realising she was being unfair. 'Well, you see, she gets on fine with Emmi, but when it comes to doing things around the house . . . Basically, I'm going to have to ring the agency and tell them things aren't working out.'

'Really? Why don't you tell me all about it over dinner?'

'Dinner?' Kate blinked. He had asked her once before, months ago, but she'd wriggled out of it. In truth, she'd been caught off guard then as she was now, and apart from that, Dick's reputation preceded him. Kate had made her gabbled excuses sound as convincing as possible. 'Commitments at home', 'the ties that bind', *et cetera.*

'Tonight?' she added, with a slight wobble in her voice.

'Why not?'

'Well, it's a bit difficult, you see, I said to Charles I'd work a couple of hours overtime to get his presentation typed up.'

'You'll have to eat afterwards, though.'

Kate had planned to phone for a pizza delivery while she was working, to waste less time. 'I want to be home before Emmeline goes to sleep,' she explained. And picturing Emmi tucked up in bed cuddling the Winnie the Pooh she'd loved since she'd been a baby, Kate's resolve strengthened. Then she remembered that the

Adonis towering over her paid her wages. 'I can't break a promise,' she murmured.

Dick ran his tongue lightly over his lips, lifting an eyebrow. 'Very admirable.'

Kate tried to look regretful, but wasn't sure if her face could be expressive enough. The last time she'd been out to dinner with a man had literally been in another century. It wasn't that she didn't want to go out, it was just that when the opportunity came her way there was always a valid reason why she couldn't. And besides, being attracted to Dick Anthony was a mistake . . . something hormonal, and everybody knew that hormones could be a pain in the—

'Lunch then.' He interrupted her train of thought.

'Lunch?' she echoed, and before her brain could shift into a different gear, her hormones answered for her: 'Lunch would be fine. Shall I book us a table at the bistro round the corner?'

They were out of the lift now and drifting through the plush reception area. Natalia, the receptionist, glanced pointedly at her watch.

Kate, surprised at herself, and hoping Natalia hadn't overheard anything, turned to Dick and said quietly, 'Of course, if you'd prefer somewhere a little further afield . . .' Now she was making it sound almost sordid.

He smiled, and looked less like a god and more like a human being. 'The bistro will be fine. It's not as if we have anything to hide.' He turned towards the corridor leading to his office, glancing over her shoulder. 'One o'clock. I'll be waiting for you downstairs.'

Kate gazed after him. When she realised that her

mouth was slightly open and that Natalia was staring at her coolly, she quickly cobbled her wits together and headed for the Ladies' loos. The expanse of mirror over the marble basins confirmed her fears. Her face was salmon pink. But then she hadn't been this hot around the collar of her best M&S blouse in ages.

Wisps of ash-blonde hair had escaped the plain black scrunchie she was wearing and were hanging limply around her ears. She pulled out the scrunchie, took a comb from her bag and set about tidying her medium-length hair, smoothing out the kinks before looping it up again and securing it at the nape of her neck.

She was just reaching for her foundation stick when the door opened and Natalia entered, kitten heels tapping across the tiled floor. 'Hi,' she said, smiling.

Kate smiled back stiffly. She hated doing her make-up with an audience, unless that audience happened to be Emmi.

'A few of us are popping down to the Cork and Cheese at lunchtime,' Natalia went on, pausing at a cubicle door. 'Do you fancy coming along?'

Anthony & Gray was as cliquey as hell; the Cork and Cheese gang had never asked her to join them in the eight months she'd been working there.

'I can't,' said Kate, realising that the receptionist *had* overheard the conversation with Dick. 'Sorry, I've already got plans.' As if Natalia didn't know.

'Shame. Never mind.'

Kate turned to leave.

'By the way,' added Natalia, 'heard the goss?'

'What goss might that be then?'

'Dick got dumped the day before yesterday.'

Kate froze, wondering what to say.

Natalia elaborated: 'Apparently he confided in Charles, who told Henry, who told—'

'I, er, didn't know he'd been seeing anyone.'

'You were the only one then.' Natalia tappety-tapped into the cubicle. When she came out again, Kate was still hanging around, kicking herself for being so obvious yet unable to leave until she knew exactly what had been going on.

'A waitress at the bistro round the corner apparently.' Natalia resumed the conversation while she washed her hands. 'Not his type at all, I would have thought. But then I suppose he can't afford to be choosy if he aims to sleep with half the women in London by the time he's forty.'

Kate squirmed visibly.

'Well, I can't stand around gassing all day,' said Natalia. 'Some of us have work to do.' And on that note, she sashayed out with a flick of her unnaturally blue-black bob.

For the rest of the morning Kate kept reminding herself to phone the No Nonsense Nanny Agency to tell them that, in fact, she *had* had enough nonsense from them, thank you very much. She'd call just as soon as she had a free moment. But it wasn't until she found herself sitting opposite Dick in the minimalist local restaurant often frequented by employees of Anthony & Gray that she realised she'd been deliberately procrastinating.

All through the meal, as she nibbled at an exotic salad

9

while wishing it was plain old-fashioned shepherd's pie, Kate tried not to dwell on the problem and instead attempted to pay attention to her surroundings. She couldn't spot any of the usual female employees today; there were only two waiters. Kate wondered if Natalia had been winding her up. She didn't want to speculate that she was being used by Dick to make his supposed ex-girlfriend regret her decision.

'So,' he broached, patting his mouth with a heavily starched napkin and settling back in his chair, 'this situation with your nanny . . .'

Kate sighed. After talking shop for over half-an-hour, he'd suddenly remembered the subject of their earlier conversation back in the office.

'I know I'm going to have to sack Paloma,' she confided reluctantly, hoping there wasn't any watercress stuck to her teeth. 'It's just . . . I was going to have a go at the woman who runs the nanny agency, but it's struck me that it's not her fault if good staff are in short supply.'

'Exactly how I feel sometimes.'

'Is it?'

'You don't know how much I rely on conscientious workers like you.'

Kate felt another hot flush coming on. 'Well I'm desperate,' she said.

'Can I help?' Dick's hand crept across the table towards hers.

'Er . . . only if you happen to know anyone who's brilliant with kids and has a few basic housekeeping skills.'

'It sounds to me as if you need a wife.'

'Mmm,' bristled Kate, who had named her daughter

after Emmeline Pankhurst, the suffragette.

'Please don't take this the wrong way,' said Dick, serious again. 'I think it's great how women can juggle bringing up a family and holding down a full-time job. Especially when they're on their own.' The pressure of his hand upon hers was strangely comforting. 'You're an amazing woman, Kate Finlay.' He said it so sincerely, and with a trace of awe in his voice.

'Amazing enough to deserve a pay rise?' she quipped, sensing that the balance had shifted and that she was now in control of the situation. Perturbed, she looked at her watch. 'We'd better be getting back, hadn't we?' Suddenly it became imperative to bring a smile to his face. He seemed uncharacteristically glum. 'Before the boss has any excuse to sack *me*.'

Everyone had gone home. Kate was alone with the hum of the air-conditioning and the tapping of her keyboard. Even Dick had dropped by her desk to say goodbye at five on the dot, scribbling his home number on a Post-it note and slipping it into her bag while she pretended to concentrate on her computer screen. Every now and again she would pause from her typing and glance at the bag, feeling sixteen again rather than a decade older.

The phone rang, making her jump. It was Paloma.

'What's wrong?' asked Kate.

'Nothing. Emmi's just having her tea. I was ringing to remind you about the costume.'

'What costume?'

'You know, we arranged it earlier this week. You were going to surprise Emmi with a costume from the fancy dress hire shop in Addenham. It's open late tonight. Are you popping in on your way home?'

Damn. The birthday party Emmi was going to tomorrow afternoon. Kate groaned. It had completely slipped her mind. 'I, um, forgot to order anything. And I'm swamped at the moment,' she muttered. 'I'll be back later than I thought. I've got to get this finished for Monday, and I can't type any faster than the laws of physics allow.'

'No.' There was a pause.

'Why don't you ring up and reserve a costume? I can pick it up tomorrow morning.'

'I suppose that's one possibility . . .'

'It'll just have to do,' said Kate. 'I'll see you later.' And she put the phone down with rather more force than was necessary.

'What are you doing?'

All Emmeline could see of Paloma was her bottom, clad in speckled grey jogging pants.

Paloma mumbled a reply, still burrowing in the wardrobe.

'Are you looking for something?' asked Emmeline.

'This!' Paloma emerged with a long, floaty, red dress with white circles all over it.

'What's that for? Are you going to a party.'

'You'll see tomorrow. As for tonight, you should be in your pyjamas ready for bed. Come on. A quick bath and then I'll read you a story.'

Paloma tossed the dress on to a chair and took Emmeline's hand, leading her down to the first floor and into the bathroom. After five minutes of splashing around in the large tub, which Paloma had filled with strawberry-scented bubbles, Emmeline had forgotten all about the dress and was more intent on other matters, such as why her mother wasn't home yet.

'She has to do what her boss tells her,' Paloma was saying. 'Just like your teachers at school tell you what to do.'

'Her big boss is called Dick Anthony. Then there's Charlie Gray, he's her littler boss.'

'I know.'

'Will she be home before I fall asleep?'

'Er, she's going to try.'

But Emmeline was too tired. After listening for a while about Charlie (not the one who kept telling her mother what to do) and the chocolate factory he longed to see inside of, she felt her eyelids grow heavier and heavier, as if a weight was pressing down on them . . .

Kate finally got home just after ten, kicking off her shoes with a groan. The train had broken down. She'd been sitting on it for almost two hours. She was starving and exhausted and there seemed to be no sign of any leftovers in the cooker. Swallowing her indignation, she grabbed a packet of crisps and tucked in voraciously.

Odd. Paloma wasn't curled up in front of the TV as usual. There seemed to be no sign of her, not even a trail of popcorn.

Kate went upstairs, peering into Emmeline's room. The little girl slept with a nightlight. Kate crept in and leaned over the bed to plant a gentle kiss on her daughter's brow. The child didn't stir. Irrationally miffed by this, Kate crept out again and climbed the second flight of stairs to the attic, which decades ago had been converted into a couple of extra rooms.

Paloma was in the junk room, frowning in concentration as she pored over some polka-dot material and Kate's grandmother's old Singer sewing machine. 'Bloody bobbin!' She glanced at her watch. 'Is that the time already?'

'What are you doing?'

'Sewing.'

'I can see that,' Kate replied tetchily. 'But what? And why?'

'It's a costume for the party tomorrow.'

'A costume for Emmi?' Kate felt a pang of guilt, which grew more acute as Paloma explained.

'I rang the fancy dress hire shop, but it's only got a limited stock. It seems as if Emmi's whole class is going to be at this party.'

Kate's heart plummeted. 'There wasn't anything left, was there?'

Paloma shook her head. 'Nothing suitable.'

'Great.' Kate sank on to a spindly chair which had seen better days.

'But I had an idea,' Paloma began tentatively. 'My mother was Spanish. I remember she made me a flamenco dress when I was a little girl, so I thought I'd give it a go myself. I'm not *too* hopeless at sewing, and it's lucky I'm a compulsive hoarder.' She gestured to the polka-dot material. 'I don't think I've worn this in years. No wonder I can never travel light.'

'Your mother was Spanish?' Kate echoed. It would explain the olive skin, the wild curly hair, like something out of *Carmen*.

Paloma nodded. 'Guillermina Alvarez Reilly.'

'Oh . . .'

'Exactly,' smiled Paloma. 'My father was Irish. Everyone just called him Paddy.'

Kate found herself grudgingly fascinated by this. 'Where are they now then? Spain? Ireland?'

'They're dead.'

Kate bit her lip.

'It's OK.' Paloma looked down. 'It was a long time ago.'

Silence filled the room. Kate watched her nanny yawn and couldn't resist doing the same. 'Listen,' she muttered at last, 'you look shattered. Why don't you leave the sewing for now and carry on with it tomorrow morning?'

Paloma shook her head. 'I don't know how long it's going to take. If Emmi's presented with the finished result she'll probably be fine about it, but we both know she'd throw a wobbly if she saw I was still working on it.'

That was true. Kate hesitated for only a second before asking, 'Is there anything I can do to help?'

Paloma looked up again, a tiny smile curling her lips. 'A coffee would be brilliant.'

'Right.' Kate nodded, heaving herself to her feet and turning to go back downstairs. Then she realised that she didn't even know if the girl who had been living in her house for an entire month took milk or sugar or

15

preferred decaff to normal coffee. Before she could ask though, Paloma settled the problem for her.

'The plainer, more undiluted caffeine, the better. Oh, and before I forget, there's some shepherd's pie in the microwave for you. Hope that's OK?'

2

At seventy-six, Edgar Finlay was still a notably hand-some man. Kate sat at the small table by the patio door and gazed at her grandfather over a mountain of triangular-shaped salmon paste sandwiches. She could hear Emmi outside, playing in the communal garden of the warden-assisted retirement flats.

'You aren't eating enough for a girl your age.' Edgar frowned at his granddaughter.

When would he realise that she wasn't partial to fish paste butties? She had already eaten three. 'You always make far too many,' she chided.

'Hmm.' He took up the main thread of their conver-sation again. 'So what had you planned to do if the agency hadn't been able to send you a replacement immediately?'

Kate shifted in the chair and set about pouring herself another cup of tea. 'Is this all the sugar you've got left, Grandad?'

'Katharine Finlay, don't beat about the bush. Yo[u] would have expected me to take care of Emmi ag[ain] wouldn't you? Albeit temporarily.'

'No, I know you don't feel up to it. I would h[ave] to have asked Mum, that's all.' She winced a[t] brushed against the hot teapot. 'It doesn't matter any more though, does it? Paloma's staying on.'

'Just as well. From the sound of it the girl's a good sort, even if she doesn't know one end of a toilet brush from the other. But then you can't expect everyone to be as perfect as you.'

'I'm not perfect!'

'Glad to see you've realised.'

She scowled and looked out through the glass door. Emmi was playing with another child now; probably the grandson or great-grandson of another resident of the retirement flats. Sometimes, mused Kate, as she watched the children's earnest attempts to do cartwheels, when her grandfather was in this sort of mood she wondered why she sought his company so much. For years she had been secure in the knowledge that she was his favourite granddaughter, but he seemed cantankerous lately, even with her. He had acted as a childminder to Emmi up until his accident earlier that year. A transit van had ploughed into his Volvo at a particularly notorious junction on the outskirts of Addenham. Although he hadn't been seriously hurt, his right leg was still giving him trouble and, as yet, he hadn't had the confidence to get behind a steering wheel again. Kate doubted he ever would. And so, rather than being indebted to her mother long-term, she had turned to the No Nonsense Nanny Agency for help.

'Emmi reminds me so much of you,' her grandfather was saying now. 'Today more than ever. I remember the Cooper fancy dress party. You wanted to wear following day, too. In fact, you would have tried to wear it to school on the Monday if you hadn't had to wear a uniform.'

Emmi's knickers were revealed in all their glory as she executed a faultless cartwheel. Her face was momentarily hidden by the frills of her flamenco-style dress before she came back up, whooping delightedly.

'Mummy, Mummy! Did you see me, did you?' She came running over to the patio door as Kate slid it open.

'Of course I did, darling. You were wonderful!' Kate tucked a stray hair into the bun Paloma had had to redo for Emmi that morning.

Beaming, the little girl ran back to join her new friend, cardigan flapping like a cape behind her.

Kate turned to face her grandfather. 'Has Mum told you about Annabel's twenty-fifth yet?' She couldn't disguise her lack of enthusiasm.

'Of course.' He sighed heavily. 'It promises to be a . . . *sedate* occasion.'

'Well, there won't be a mobile disco if that's what you mean.'

Her grandfather paused to lick his lips, as if gearing up to make a remark that she might not want to hear. 'Are you planning on bringing anyone?'

Not *this* again. Kate looked at him askance. 'Unlike my sister, I haven't had the good fortune of meeting the man of my dreams yet, as she's so fond of reminding everyone. When I do, Grandad, you'll be the first to know.'

'I'm glad to hear you've still got some room in your dreams for Mr Right.'

Kate reached for her cup of tea and took a few sips, racking her brain for an apt reply. It would be churlish to sneer that Mr Right was an out-of-date, romantic cliché. 'I'm not really after anything serious,' she said eventually. 'It's safer that way.'

Her thoughts flew to Dick Anthony, but she could hardly ignore where living for the moment had landed her the last time round. Yet it wasn't as if she was that teenager from the sticks any more. She was a confident twenty-first century woman with a career path mapped out ahead of her; not the naïve girl who in an attempt to escape home had found herself at university, raving about modern art – while loathing it in reality – and downing vodka after vodka in the student bar.

She looked her grandfather squarely in the eye. 'I'm not like Annabel. She always had to have a boy dangling from her arm, and she was barely even eighteen when she got married. I don't need a man to make me complete.'

'Maybe not.' Her grandfather began the mundane task of clearing the table. 'But as I said to your grandmother once, why can't you bring yourself to consider that a man might actually need *you*?'

It was a Saturday in mid-October. The bar or club, or whatever people wanted to call the only place for miles around with a DJ, was heaving. The mass of bodies which had spilled on to the terrace at the rear of the building was generating a welcome heat. Paloma sat hunched on top of a picnic table, poking her fingers – to see how many would fit in one go – through the hole in the middle where the sun umbrella normally went. The experiment ceased abruptly when she acquired a splinter. She picked the tiny sliver of wood out of her finger and reached for her Bacardi Breezer.

'Even with all these people, it's boring here tonight,' she moaned, pouting at her friend Lottie, who was sitting rather more conventionally on a bench.

'You get bored far to easily.'

'Do not!' bridled Paloma.

Just then a slurred male voice interrupted them: 'Would you mind if we joined you?'

Paloma frowned and looked over her shoulder at a gaggle of young men who already looked the worse for wear, even though it was only nine o'clock. Her frown dissolved into a smile. 'Lads' night out, is it?' The evening might not be such a dead loss after all.

'Stag night,' said one. 'Old Scottie Boy here is getting himself hitched.' And he thrust forward a lanky, dark-haired young man in his late twenties who gave Paloma a lopsided smile before emitting a loud belch.

Paloma, who was on her third – or was it fourth? – drink, heard herself giggle as if it was an out-of-body experience. 'Scottie meet Lottie. I'm Paloma, by the way.' She cocked an eyebrow at the bridegroom-to-be. 'And I don't suppose your name really is Scottie Boy?'

'Scott Llewellyn.' He shook her hand soberly, even though his sobriety was definitely in question. 'Pleased to meet you.'

'Paloma, I think it's time we went home,' whined Lottie, tugging her cardigan around her bust in a vain attempt to conceal the fact that she was a 38D.

But there was no way Paloma was going to leave now that the night had got interesting. Lottie, however, who was shy in the company of men even when she was drunk, was obstinately swinging her legs over the bench. Paloma grabbed her sleeve. 'Stick around a bit longer. Go on! It'll be a laugh.'

'Aren't you coming with me?'

''Course she's not!' The stag party, aware that they were on the verge of losing one girl, were determined not to lose another.

'I'm going to stay and chat to my new friend Scott here,' said Paloma. 'He's about to embark on a very big step in life. I just want to make sure he knows what he's letting himself in for.'

'I hope you know what *you're* letting yourself in for,' muttered Lottie. As a tall, muscular lad, who looked as though he played rugby, lurched towards her, she bolted.

'Lottie nearly always goes home before closing time.' Paloma sighed, glancing around at the sea of male faces. They seemed to have multiplied. 'Right then.' She bucked up and grinned, brandishing her empty bottle. 'Whose round is it next?'

Kate was determined not to go to bed early. If popular culture was to be believed, she ought to be drowning her pre-menstrual sorrows in something alcoholic while watching a girly video and eating ice cream or chocolate or both . . . But what was she doing? She was reading a book. Which was all very well as pastimes went, yet it didn't seem right when you were only in your mid twenties and it happened to be a Saturday evening. It wasn't as if she could concentrate properly either. Her mind was going round and round in circles; she'd read the last paragraph four times already.

Enough was enough. She put the book to one side and went to find a corkscrew. A while later she was drinking Chablis, watching *The Little Mermaid* (a Disney video was all she could lay her hands on at such short notice) and gorging on chocolate ice cream. She would probably have a headache in the morning, but at least she didn't have to get up for work.

As she slouched on the sofa, her mind wandered from the video, too. However much she tried not to, she couldn't help stewing over the envy she'd felt earlier that evening when Paloma had been preening in front of the hall mirror, on the verge of going out. Kate had looked up from slicing a toffee apple for Emmi. 'Bye then.'

Paloma had hesitated. 'Is it still OK?'

Kate had been confused. 'Is what still OK?'

'If I go out tonight?'

'Oh – that. Why shouldn't it be?'

'If you ever need me to babysit on a Saturday . . .'

'I don't. Not tonight, at least. Go on, don't waste time hanging around here.'

Kate had peered out of the corner of her eye as Paloma had smoothed a hand over sleek black trousers and tottered out of the front door in gravity-defying heels. Staring down at her own attire of faded sweatshirt and equally faded combat pants (why should she dress up when there was no one special to notice?), Kate had felt an urge to reach for the phone and punch out a number she had memorised, even though she'd never dared ring it. But her daughter had still been up, so Kate had waited until later. The problem was, by the time Emmi had gone to bed, the wild impulse to phone Dick was no longer wild or impulsive but a stomach-churning ordeal she had lost the nerve to go through with.

Going to lunch with someone a few times, even being a little vulnerable in a flirtatious manner over a glass of wine, was not the same as calling them up at the weekend and letting them know what a sad, desperate and lonely individual you really were. He had given her his home number a couple of weeks ago, yes. But he hadn't seemed disappointed that she hadn't called.

What was their relationship exactly? Kate tried to be analytical and detached about it. She fancied him. She assumed that he fancied her. It was the old scenario of boss and secretary, done to death in countless novels, and yet, when it was happening to *you* . . .

Perhaps he was worried about the consequences at work, thought Kate. In larger companies, such as the financial institutions she had slaved in before joining Anthony & Gray, there were policies against employee dating. Safeguards, really. In this age of sexual harassment suits and political correctness, Kate supposed it was necessary.

She was aware that Dick had gone out with employees in the past, though. Why should she be any different? And she *wasn't* looking for anything serious. Just something she could keep as separate as possible from her life here at home.

'Mummeee!'

Kate leapt guiltily into Mum Mode. Hiding the bowl of ice cream behind the sofa, she hurried into the hall. Her daughter was at the top of the first flight of stairs.

'Mummy . . .'

'What is it, darling?'

'I had a bad dream . . . Can I have some hot milk?'

'Come on down then and tell me all about it.' Kate held out a hand to her.

'Could you make the milk chocolate flavoured?'

'Hmm. Maybe.'

'What are you watching?' The little girl paused to look through the lounge door.

'Er . . .'

'*The Little Mermaid!*' Emmi jumped up and down, the nightmare seemingly forgotten. 'Can I watch it too? Can I?'

'It's late, darling . . .'

'But it *is* a Saturday.'

'Well, all right then.' Kate didn't need much persuading. 'Just this once, though,' she said sternly, knowing that 'just this once' didn't exist in Emmi's vocabulary but prepared to face the consequences in return for some company.

Paloma had never been in a situation quite like this. But then, she had never been arrested, so that narrowed the chances of ever having been handcuffed. The last thing she could recall was stumbling through a small garden full of crunching gravel. Now she blinked around a conservatory taking on texture and colour in the watery light of dawn, and finally focused on the young man slumped beside her on a wicker sofa.

Further snatches of memory returned with a jolt, making her wince . . . Dancing on a table to 'Living La Vida Loca' . . . Juggling empty Bacardi Breezer bottles until one of them smashed . . . Falling off the table and being caught rather awkwardly . . . Wondering if her ankle was broken and demanding that someone call an ambulance – until she'd realised that the rugby-player-sized bloke was just stepping on her foot and she didn't have a sprain, let alone a fracture . . .

It wasn't a shock that she was now feeling queasy, that her head was aching and throbbing and that, seemingly, something furry had set up home in her mouth during the night. Aside from that, she was also in desperate need of a toilet.

'Scott,' she moaned, remembering his name. 'Scott, please wake up . . .' The young man didn't stir. Paloma nudged him harder. 'I have to go for a wee.'

He shuddered awake, turning his head to look at her. At first there was no recognition, just a puzzled gaze. Then his bleary eyes widened.

'No, you didn't pull,' she informed him, injecting her voice with firmness. 'I don't steal other women's husbands. Or fiancés, come to that. And I don't go in for one-night stands.'

He blinked downwards. They were both fully clothed.

'Well, just in case,' Paloma went on lamely. 'I didn't

intend for any of this to happen.' She lifted her arm. His own came along for the ride.

He closed his eyes with a groan. 'The sodding hand-cuffs!'

'I'm sorry, but I need to use your toilet,' she mumbled, realising for the first time through the fog of her hang-over that this was going to be the most embarrassing moment of her life so far.

'Bollocks.' He groaned again. 'So do I.'

At the insistent bleating of the telephone, the man lying beneath the 1955 MG emerged legs first and groped around on the ground for his mobile. 'Llewellyn Limos.'

He sensed the shudder of distaste at the other end of the line and reciprocated with a shudder himself.

'Thomas,' said an all-too-familiar voice, 'it's your mother.'

'Yes. Hello.' It struck him that he'd made the simple greeting sound like 'What do you want? I'm busy'. Sheepishly he added, 'How are you?'

'Concerned,' she stated.

'Really? What about?'

'Your brother.'

Thomas Llewellyn leaned back against the classic sports car, stretching out his legs and reaching for the coffee he had made five minutes ago. But as soon as he took a sip, he realised that what had seemed like five minutes must have been closer to twenty-five. 'Urgh!'

'What's wrong?'

'Um, nothing. My coffee's gone cold, that's all.'

His mother sighed in exasperation.

'Sorry.' Thomas was sheepish again, although he couldn't entirely batten down the sardonic tone that usually crept into conversations with her. 'You've got my unfailing attention. What's Scott been up to this time?'

'He drove me mad yesterday going on about the wedding.'

'Oh? And how is Viennetta these days?'

'Violetta,' corrected his mother crisply, 'is every bit as excited and nervous as a bride should be.'

'Nervous? You mean she's got cold feet?'

'It's not Violetta who's got cold feet to any worrying extent – it's Scott!'

Thomas snorted. 'Is that what's worrying you? Perfectly natural for the groom. I know I'd be crapping in my pants.'

'Thomas Llewellyn!'

'Sorry.' He sighed. 'But really, I don't think it's anything to worry about.'

'He's met a girl. A nanny, apparently. From Beckton Lacey.'

Thomas took it all in. 'I see. When did this happen?'

'On his stag night. Where on earth were you, Thomas? Your own brother for goodness sake, and you couldn't even be bothered—'

'*Which* stag night? He seems to have had one every other night for the past three weeks. I managed to make it to the official one, with the stripper.'

She coughed, to mark her disapproval. 'This was last Saturday.'

'I was busy at the weekend.' Until Sunday afternoon, that was, when Jem had packed her bags and stormed out. And in return for four months of putting up with him in his miserable sodding house (her own words) she'd taken back the Beatles compilation she'd given him for his birthday.

'You've got to do something about it,' stated his mother.

'Er . . . why me?'

'Because Scott listens to you. You told him not to let Violetta get away, and he went ahead and proposed to her. She's so good for him. Such a lovely girl.'

'I know,' agreed Thomas, who only called her Viennetta because she thought it was funny and didn't mind. 'But Scott doesn't always listen to me. And I really don't think this girl he's met is a threat, just a minor distraction. You know what Scott's like. Remember when he wanted half the occupants of Battersea Dogs' Home for his eighth birthday?'

'What on earth does that have to do with it? Really, Thomas, whenever you witter on like this I know it's because you don't believe what you're saying.'

Thomas felt chastised, and caught out. 'OK,' he sighed, 'I'll have a word with him.'

'He's talking about postponing the wedding, "giving himself more time". Do you know how much effort I've put into organising everything?'

'Listen.' Thomas tried to placate his mother. 'I'll explain to him that weddings on this scale can't be postponed and that he's never going to get another chance. He loves Vie. He's not going to blow it. Not when I make him see that it's now or never.' Thomas managed to hit the verbal brakes before he could be accused of wittering again.

Of course, he wouldn't know the extent of the problem until he spoke to Scott. Their mother was renowned for being melodramatic, and he was already beginning to imagine the worst himself. What if he was going to grow more like her in his dotage? Not that thirty-four was old. It just wasn't the first flush of youth, either.

'The only blessing in all this,' grunted Thomas to himself, ending the call and beginning another, 'is an excuse to go down the pub.'

And this was how all pubs ought to be, he thought, three hours later, admiring the inglenook fireplace and the decorative toby jugs and brass ornaments dotted around it. There was no juke box blaring out; no quiz; no karaoke; no rump steak and onion rings on the menu. The Abbot Inn didn't belong to any chain of pubs or any particular brewery. It only had itself to answer to.

Thomas's beer was a little on the warm side, but the atmosphere more than made up for that. The bar he was propped up against was suitably scratched, the light was dim, the air smelled stale and yeasty, and Jim, the old man beside him, had been droning on for the past ten minutes about how he'd won the Second World War apparently single-handed.

Bliss, thought Thomas, then wondered if that wasn't perhaps a bit of a girly word. Orgasmic, he thought instead, but realised that was taking it too far. And I used to call myself a journalist, he scoffed, straightening up as his brother entered through the far door.

Scott grinned, stooping to avoid hitting a beam before striding over to the bar with all the panache of a puppy. Brotherly back-patting ensued, a couple more pints were purchased, and the old man's wartime yarns were politely curtailed as Thomas and Scott settled at a table near a window.

'It's dead in here,' commented Scott, casting a glance around.

'Just how I like it.' Thomas couldn't stand the kind of bars his brother frequented. But that was what came of working in the City. Scott was an Armani man, with everything that went with it. Thomas favoured the Oxfam shop in Addenham High Street. Their mother drew attention to their differences more often than they did, yet over the years this had only served to bring them closer, in solidarity against her.

'What's so urgent?' asked Scott. 'I was supposed to be going out for a drink after work.'

Thomas arched an eyebrow at his brother's pint. 'So what are you doing right now then?'

'You know what I mean.'

'I just wanted to discuss a certain young lady I've been hearing about.'

'Mother told you then.'

'Making mountains out of molehills. I don't suppose it's anything serious . . .'

'I think I'd like it to be.' Scott leaned forwards. 'She's amazing, Tom.'

'What about Vie? Your fiancée.'

Scott slumped back in the chair again. 'I don't want to hurt her. I just can't stop thinking about Paloma.'

'Paloma . . . ?'

'Reilly. She's a nanny. Lives in Beckton Lacey.'

'Mother said it happened on Saturday.'

'At the stag do. Oz handcuffed us together for a laugh when we were plastered and only came round with the key on Sunday afternoon. Paloma ended up back at mine, you see. I suppose she had little choice. But before you leap to conclusions, nothing happened. Anyway, by the time Oz turned up we'd found some cutters and Paloma had shot off.'

'Always knew Oswald wasn't the best man for the job.'

Scott groaned at the pun. 'Just because *you* didn't want to do it, doesn't mean you can take the piss.'

Thomas fished in his pockets for cigarettes and matches, buying time to consider his next move.

'I thought you'd given up,' frowned Scott.

'I'm always giving up.' Thomas shook his match to extinguish the flame, dropping it into a chipped ashtray. 'One of these days I'll manage it. Probably when I come across a decent reason for living.'

'You're not a hack any more, hunched over your laptop. There's no excuse, it does nothing for your image.'

Thomas shrugged. 'I never said it did.'

'So how's Jem? Any chance of wedding bells? I'd like to get Mother off my back.'

'I haven't a clue how Jem is.' Thomas realised he was

going to have to come clean. 'She moved out over the weekend.'

Scott said nothing for a moment, then shook his head grimly. 'Another one bites the dust.'

'She accused me of paying more attention to my cars than to her.'

'Well, when was the last time you went out together?'

'I took her to that golf tournament a fortnight ago.'

'There you have it. Cars and golf. Women don't even feature in your top three. Not if you count that music you always have to have blaring out.'

Thomas took a drag of his cigarette. It was an exaggeration about the latter, but, come to think of it, he could have done with drowning his sorrows to 'Yesterday' or 'Hey Jude'. Bugger Jemma Whitelace. 'Women come a close fourth,' he muttered. 'And at least I don't let them screw up my head.'

'If that's a dig about Paloma, you don't understand. She's got me thinking, Tom. Wondering if I'm doing the right thing marrying Vie. That isn't screwing me up, it's helping me reach the most important decision of my life. If I can have doubts like these, if I can be so attracted to other women . . .'

'There'll always be other women. The question you have to ask yourself is whether you love Vie enough to resist them.'

'That's the writer talking,' snorted Scott. 'It can't be the man. Not with your track record.'

'One woman at a time,' corrected Thomas.

'And now you're going to say they've all been "relationships" too.'

Thomas stared at his cigarette. 'Of a sort,' he said at last. 'I'm just not very good at them.'

'It shows.'

'So . . .' Thomas faced his brother squarely '. . . you're going to call off the wedding then?'

Scott raked his fingers through his hair. 'If only I could have more time . . .'

'Do you have any idea how much money's been spent? Not to mention all the energy Mother's invested. You've had everything booked for nearly a year. It's practically all organised. Vie's dress, the church, the reception—'

'That's what I mean. It's so . . . stifling. I suppose I feel trapped. Part of me feels it has every right to back out. This is my life we're talking about. And then the other part hates itself for wanting to see more of Paloma. I've sent her flowers. She's pretending to be really cool about the whole thing. But I know she fancies me. I knew it the night we met.'

Thomas shook his head. His brother was many things: spoilt, selfish, immature. He was also young, vulnerable and, at this moment in time, disastrously confused. Vie on the other hand was mature for her age, sweet-natured, charming, quick-witted and not bad to look at. Thomas had encouraged the romance because he'd appreciated how good she was for Scott. To stand back and watch that thrown away now . . .

There was nothing else for it, Thomas decided, recognising that it wasn't the waste of a wedding day that he ought to be concentrating on but the waste of what might be a half-decent marriage. He was going to have to go straight to the heart of the problem to see what all the fuss was about. He was going to have to confront Paloma Reilly herself.

3

Thomas had to knock on the door of the Old Parsonage, seeing as there wasn't a bell. He waited a while, but no one came to answer it. Someone was home, though, or so it would appear. The bay window overlooking the small front garden was open slightly, the voile nets twitching in the breeze. For October, the weather was surprisingly benign.

Thomas took a few steps back, staring up at the house, recalling what he'd managed to glean in the village shop about the three female occupants, one of whom was only six.

He appraised their home as if he was an estate agent. It had to be worth a tidy sum; it was the kind of attractive nineteenth-century property that always seemed to be in demand. Picturesque was the best word Thomas could use to describe the setting. The small church of Mary Magdalene nestled across the road, its stone walls a pale honey colour in the midday sun. To the right of the church was Beckton Lacey's village green, with a traditional whitewashed pub at the far end that would definitely be worth a visit later.

With an impatient sigh, Thomas strode back up the path and knocked again, more emphatically this time.

'OK, OK,' came a voice from inside. 'I'm coming!' The door was flung open. 'Yes?'

'Um . . .' Thomas blinked at the plastic hairbrush dangling from the young woman's hair.

'It's knotted,' she said brusquely, trying to ease it out. 'There . . .' She managed it, contorting her face as she did so. Tossing the brush on to the hall table, she looked at Thomas again. 'Sorry, you caught me at a bad moment.'

It didn't seem so bad from where he was standing.

She wasn't the type he would usually go for. He had a thing for brunettes with Barbie doll legs. This girl was short, but she had a trim figure visible beneath the old blue jeans and clingy white top. She looked freshly scrubbed, her blonde hair shiny and fluffy. It was no wonder the brush had got tangled up. He wouldn't mind getting his fingers tangled up in hair like that, too. With his eyes closed he could always pretend it was brown.

'Can I help you?' She frowned.

Thomas realised that all he'd said so far had been 'Um'.

'Er' – he kicked himself mentally, recalling why he was there – 'we need to talk.'

'Sorry, but who are you?'

'Thomas Llewellyn.' He waited a second for the name to sink in before steaming on. 'Scott's my brother. I'm here because I'm worried about him.'

'I think you've come to the—'

'You ought to know that he's always had a weakness when it comes to women. Not that I haven't, if you understand what I mean, but Scott's fickle about it. And

37

this time he was all set to marry Vie. She's perfect for him. Which isn't to say that you wouldn't be, but Vie's from the same sort of background.'

The girl looked thrown. He could hardly blame her.

'Miss Reilly,' he went on, 'I don't intend to come on all heavy . . .'

'No,' she said after a pause. 'You don't strike me as the type. You've got too much hair.'

'Sorry?'

She cocked an eyebrow. 'Most of the "heavies" on TV look as if they've had a nasty encounter with some hair clippers.'

'Oh. Oh, right.' He felt himself losing ground rapidly. She wasn't what he'd been expecting. 'I'm sure you understand the position I'm in; you seem like a reasonable girl.'

'Really?'

'You can see, can't you, that there's only one decent thing for you to do?'

'And that would be . . . ?' Suddenly she seemed almost bimbo-ish, gazing up at him enquiringly through dark gold lashes.

'To tell Scott that it's over between you. That he should go ahead and marry Vie.'

'Oh.' She pursed her lips thoughtfully. 'You think I hold that much sway?'

'Well, if he knows there's no future for the both of you, there's no real reason why he can't go ahead with the wedding as planned.'

'Hi,' came a voice behind him, making him jump. He looked round. This was the variety of female that usually sent his pulse racing. Tall, olive-skinned, with a mop of dark ringlets and a wide, voluptuous mouth. Sidling past him, she stepped into the house as Paloma Reilly moved aside to let her through.

'Good thing you were home,' the new arrival said to Paloma. 'I forgot my key.'

'Just as well then. And you've arrived at an opportune time. Paloma, I'd like you to meet Thomas Llewellyn. Apparently you know his brother Scott.'

Thomas's mouth dropped open, but no words came out. He stood looking at both women.

'I'm sorry.' The blonde had a defensive glint in her clear grey eyes. 'But you really asked for it.'

Kate couldn't help overhearing the conversation that followed. She was peeling spuds for lunch, and the door between the kitchen and the lounge didn't shut properly. Of course, she could have gone out into the garden to play with Emmi, who was on her half-term break, but the potatoes honestly did need peeling.

The gall of the man! she thought huffily, recalling how Thomas Llewellyn had looked down his nose at her from his great height of six-foot-something. He had a crooked nose at that, and penetrating hazel eyes beneath a thatch of unkempt dark hair. A cross between Heathcliff, Mr Darcy and a flustered Hugh Grant.

As for Paloma, she was sounding frustrated as she tried to convince him that there was nothing going on between her and his brother.

'Then why do you keep seeing him?' demanded Thomas.

'I don't! I've only met up with him twice since that night in Addenham. The first time was to pick up something I'd left behind, the second was to tell him to stop this before it all gets out of hand. He'd sent me a bunch of flowers—'

So that was who the bouquet had been from, thought Kate, who had initially presumed that it might have been meant for her, from Dick.

'—and I realised I was going to have to be blunt with him,' Paloma went on. 'He just won't listen, though.'

Kate heard Thomas Llewellyn sigh. 'That sounds like my brother.'

'So you see,' the insistence in Paloma's voice subsided, 'I'm not the villain around here. In fact, if this carries on, I could easily claim to be the victim.'

'Have you got a boyfriend?' asked Thomas.

Kate almost snorted. He sounded as if he was chatting her up in a pub.

'Er . . .' Paloma seemed caught off guard. 'Not at the moment.'

'Well at least Scott can't mess up any relationships besides his own.'

Kate squirmed. Perhaps Thomas wasn't making advances towards Paloma. Perhaps he was genuinely concerned.

'Perhaps we could go out for a drink sometime . . . ?' he continued.

Kate caught her finger on the potato peeler and gritted her teeth. Men!

Paloma sounded wary. 'I don't think that's the solution to the problem.'

'No. I don't think I intended it to be. I'm sorry.'

'I'd appreciate it if you could have another word with your brother.' Paloma was being firm again. 'If he does call a halt to the wedding, it really has nothing to do with me. I'm not going to suddenly start fancying him just because he's a free man. I can't help it if he's having second thoughts.'

'No. I understand.'

'Good,' said Paloma, with finality.

There was a long silence. Kate – conscience pricking her for listening in on the conversation – stooped to scrape the potato peelings into the bin. As the bin was inside a cupboard, and as she managed to spill a few shreds of potato skin amongst various cleaning utensils, she didn't catch the next snippet of conversation while she cleared up the mess. She was just emerging when someone spoke directly behind her. Banging her head, she straightened up with a curse. 'Shit.'

'Are you all right?'

She glared at Thomas Llewellyn.

'Sorry if I startled you,' he smiled.

'Yes, well,' her guilty conscience battled with her annoyance, 'what do you want?'

'To apologise for steaming in like that before.'

'I suppose you felt you had every reason to.'

'It's just . . . you should have corrected me.'

'You didn't let me get a word in edgeways to begin with, and then when I realised what was going on . . .' She wouldn't normally have misled someone like that, but the temptation had been too great. He had deserved it. 'I don't know what came over me.'

'*Touché.*' A shaggy dark eyebrow twitched. 'It *was* my own fault.'

'Yes,' mumbled Kate, pushing back the hair from her face.

'I assumed you were the nanny. As it's a Monday—'

'Half-term,' she pointed out.

'Thought I'd seen rather a lot of kids about. I suppose that's why you're off yourself.'

Kate wasn't about to explain that it was technically a sickie, although the fact that it was half-term had given her an incentive. The painkillers she'd taken earlier that morning were already losing their effectiveness, and she couldn't take another dose for at least an hour. She felt achy, bloated and spotty and wanted nothing more than for Thomas Llewellyn to bugger off.

'Well, um,' he was saying, 'I couldn't leave without apologising.'

'And you have,' Kate pointed out.

'Actually, I was also wondering . . .'

'What?' she frowned.

'If you'd like to come over to that pub across the green with me, for a drink.'

Kate's frown deepened in disbelief.

'I take it that's a no,' he said, just as Emmi ran in from the garden.

'Mummy, can I have some Ribena?'

Thomas Llewellyn gazed down at the little girl in fascination. 'She looks just like you!' He grinned at Kate.

She felt herself blush, and was more annoyed with him for that than anything else.

42

'Mr Llewellyn,' she said briskly, before Emmi could start interrogating him in her usual manner, 'I'm very busy and if you've said all you had to say—'

'I get the hint.' He was still grinning, damn him. 'It was a pleasure meeting you – when I finally did get to meet you, rather than who I assumed you were. If you get my drift.'

'I get it.'

'I'll see myself out . . .'

'Mummy,' Emmi stared after him with wide eyes, 'who was that man?'

'No one important.' Kate reached for the Ribena. 'Just someone Paloma knows. He won't be bothering us again.'

Paloma poked her head around the lounge door. 'I'm sorry about what happened.'

Kate was lying on the sofa with a hot water bottle on her stomach. 'It's not your fault.'

Paloma perched on an armchair. 'I'd like to explain, though.'

'There's no need.'

'I met Scott Llewellyn on his stag night. His best man handcuffed us together.'

'I don't want to know any details. Just as long as you don't bring your private life into this house again.'

'But I didn't . . .' Her face fell.

Kate softened, in spite of her bad mood. 'It's not as if you asked Thomas Llewellyn to come here, I know.'

'It's weird,' said Paloma, wrinkling her nose. 'Thomas

is nothing like his brother. Scott's so refined, and he's always really well dressed.'

'I bet they're both still Neanderthals underneath. It just showed more with our uninvited guest.'

Paloma blinked at Kate. 'Probably. Would you like me to pop down to the shop and get you some Guinness?'

'Sorry?'

'An old friend of mine used to swear by it when she had bad periods.'

'Oh, er, I'd prefer a cup of tea.' Kate was embarrassed to discuss her affliction. As a teenager, her GP had more or less assured her that the painful periods would ease off when – or if – she had a baby; in the meantime, he'd put her on the Pill. Perhaps because she'd found it didn't really make that much difference to her, she hadn't been very good at remembering to take it. Obviously. Not that she resented her daughter's existence, not even in her darkest moments, but having had an emergency Caesarian at thirty-seven weeks, her cervix hadn't had a chance to dilate. Apparently, if it had, she wouldn't be struck down like this once a month.

'I wonder how they found me,' Paloma was saying.

'Huh?'

'Scott – when he sent me those flowers, I wondered about it then. As far as I can remember I never gave him this address. I only said I lived in Beckton Lacey. And then Thomas turning up like that – though I suppose he might have found out from Scott, but why—'

'You haven't been here long enough to know.'

'Know what?'

'That you can't keep a secret in Beckton Lacey. Ask anyone. Which,' Kate pointed out crabbily, 'is presumably what the Llewellyn brothers did.'

4

Despite the fact that she came to Addenham Library often, although usually on a Saturday afternoon with Emmi, Kate had never been in this particular section. She wasn't into sport much, steering well clear of *Grandstand* and *Match of the Day*, or whatever that football thing was called now. She ran her finger across the top shelf until she came to the Gs. With a determined sigh, she pulled out *Golfing for Beginners* and flicked through it. This was ideal, the extent of her experience stretching to a few games of pitch and putt in Bowness-on-Windermere and a round of crazy golf in Southend-on-Sea. Hardly on a par with Tiger Woods. She fished out her ticket and headed for the counter, thankful that the library closed at eight on a Wednesday.

A while later, at home, when Emmi was asleep, Kate dared to venture into the Old Parsonage's spare room. Wading through the junk, she spotted what she was after – the set of old golf clubs that had been one of her grandfather's many fads. They needed a thorough clean, but apart from that they were probably good as new. She hauled them out, complete with bag and trolley, and took them downstairs.

The next step, apart from studying the library book,

was to go to the driving range on the outskirts of Addenham to practise her swing. She could just about fit the clubs in the boot of her small hatchback. Saturday morning would be best, while Emmi was at ballet. Kate was sure she could master it, and come Anthony & Gray's Company Golf Day in three weeks' time, she would knock Dick's socks off. Perhaps he would ask her out for a romantic dinner then, rather than just another casual lunch. Acquiring some skill in golf was no longer a matter of saving herself from looking stupid. Although why the firm couldn't simply stick to the one corporate event in the summer, when it wasn't freezing and miserable, Kate had no idea. She had conveniently been on holiday for the one in July, spending a few halcyon days with her grandfather and Emmi in a little whitewashed cottage by the sea in Cornwall.

Bugger, bugger, bugger. She'd never thought it would be so hard to hit the ball. In the past when she had set about learning something new, she had achieved a satisfying enough result after practising hard at it for a while. This was different, though. She had been here almost an hour and she seemed to be getting worse rather than better. In twenty minutes she had to leave to pick up Emmi, and she would feel a failure if she didn't manage to whack a few balls past the fifty-yard mark; or at least knock them off the little black rubber bit of tubing that represented the tee.

Eleven minutes and a bucket of balls later, she shoved the five wood back into the bag and scowled. It was no good. She couldn't waste any more time and money.

Golf stank. It was boring and pointless and—

Heading towards the exit, she came to an abrupt halt. The fifteen bays at the driving range were nearly all occupied, and there, in the one she was about to walk past, was Thomas Llewellyn.

Admittedly he looked different from the last time she had seen him, but there was no mistaking his profile and the tousled dark hair. Could the day get any worse? She wasn't in the mood to speak to him. Frankly, she wasn't in the mood to talk to anyone. He probably wouldn't even notice her, though, she reassured herself, putting one foot in front of the other again. And even if he did, he was hardly likely to act on it.

'Hello.'

Dammit. Just as she'd been passing quietly behind him he had turned round to reach into his bucket of balls. She blinked at him over her shoulder, pretending not to recognise him.

'Remember me?' he grinned.

She frowned as he came towards her. 'Oh. Of course.'

'I wouldn't have had you down as a golfer,' he said. 'Although you don't seem to be having a good day.'

Had he been spying on her? Kate was mortified, recalling her abysmal efforts. She hadn't spotted him before. Then again, she had tried to shut out the fact that she was in a public place and had pretended she was the only person there. It was her way of coping. If she were to meet anyone's eye, embarrassment would get the better of her.

'I, er, don't play,' she mumbled. 'At least, I've only taken it up recently.' I.e. Wednesday, when she'd borrowed the book from the library, but he didn't need to know that.

'I'm sorry, it's just that when I first arrived I was giving a lesson a couple of stalls away . . .' He paused and then went on. 'Your main problem is that those clubs are too long and heavy for you.'

Kate bit her lip.

'They're not yours, are they?' he continued. 'Did you borrow them from your boyfriend?'

'I haven't got—' she stopped, then added tetchily, 'They used to belong to my grandfather.'

'Well then.' Thomas Llewellyn narrowed his eyes in a critical fashion as he looked at her. 'He was probably taller than you.'

'He still is.'

'Right . . .' Thomas must have assumed that her grandfather was dead. 'Well, because you're shorter, and a woman—'

Her spine stiffened. 'What's that got to do with anything?'

'Plenty. Look, I'm not being sexist, but you've got to admit that women are shaped differently from men.'

She replied with the merest hint of a nod.

'They've got a different centre of gravity. If you're serious about this game then you can't use hand-me-down clubs like that. You need to be fitted out properly, or you'll just pick up bad habits and mess up your swing.'

'And how come you know so much about it?' she demanded, before remembering what he'd said earlier.

49

'Because I give lessons professionally. If you're interested, you can have my card. I only do it part-time—'

'No, thank you. I've already got an instructor.' The lie rolled glibly off her tongue before she could think it through.

'Really?' Thomas glanced around pointedly.

'Well, not here, right now,' Kate muttered, finding herself in a verbal pickle. 'I just thought I'd get some practice in. Anthony & Gray have a Golf Day—'

'Anthony & Gray?' Thomas interrupted.

'The firm I work for. It's a design consultancy.'

'Yes, I know.'

'Oh . . .' Kate was lost for words.

'I went to school with Dick Anthony,' Thomas elaborated. 'I haven't actually run into him in ages, but I've heard about his conquests. In business, I mean. He's made a name for himself very quickly – basically because he has an eye for hiring the best employees.'

This conversation was providing too much information to take in all at once. She would have to let each snippet sink in slowly.

'There was supposed to be a compliment in there,' Thomas was prompting. 'To make up for getting off on the wrong foot the other day.'

'Sorry?'

He shook his head. 'Never mind. This Golf Day,' he continued, rather tentatively for her liking, 'are you sure you'll be playing?'

'Why?'

'Nothing. It's just . . .' He shrugged. 'You must know better than me.'

'Know what? I missed the last one, and I haven't got anything to do with organising it. Natalia the receptionist always takes care of it. She's a huge golf fan, and really good at it, too. She said so,' Kate added lamely.

'Well, whatever. As I recall, Dick's a fanatic. Worse than me even. He used to go to the British Open, without fail. Although, I admit, I don't know if he still does.'

Kate was beginning to feel more than just a little uneasy, suspecting that she had fallen into a trap, although not sure what the trap was precisely, or who had laid it. She was also aware that part of her discomfort was due to another reason. Thomas Llewellyn's physical presence was arresting today; more so than on their first meeting when, ironically, he had tried to come across as intimidating in worn suede jacket and scruffy black jeans but in her opinion had failed dismally. He looked smart and suave now in a polo shirt and jumper teamed with khaki trousers.

'Are you sure you don't want my card?' he was asking. 'If you really *are* playing on this Golf Day, then I might be able to give you a few pointers.'

She fiddled with the toggle at the bottom of her fleece as he reached into his back pocket and casually extracted a business card. He held it out to her. She hesitated, and then took it.

'"Llewellyn Limos"?' She stared down at it, bemused.

'Wrong one. Sorry.' He fished out another and swapped them over. 'One's my mobile, the other's my home line. You can get hold of me both ways, of course, but it's a bit unprofessional to muddle them up.'

His smile, which crinkled up his eyes, was mildly self-deprecating.

'After all,' retorted Kate, 'I don't think a "chauffeur-driven vintage automobile" will really help me much with my swing.'

'The wrong sort of driving,' he nodded, with a small chuckle that made him seem rather boyish.

So he juggled two businesses, did he? Kate was grudgingly intrigued. The golf lessons had to be more of a hobby, though; something he did for pleasure. She wondered how many cars he owned and how many chauffeurs he had working for him. His upbringing was more evident today; in fact, it was easy to see how he could have gone to school with Dick.

'My brother came to his senses, by the way,' he was saying.

'Senses?'

'Before Vie got a whiff of how close he'd come to calling off the wedding. Lucky sod. But then he always did lead a charmed life.'

'When's the big day then?'

'Next weekend.'

'Really?' Her eyes widened. 'I didn't realise it was that close.'

'He was cutting it a bit fine, yes.'

'And is he keeping it in the family?'

Thomas's brow wrinkled. 'Sorry?'

'These vintage cars of yours, are they all lined up and polished, raring to go? All the chauffeurs' uniforms starched and pressed?'

'Er . . . Scott and Vie only asked for the ivory

Studebaker. They wanted the bridal car to stand out among all the guests' spanking new Mercs and Jags. And I had to hire a chauffeur for the day.'

'So you don't employ one on a permanent basis then?' asked Kate, surprised.

'I do, actually,' said Thomas. '*Me.*' He was grinning again. 'Mother didn't think it would be appropriate that I don the peaked cap on this occasion. Then again' – his smile wavered – 'the old bat never does.'

It hadn't been a good idea calling his mother an old bat, thought Thomas grimly, half-an-hour later, as he turned his MG down a road marked 'PRIVATE – ACCESS ONLY'. Kate Finlay had cooled radically following that slip of the tongue, and even though he had tried to explain that it was a term of endearment both he and his brother used, she hadn't seemed convinced.

He slowed the car as he turned a sharp left between two brick gateposts. There had been a gate here originally, but by all accounts it had been spirited away for scrap metal during World War Two and no one had bothered replacing it. Thomas followed the overgrown drive up to the house. Several generations of the same family had lived here once, but the lineage had died off in the early 1960s. Since then there seemed to have been a variety of owners, Thomas himself having bought it six years ago from a couple who had intended to renovate the whole place but had run into financial difficulties after simply having the roof fixed.

The original sign was still nailed to a gatepost, albeit hidden by a tangle of ivy: 'The Croft'. Thomas used to joke with Jem and with previous girlfriends that he'd often been tempted to cross out 'The' and spray-paint 'Lara' instead, as a tribute to his favourite heroine. Telling them that probably wouldn't have been a good idea either, he thought now, sighing as he parked the car in the gravelled courtyard.

A familiar face appeared at a downstairs window. Someone looked pleased to see him. Thomas opened the front door and was immediately pounced upon.

'Down, Tina!'

The Yorkshire terrier jumped off the floor as if she had a spring built into each leg. She hopped dementedly around his knees. Thomas crouched down but had trouble pinning her to one spot in order to ruffle the tufted grey ears. A tongue dragged itself roughly across his jaw.

'Hungry? I am home later than usual. The thing is, it's all because of a woman. Again.' He pulled a face as he followed the dog into the kitchen. 'I know I'm a predictable sod, but it's in my genes, I can't help it.' He rummaged around on the bottom shelf of the larder and pulled out the Pedigree Chum. 'And you're right, I'm on the rebound from Jem. I've got to be . . . It's been less than a month. Do you miss her too?'

Tina cocked her head, entranced by the tin in Thomas's hand.

'Then again,' Thomas scooped out some of the contents into Tina's bowl by the back door, 'you and Jem weren't exactly bosom buddies.' In fact, Thomas could recall the day Tina had run off with Jem's only true bosom buddy – her Wonderbra. 'Maybe you're not that bothered.' He doubted Jem was.

He sank down on to a kitchen chair, feeling it wobble slightly on the uneven terracotta tiles, and deliberated whether to have a coffee or not. Tina made slurping noises as she ate. Thomas turned to watch her.

'The thing is,' he said slowly, 'I don't know what it is about Kate Finlay exactly. She's like . . . Like a square peg in a round hole. Something about her doesn't seem to fit.' He frowned, sensing that his train of thought was getting somewhere at last. 'As if—' But his psychological analysis lacked an audience. Tina was scraping urgently at the back door.

Thomas rose to let her out into the yard before switching on the kettle.

Kate was only in her mid-twenties, he would guess. And she was a mother. He'd never been out with anyone who had a kid before. It made her . . . unusual. The women he normally dated weren't exactly the type he would call maternal. They had careers rather than jobs. They did *want* children, but not until they were late-thirty-something and had acquired a suitable husband and a decent house rather than the flats they always seemed to congregate in during their bachelorette years. He acknowledged now that perhaps these women went out with him, even cohabited with him for a time, because he was their last chance to experience a Bohemian existence before they settled down with Mr Conventionally Right, who would probably be a banker or a barrister, or something along those lines.

What was Kate's daughter's name again? Amelia? Emma? Whatever. She'd looked a sweet little thing.

Very like her mother, but harmless. Whereas Kate . . . Kate had attitude. Not that Thomas wasn't used to women who bit back, but somehow part of her appeal lay in the fact that she didn't look comfortable doing so.

He made himself a coffee and sat down at the stripped-pine table, stretching out to push the back door shut with his foot. A cold gust of wind had thrust its way into the large kitchen and was circling restlessly, as if it didn't know where to go next. Thomas shivered and cupped his hands loosely around the cracked mug.

Would it be awkward, though, with a child in the equation? He was only used to A plus B, without a C involved. Then again, what he was used to had never worked out particularly well. It wasn't as if he minded kids. He'd always imagined he'd have a brood one day, although oddly enough this 'one day' never appeared to get any nearer. It was always the same distance into the future: just over the horizon.

He wasn't incompetent at picking up women; it was keeping them that was the problem. Some people considered him charming when he wanted to be, but would charm alone work on Kate? Somehow, he had to make her sit up and take notice – which, it struck him a moment later, was something he'd already succeeded in doing, but in a far from ideal way.

5

Kate sat at her desk in the office, not so much staring into space as into the murky depths of her coffee. Mesmerised by a couple of granules that hadn't dissolved properly, she gave a start when the phone began to purr.

'Hello.' She answered it croakily, and coughed before adding, 'Anthony & Gray, Kate Finlay speaking.'

'Have you got a cold?'

Kate rolled her eyes. Great. It was her sister Annabel. 'No, um . . .' She paused. 'This is . . .' She couldn't bring herself to say 'nice'. 'This is a surprise,' she compromised.

'Hard at work?'

Kate glanced at her in-tray. 'Rushed off my feet.' Actually, she was bored silly, although there was rarely a lull like this. Lately, she seemed to have been busier than ever, and there was less of a support network than she'd been used to in her previous jobs. Which was why she needed Paloma's help at home to tackle the chores she didn't have time for any more.

'I'm up in town today,' Annabel swept on in that slightly breathless manner of hers, 'for a spot of shopping and a rest from the twins, and I was wondering if you fancied doing lunch.'

'Well . . .' Kate studied her nails. She had a chip in one. She'd file it in a mo. 'As I said, I really am rather busy . . .'

'Surely you've got to have a break. They can't expect you to turn into an anorexic.'

'Paloma made me a packed lunch,' Kate lied, recalling the spread she'd seen her nanny pack into Emmi's lunchbox.

'So?'

'So I can't let it go to waste, can I? Besides, I can eat it at my desk while I carry on working.'

Annabel sighed. 'You'll burn out before you're thirty.'

'No I won't. I love my job.' Kate wished she sounded more convincing.

Annabel's mobile phone line was beginning to crackle. 'I was hoping we could have a chat about my birthday.'

Kate spoke louder, above the interference. 'I thought Mum had it all in hand?'

'She has, but there's no harm in trying to help, is there? And you know you're always so good with decorations and things like that. You made your village hall look gorgeous for Emmi's party.'

'Emmi was only turning six,' Kate pointed out. 'You're not after balloons too, are you? Because you know what Mum thinks about those. And if you're having it at Mum and Dad's place you've got to respect their wishes.'

'Stop being so sanctimonious.'

Kate sighed. 'I'm only teasing.'

'Mum insisted on throwing this "party". And Oliver thought it was a good idea. Don't you think I would have preferred something a bit more . . . a bit more my age, rather than tea-time on a Sunday?'

Kate hesitated. She'd never heard her sister talk this way. 'Well . . . what exactly were you thinking of?'

'Going clubbing . . . perhaps.'

'Oh . . . Why did you want to talk about decorations if—'

'Maybe I didn't. Maybe – Maybe I was just wondering if you'd fancy going clubbing, too?'

The conversation was growing increasingly bizarre.

'But I haven't set foot in a club since . . .' Kate couldn't even remember. It was probably when she'd been at university, which seemed another era entirely. 'I – I suppose there's no harm in doing both,' she stammered. 'The party's on the Sunday, so we could always go out the Friday before . . .'

'Would you honestly like to?'

'We could round up a few friends between us who might fancy it,' Kate ploughed on diplomatically, not wanting to have to lie again, but then hearing herself say, 'It'll be fun.'

'Well, then, I suppose that's settled.'

'I suppose so,' said Kate, her brow furrowed.

'We can speak again nearer the time.'

Kate wondered if she ought to say she *could* make lunch after all, but decided against it. They would probably end up having a row. She could cope with her sister in small doses, and she'd had more than enough already for one day. Annabel was exhausting, and Kate didn't feel up to offering any sympathy or advice – not without saying something she'd regret. Apparently, Annabel's perfect little life had developed a flaw, but Kate couldn't bear to hear about it today.

'Does that make me a selfish bitch?' she whispered into her coffee, after she'd hung up.

The purr of the phone made Kate jump again, as if it were answering her question instead.

'Yes?'

'Kate, it's Dick. Would you mind popping into my office?'

'Now?'

'You're not too busy, are you?'

She looked at her chipped nail. 'No.'

'Good. I'll see you in a minute then.'

She put the phone down again and glanced around furtively. From her small screened-off corner she could make out part of the main corridor and the edge of a desk in the art department. Taking out a small mirror from her bag, she peered into it, smoothing back any stray tendrils of hair and tucking them into her scrunchie. She didn't have to use the loo, so there was no need to go to the Ladies'. Besides, she didn't want to be caught preening in the large mirror there prior to entering Dick's office.

A flush was creeping upwards from her throat. She could feel it betraying her as she started making her way towards the corridor. Her pulse was already racing. Turning a corner, she caught sight of the closed door to Dick's inner sanctum and realised that maybe she did need to pee after all. The Ladies', though, was in the opposite direction. Dammit. How was she supposed to act cool and poised when she felt like a quivering adolescent inside?

She knocked on Dick's plain, pine-effect door, and waited.

'Come on in,' he called.

Kate turned the chrome handle and entered. But instantly she noticed that Dick wasn't alone. There was a client here, too, sitting in the visitor's chair with his back to her. Kate's heart sank. She had been summoned for business, not—

The client swivelled his chair round.

'Oh, bugger,' gasped Kate.

'I seem to have come as something of a shock,' said Thomas Llewellyn.

Dick raised his eyebrows at Kate. 'Tom here says that you know each other.'

Kate looked from her boss to Thomas, and then back again. 'Er . . .' Her blush seemed to have shot straight up past her hairline; her entire scalp was tingling. She couldn't tell whether she was outraged, alarmed, embarrassed or a mixture of all three. Disbelief had frozen her ability to think straight.

Thomas was casting an appraising eye over her short taupe suit. In fidget mode she smoothed the lapel of her blouse and straightened an earring.

'Tom and I were at school together,' Dick was saying.

'Yes, I, er, know.' She frowned at Thomas. 'What . . . ?' she stuttered inanely. 'Why . . . ?'

'I decided to look up my old friend,' he said. 'To see if he could help with a spot of corporate identity.' He nodded towards Dick, then smiled at Kate. 'Knowing where you work, I thought I'd give you a go.'

'So how did you two meet?' Dick was asking.

'Oh...' Thomas shrugged. 'My old pile of bricks isn't too far from Beckton Lacey. And everyone in Beckton Lacey knows Kate Finlay.' He gave her another smile, more enigmatic this time, then swung back round to Dick. 'Could you spare her for an hour or so later? I'd like to take her to lunch.'

Kate looked helplessly at her boss. Why couldn't he stand up and declare in heroic fashion: 'Kate's mine. You can't have her!'? Why was he just lolling in his big, black leather chair, seemingly undaunted?

Because, Kate realised – the consciousness sweeping over her with a sudden painful clarity – she wasn't Dick's. She wasn't anybody's.

'I'm sure I can spare her. You're not too busy, are you, Kate?'

'Um...'

'Great.' Thomas winked at her. 'I'll meet you in reception then, about one o'clock?' He glanced at his watch. 'That should give us enough time to go over my briefs.'

'Briefs?' croaked Kate, then realised that the last part had been addressed to Dick.

'My various design briefs,' said Thomas, 'for Llewellyn Limos.'

'Of course. One o'clock then.' Her knees felt jelly-like as she made her exit.

'Small world,' she heard Dick chuckle as she closed the door behind her.

'Sod it,' she muttered, panic digging its claws in.

'I thought we agreed – one o'clock, in reception?'

Kate flinched as a shadow fell across her desk. She peered upwards. 'Is that the time already?'

'It's ten-past, actually.' Thomas tapped his watch.

'I really am rather busy . . .'

He cast a hawk-like eye over her desk as she cursed herself for not having the foresight to provide some props, such as reams of paper spilling over on to the floor.

'You don't look particularly industrious,' he observed, picking up her nail file.

'Looks can be deceiving,' she huffed, snatching it back from him.

'Listen.' He bent down, spreading his hands on her desk, his face almost level with her own. 'I'm not a stalker, or any other kind of psycho. I honestly *had* been thinking about pulling the limo business into the twenty-first century with some clever corporate design. New business cards, a glossy brochure with photos of all the cars . . . It's a cut-throat industry. I've got to keep up.'

'But . . .' Kate rubbed a hand across her brow.

'Let me take you to lunch and we can talk then. Somewhere more private.' Her face must have betrayed her qualms. 'In public,' he went on quickly. 'If that makes sense . . .' Any moment now he would start to get Hugh Grant-ish again.

Kate felt her panic begin to dissipate. He really was attractive, especially in those khaki trousers again, this time with a shirt and tailored jacket. Not exactly Savile Row, but the look suited him. Was there any harm in lunch? Other women would be flattered by the lengths he was going to.

She picked up her bag and unhooked her raincoat from a nearby stand. 'OK, then.' She took a deep breath. 'Let's go.'

Neither of them spoke in the lift. It wasn't until Kate walked straight past the Cork and Cheese, the wine bar which occupied most of the ground floor, that Thomas asked, 'Do you want to avoid being seen with me socially? By your colleagues, at least.'

Kate shook her head. 'That place isn't really my scene. There's a pub nearby—'

'Fine by me.' Thomas grinned.

Kate led the way along a narrow, Dickensian alley and down some steps into a small, dark basement pub with sawdust on the floor. The type of place that seemed incongruous among the angular, glinting office buildings.

'They do great baguettes,' she recommended, as they stood at the bar waiting to place an order. 'Duck and orange paté's the best.'

Thomas pulled out his wallet. 'This is on me, OK?'

'If you insist. It's hardly Langan's.' She went off to find a space to sit down.

'You still think I'm a bit full-on, don't you?' he asked, a short while later, as they faced each other across a ridiculously small, round table.

As she tried to ensure that their knees didn't touch, Kate said insouciantly, 'I'm not sure what I think.'

'You never rang me for golf lessons,' he pointed out.

'Yes, well,' she muttered, 'I've decided golf isn't really me.' She hesitated a second, then added sheepishly, 'I won't be playing on the Golf Day, after all. Apparently the only thing I'll be playing is hostess. The other girls were having a laugh, winding me up. Natalia is as hot on golf as she is on bacon sarnies.'

Thomas looked blank.

'She's a vegetarian,' explained Kate.

He nodded comprehendingly.

'By the way,' she went on, 'you didn't say anything to Dick about seeing me at the driving range, did you? Only I'd rather he didn't know anything about all that.'

'Your secret's safe.' Thomas stared into his beer. 'It's a pity you've given up, though. I was looking forward to teaching you.'

'Well, I've saved you the bother.'

'I would have done it for free,' he said defiantly. He stared at her with an earnestness that made her wriggle in her chair. 'Kate, listen, there's something I want to ask you.'

She intended to just sip her wine, but ended up taking a gulp. 'What?'

'I'm having a party this Saturday. Not massive, just a few mates. It's a long-standing tradition. I usually build a Bonfire—'

'Guy Fawkes' was last weekend.'

'I know. I couldn't do it then, it was my brother's wedding.'

She raised her eyebrows. 'Of course. How did it go?'

'With a bang. Or at least the fireworks did.'

'No. I mean, seriously – how was it?'

'Fine, under the circumstances.' He lifted his glass. 'A fun time had by one and all.'

He was being sarcastic. Kate didn't understand why. 'Considering the lengths you went to to make sure it went ahead, you don't seem very enthusiastic now.'

'Oh, I am. About the marriage, that is. I just hate big weddings.'

'In your line of business? The cars, not the golf, obviously.'

'I just get on with the job.' He shrugged. 'It's not ideal, but it pays some bills. Besides, I love old motors, as do other people. If I share the cars in this way I feel less guilty about owning so many of them.'

Kate glanced up as a barman brought over their baguettes. 'So,' she said after a pause, conscious that she was actually about to start flirting with Thomas Llewellyn and feeling a frisson pass through her as she realised she was going to enjoy it, 'this party you're throwing, what does it have to do with me?'

He examined the contents of his lunch and nodded approvingly. 'Good choice.'

'The party?' she prompted, aware that he was flirting too by pretending to be evasive.

'I was wondering if you'd like to come along.'

His very nonchalance was disarming. Kate stared at him and suddenly realised that she wasn't very hungry.

'Maybe I will,' she murmured. 'I'll have to check if Paloma can babysit.'

'And if she can't?'

Kate wasn't about to admit that she'd be willing to pay Paloma triple-time-and-a-half. 'We'll have to see,' she shrugged, heady with something, she wasn't sure what. How could her emotions charge from panic to . . . to this?'

Thomas nodded. 'I'll give you directions. It's really not far from you.'

Kate wondered what sort of a place it was. 'If you're building a bonfire you must have a fairly big garden?'

'It's more a paddock. The *Ground Force* team would have a field day.' He grunted at his own pun. 'Or run a mile in the opposite direction.'

'Have you got a large house to go with it then?'

'What would you classify as large exactly? I've a few rooms I hardly ever venture into. My dog knows the place better than I do on that score.'

Kate picked at her baguette, while Thomas set about describing 'Tina', who by the sound of it was a rather spoilt terrier. Kate would have preferred it if he'd described his home rather than his pet, but then Thomas Llewellyn was consistently surprising.

He devoured what was left of his baguette, then picked up a beer mat. Selecting the side with more blank space, he set about drawing a map, explaining it as he did so.

Kate paid careful attention. But at one point when she glanced up, she caught sight of Natalia and her cronies at the other end of the pub, goggling in her direction. They looked away as she spotted them. Kate scowled. It was obvious that Natalia and co. had followed her here. The Cork and Cheese had lost some of its best patrons today.

Kate suddenly wanted to get back to the refuge of her desk. Thomas was handing over the beer mat.

'Around eight-ish?' he said.

She nodded distractedly. 'Definitely.'

'I thought you said "maybe" before?' His tone was playful.

'Oh.' Kate had forgotten to be coquettish. 'Well, maybe definitely. Look, would you mind if we left now? I've a spot of shopping to do before I get back to the office.'

He regarded her for a long moment, then nodded. 'Sure.'

Kate led the way out, avoiding even looking at the Cork and Cheese Gang. On the main road, bustling with activity, she turned to Thomas and gave him a half-smile. 'Thanks for lunch. Sorry I had to cut it short.'

'And not that you ate much of it.'

'No . . . I wasn't particularly hungry.'

They shuffled about on the spot. An awkwardness had descended.

'Do you want help carrying your shopping?' he asked.

'Oh, not really, don't worry.' She would have to think of something to buy then. 'I'll be fine. Just a few girlie bits and bobs, you know. Nothing too heavy.'

'Well, then,' he leaned down and brushed his lips against her cheek, 'I'll be seeing you.'

Her heart was thumping madly. She nodded. 'I'll do my best to make it to your bonfire thing.'

'You'd better,' he murmured. 'Because I don't give up that easily. I just thought you ought to know.'

'I'm beginning to get the idea.' And she stood and watched as he turned on his heel and strode away from her towards the nearest Tube station.

6

Paloma tried to conceal her amusement as she watched Kate fussing in front of the hall mirror. Emmi, her hair still knotted in a high bun from ballet that morning, danced with little skids around the varnished floorboards, while also keeping an eye on her mother.

'Do you think my hair looks better up or down?' asked Kate, wielding a lethally long tortoiseshell hair-clip.

'Up,' said Emmi.

'Down,' said Paloma.

Kate looked at them, confused.

'Wear it up like mine, Mummy.'

'Don't you think it would make a change if she wore it loose?' Paloma remonstrated gently.

'No.' Kate shook her head. 'Emmi's right. Besides, it ends up all over the place when it's down.'

Paloma pursed her lips. 'Just a suggestion.'

'Right,' said Kate a minute later, her hair securely twisted up and fastened in position. 'I'm off. I won't be too late.' She gave Emmi a kiss before zipping on her ankle boots.

'Be as late as you like, and have a good time,' stressed Paloma. 'There's no point hurrying back. Emmi'll be in bed soon anyway.'

Kate nodded gratefully, then glanced at the hall clock. Paloma followed her gaze. It was five-past-eight. Kate frowned, tugging on her thickest jacket and coiling a scarf around her neck. Yanking open the front door, she let in an icy draught and then shut it out again behind her. Paloma and Emmi watched from the lounge window as the bundled-up figure hurried down the path towards her car.

'I think Mummy's late for her date,' said Emmi sagely.

'It seems that way.' Paloma put an arm around the girl. The skinny little shoulders stiffened for a second and then relaxed. 'Do you mind if your mum has a boyfriend?'

'A bit,' said Emmi, with an honesty Paloma found painful. 'She just said she was going to a party tonight, but she looks like Alison Pearce did when Jamie Heswall asked her out to McDonald's.'

Paloma suppressed a smile. 'She hasn't said anything to me about a boyfriend, but I think you're right.'

'So you don't know who he might be?' Emmi fixed earnest grey eyes on her.

'I haven't a clue. But I'm sure your mum will tell us all about him when the time is right. You see, sometimes you might meet someone and go out with him a couple of times before realising that they're not right for you after all. So, rather than look silly, you just pretend it's not important until you know one way or the other.'

Emmi nodded.

'Have you ever wondered what it would be like to have a dad?' Paloma asked cautiously.

The little girl shrugged. 'Lots of people don't have

71

dads. Some people don't even have mums.'

'True.' Paloma sighed. 'But wouldn't you like to have both?'

Emmi shrugged again. 'It would depend.'

'On what?'

'On whether Mummy wanted a husband. Great-Grampa told me that. And he knows everything,' Emmi assured her. 'That's what happens when you're old. You don't have to learn anything because you already know it.'

Paloma couldn't resist smiling this time.

'Can we have some ice cream now?' asked Emmi. 'My tummy's still grumbling and I won't be able to sleep.'

Thomas stared out of his kitchen window. Normally at night the paddock that lay beyond the yard was lost in a seemingly endless gloom. Tonight it was illuminated by a frenzy of orange and gold flames. Dark silhouettes passed in front, or stood huddled in groups, revelling in the heat generated by the bonfire. The party was going well – except for one thing. Looking at his watch, Thomas sighed. She wasn't coming. 'Maybe definitely' was now 'definitely not'. He might as well have stuffed himself on garlic bread after all.

'There you are.'

A male voice made him turn with a jolt. 'Dick . . . Hi.'

'Just fetching more wine. What are you doing in here on your own? You're not about to produce more grub, are you?'

Thomas shook his head. 'No . . . I got side-tracked by the mess. I only came to fetch more wine myself.' He mustered a smile and started clearing empty bottles from the table, clinking them into a box on the floor for recycling.

Dick looked amused. 'You thought you'd invited guests, didn't you? Not parasites.'

'Something like that.' Thomas poured himself a glass of Burgundy. He looked questioningly at Dick, who nodded.

'Cheers.'

'It was good of you to make it at short notice.' Thomas took a sip of wine. He'd move on to beer next, even if he did feel odd man out.

'Thanks for asking me. It was good catching up the other day. We should do it more often.'

'Mmm.' Thomas stared soulfully into his glass. An evening's worth of alcohol was beginning to take effect. He'd started drinking before anyone had even arrived, but he'd never felt the need for this much Dutch courage in the past.

In an attempt to shake off his despondency, he diverted his attention back to Dick. 'Didn't you say you were going to bring someone?' He looked up as he spoke, just in time to see a shadow cross his old friend's face.

'You know how these things are . . . It fell through. As always.' Then Dick seemed to buck up, gesturing around him. 'I'd forgotten how rustic this place was.' His tone was dry but good-natured.

'You always did have a way with words.'

'You were the writer, though,' Dick pointed out. 'And you didn't explain properly the other day – what

73

happened in that department? Why did you give it up?'

'Because I was crap,' said Thomas flatly.

Dick seemed perplexed. 'No you weren't. Your column was a hoot. And I always used to look out for your more serious stuff. You seemed to be able to get right down to the bare bones—'

'And it didn't exactly make me popular.' Thomas jerked his head round. Someone was knocking on the front door. A rush of heat surged through him. He wasn't expecting anyone else apart from . . . 'Excuse me,' he muttered, hurrying to answer it.

On the step, flushed and frozen and grasping a bottle of lemonade, was a small figure wearing a puffy anorak two sizes too big for her. Or perhaps that was just an illusion, the jacket contrasting against sleek, dark trousers. 'Hi,' she murmured. A watery smile materialised above a bright red scarf. 'Sorry I'm so late.'

'Is everything OK?' Thomas beckoned Kate into the hall, closing the door behind her.

'I had trouble finding this place in the dark,' she sniffed. 'And I had to go via a shop on the way, for the lemonade. The heating in my car's playing up, too. It's like the Arctic in there.' She paused. 'I'm sorry. You probably thought I wasn't coming.'

'No, er,' Thomas took the lemonade from her, 'I just thought you'd been held up.'

'I didn't say for certain that I'd be here,' she reminded him archly.

'Your *precise* words were—'

'Dick!' She sounded surprised. 'I didn't realise you were coming.'

Thomas twisted round and saw his friend leaning against the kitchen door frame with a grin on his face that struck Thomas as ominous.

'Hello, Kate. Tom mentioned he'd invited you.'

Thomas frowned. He'd mentioned nothing of the sort. And Dick had never asked.

Kate was looking from one man to the other. But just then there was another interruption. Tina came bobbing down the stairs and started snuffling around Kate's feet, her ears moving up and down like antennae.

'I bet I can guess who this is.' Kate smiled at Thomas. 'And you're right, she does look like a Tina Turner wig on a bad hair day.'

'On *any* hair day, surely?' interjected Dick.

'She's also the main reason I don't have fireworks,' Thomas explained.

'Most pets don't like them.' Kate sounded genuinely sympathetic as she stooped to ruffle the dog's mottled grey fur.

'She also doesn't like too many people invading her space.'

'So that's why she hasn't made an appearance before,' smirked Dick. 'I didn't know you had a dog, Tom. And such a small one at that.'

'I think she's cute!' said Kate.

Thomas glowed at her defensiveness. She had won over the temperamental terrier with hardly any effort. Surely this was a sign . . .

'Would you like a drink, Kate?' piped up Dick.

Thomas's smile dropped from his lips. Who was the host around here?

75

'I'll just have a glass of lemonade, thanks.'

'Wouldn't you prefer wine?' Thomas tempted her.

'I can't.' She shook her head. 'I'm driving, remember? I left it too late to book a taxi, and you know how it is in these parts on a Saturday night – cabs are like gold-dust.'

Thomas suddenly wished he felt sober himself. 'You're welcome to stay over. A few people are. I've loads of space.'

Kate hesitated. 'I'm expected home.'

'You could phone Paloma . . .' He tailed off, not wanting to sound as if he had an ulterior motive. He was human, wasn't he? Even worse, he was a man.

'I've got lots to do tomorrow, and I really don't want to be hung-over,' she explained.

Thomas nodded. 'Fair enough.'

'Are you going to pour the lady a lemonade or not?' demanded Dick.

'Er, yes, of course.' Thomas retreated to the kitchen.

What was Dick playing at? He hadn't been possessive over Kate the other day in London, hadn't acted as if he was interested in her. Why the sudden change? Was it because they were out of the office?

Thomas poured the lemonade and went back into the hall. Dick was already showing Kate into the yard through the double doors at the far end. Grumbling under his breath, Thomas followed, observed by a pair of canine eyes peering devotedly through the banisters.

The warmth of the bonfire pressed itself into Kate's body. She stood as close as she dared, becoming more bewildered as the party wore on. There were about fifteen people there. Given half a chance she would have liked to have mingled more, but Dick seemed determined to monopolise her. And the more he monopolised, the more distance Thomas put between them. Now he was leaning against the stone wall separating the field from the yard, a can of beer in one hand and his head bent to listen to the woman at his side, who by the look of it couldn't speak any louder than a whisper.

One of the things puzzling Kate most was her own reaction to it. Only days ago she had wanted Dick to show an interest in her again. She wondered now if his indifference had been a cunning variant of the 'treat 'em mean, keep 'em keen' philosophy, because now that he was being 'nice' to her again her keenness seemed to be wearing off.

She frowned, and glanced back at the house rising from the shadows. It was tinted with an eerie amber glow from the bonfire. Houses with a long history had always fascinated her. But as she stared, memories of her own past fluttered out to greet her like ghouls and skeletons on a ghost train ride. Arguments . . . tirades . . . recriminations . . . When she had been only nineteen and had discovered she was pregnant with Emmi, she had known she could never be happy in the long run with her boyfriend Harry. Ironically, the reason she was going out with him had only hit home when she'd stared down in shock at the fuzzy blue line on the pregnancy test stick. She had been rebelling against her parents. Harry Barrett – scraping through university and sporting bleached blond hair and a nose stud – had been everything her mother and father disapproved of.

Now, years later, was she about to rebel in a similar way? Here was Dick, after all: rich, successful and oozing 'your-mother-would-worship-me' from every pore. And slouched over there, looking more like Heathcliff with every passing second, was Thomas. Against common sense and practicality, Kate wanted to be Catherine Earnshaw. She wanted to understand how a man with Thomas's privileged background had ended up living in a run-down farmhouse with a dog for company and a barnful of romantic old cars. Admittedly, he had told her and Dick on his brief tour that he had converted the barn into a proper working garage, but to Kate it still looked like a barn, full stop.

She sighed.

Irony of ironies, Dick was now waffling on about golf. She could smell stale garlic on his breath as he leaned closer. She had to slip away somehow. At last an idea came to her. She interrupted him just as he'd been about to describe a game he'd played in Valderama. He seemed surprised as she excused herself, probably unable to comprehend why her bladder wouldn't hold on until he'd reached the eighteenth hole.

Kate hurried across the yard, hoping that by the time she returned Dick would have been accosted by another guest and might be receiving a taste of his own medicine. She couldn't help glancing back as she reached the house, but it wasn't in Dick's direction. Thomas – sod him – was still deep in conversation with the leggy brunette.

A few moments later, staring indignantly into a small tarnished mirror in the downstairs toilet, Kate zipped up her jacket. It was colder inside the house than it was out by the bonfire. She scrutinised her make-up. Her lipstick had rubbed off, except around the edges, as if she'd only remembered to put on liner. Typical. Reaching into her pocket, she pulled out her favourite shade and applied another coat, although why was she bothering? What was Thomas playing at? Why had he invited her in the first place? She checked her watch. Four minutes had passed. Not long enough. She waited another two before unlatching the door and creaking it open.

She gasped as someone grabbed her sleeve and steered her into the alcove beneath the stairs. 'What the hell— *Tom!*'

'Do you know,' he said triumphantly, 'that's the first time you've called me that. I like it. Sorry if I startled you. I wanted to get your attention.'

'Why do you seem to think you can only get it by being dramatic?' she bristled. 'If it isn't turning up at work unannounced—'

'I know. I'm sorry. Really. And speaking of work, what's the story with you and Dick?'

'Nothing.' She squirmed. 'I don't know what's got into him.'

'Too much Burgundy? Although I can hardly talk. And by the way, there's nothing going on between Sylvia and me, either. She's like that with all her male friends. I'm immune to it by now.'

'Sylvia?'

'The girl who's been bending my ear for the last hour.'

'Oh,' said Kate. 'Her.'

He chuckled, which instantly made her bridle.

'Listen,' she said testily. 'It's time I went home. Maybe you could tell Dick my nanny rang with a problem. Nothing serious, just say I was being an overprotective mum or something.'

'Can't we speak before you rush off?' He had reached out for her hand and was now holding it in his large, warm palm.

'I thought that's what we were doing?' she contested.

'I want to talk properly, where we won't be interrupted. Any moment now someone's liable to turn up for a slash.'

'Great vocabulary you've got.'

'I know.'

She felt ridiculously light-headed as he pulled her up the stairs. Nothing was going to happen, she told herself sternly and a touch naïvely. It was too soon for anything like that. They were just going to talk. Thomas had said so.

'Sorry, Tina.' He grinned at his dog, who was perched on an old ottoman, wagging her tail ecstatically. 'This is private.' And he opened the first door on the left and ushered Kate inside, flicking on the light.

She blinked a moment then looked around. They were in a moderate-sized room which seemed to contain nothing but books. On second glance, however, she saw that there was a desk over by the window and a large antique chair in front of it. And the books weren't suspended in mid-air, of course, but were stacked on row upon row of shelves spanning the two walls on either side of her.

'The study,' announced Thomas grandly, as if he was the butler.

'I can see that,' she said pertly. 'It's also your favourite room.'

A frown crossed his face. 'Oh? How's that?'

Kate gestured at the heavy green curtains, and the oil lamp on the leather-topped desk. 'The attention to detail,' she explained, trailing a hand over the mahogany arm of the chair and along the edge of the nearest shelf. 'And the absence of any tell-tale dust. Also, why bring me all the way up here?'

'Ah . . . Well, I'm afraid to say that if you'd bothered to examine any of the other rooms closely, you wouldn't have found much grime there, either. I've a woman who comes in once a week and waves a feather duster around a bit along with some furniture polish. She's very adept at tackling limescale in toilet bowls, too.'

'Oh,' said Kate. 'So I've got it wrong?'

He leaned against the desk and folded his arms. 'Partly. I *used* to spend more time in this room, but now I'm busier elsewhere. Like I said before, I wanted to talk, and I thought there'd be more risk of being interrupted downstairs. Apart from the bathroom, every other room up here is a bedroom.' A smile hovered around his lips. 'I didn't want you getting the wrong idea.'

'Right.' Kate looked away, pretending to read the spine of a nearby book. 'That makes sense.'

'What? The title of that novel or what I just said?'

She looked back at him again and pulled a face.

Thomas sighed. 'I know most of this house probably seems rather . . . neglected.' He was almost apologetic. 'But it was only partially renovated when I moved in, and besides converting the barn, I haven't got around to doing much myself.'

'It's got potential, though,' Kate pointed out quickly. 'And it would be easy to go over the top. You don't want to work against a house like this, you've got to work *with* it.'

He looked at her appraisingly for a long moment. 'Can I ask you a question? Did you decorate your own place or did you get a designer in? From what I saw, it looked as if you'd had one of those TV makeovers, only better.'

Kate felt as if she'd won the lottery. 'I – um – did it myself.'

'The whole house?'

She nodded. 'It took a couple of years, of course, until it was exactly how I wanted. But redecorating was one of the stipulations of the rental agreement.'

'Oh? I thought you owned the place.'

'My grandfather's my landlord, so I suppose I do think of it as my own. He's hardly likely to throw me out on the street. After my grandmother died seven years ago, he went to live in a retirement flat. He couldn't bear to part with the house; he'd lived there with my gran for most of their married life. It's not as if he wasn't able to afford to do all this – Grandad's never been exactly poor – but my father kept saying he was mad.' She heard the edge creep into her voice and couldn't look Thomas in the eye. 'When Emmi was a baby, I was stifled living with my parents, so my grandad asked if I wanted to rent the Old Parsonage. It seemed a waste to have it empty. Dad was fuming. Deep down, he probably still is. The rent was nominal five years ago and it hasn't ever gone up.'

'You've been very lucky.'

She lifted her gaze again. Thomas didn't seem to be patronising her. 'I know,' she nodded. 'Like I said before, the only stipulation my grandad made was that I had to redecorate the place. The structure was sound enough – he'd invested a lot in it over the years, new windows and so on – but the wallpaper was beginning to look tired.'

'You love that house almost as much as your grand-father does, don't you?'

Thomas was more perceptive than she'd given him credit for. 'I do. Even though I didn't live at the Old Parsonage as a child, I spent a lot of time there.'

'Where did you live?'

'Pagelton. My parents are still there.'

He nodded. 'I know it. It's not even large enough to be called a village.'

'Blink and you miss it,' agreed Kate. 'They've got a nice enough house, but I don't think it's ever felt like home . . .' She tailed off. Her mouth ought to be clamped. She'd lost a couple of potential boyfriends by unloading herself like this. Before they could even imagine a future with her they'd been totally put off by her past.

Thomas was regarding her thoughtfully. 'If you enjoy interior design so much, why don't you do it professionally? Have you ever had formal training?'

This was another subject to steer clear of. 'I was doing art at university before I dropped out. To be honest, I wasn't enjoying it. The modern stuff isn't my scene. Although it wasn't planned, getting pregnant was my excuse to quit.' She chewed her lip, again having said more than she'd intended.

'Surely there's a demand for designers to work with the past? There are so many houses like yours, and mine, that wouldn't suit a contemporary look.'

Why was he probing and provoking her this way? And how come he was so good at it? Agitated, Kate rubbed the back of her neck. She wanted to snap at him to shut up, but his eyes were fixed on her with such empathy . . . She stared back, wondering how he could understand her so well.

'I'm a secretary,' she said at last, 'a personal assistant. It's what I ended up training for. It was safe. I couldn't afford to take risks. I've got a daughter who depends on me, I wanted to support her myself as much as possible. Is that so wrong?' Horror of horrors, there was a tremor in her voice.

'Kate, I'm sorry – again. I didn't mean to interrogate you. It's a bloody awful habit I've got.' His tone was sardonic. 'It's just . . . I want to get to know you. I've asked lots of questions in the past when I've first met a woman, but I'm not sure I've ever really listened to the answers. This probably isn't making sense . . . It's just, you're not what I'm used to. Oh, shit,' he groaned, throwing his head back. 'I could kill for a cigarette right now.'

'Tom . . .' She put a hand to his mouth, then quickly pulled away, as if she'd been stung. 'I . . .'

His lips bounced against hers and then pressed down more firmly. Kate felt as if the temperature in the house had shot up twenty degrees. Before she could even issue a protest, he had released her hair-clip. She heard a muffled thud as it hit the floor. 'Much better that way,' he managed to whisper between kisses.

The walls seemed to cave in towards her as his hands cradled her face. To be touched this way after so long only intensified the sudden cinematic sensation that nothing was real outside of this room. There was only here, only now, only this overwhelming urge to behave like a rampant teenager.

It was Thomas who drew back, slightly breathless, grinning dazedly. 'Have dinner with me this week,' he murmured. 'I want to take you out, I want to keep on seeing you.'

'Yes.' She didn't need to think twice. 'OK.' She stared at him self-consciously. 'I . . . I'd better go.'

'Probably a good idea.' Looking frazzled, he raked his fingers through his hair. 'I don't trust you to keep your hands off me.'

It was intended as a joke, but Kate wasn't laughing. She fumbled to open the door, then half-ran along the landing towards the stairs, reminded of Cinderella as she charged down them. That stroke of midnight, coach-into-pumpkin business would probably be analysed these days by some expert or other as fear; fear of what might have happened in an adult version of the fairytale if she'd stayed dancing with the prince too long. Kate needed some distance of her own now, too. Instead of a glass slipper she could leave behind a mud-caked boot; the carpet was threadbare and stained anyway, so Thomas couldn't complain.

Thomas. *Tom*. Just saying his name in her head made her stomach lurch.

'Kate . . .'

She glanced up from the bottom of the stairs, both boots still firmly on her feet (zips obviously hadn't been fashionable in Cinderella's day).

He was leaning over the banisters, holding out her tortoiseshell hair-clip. 'You were forgetting this.'

She hesitated, mesmerised by the potent combination of a man's slightly time-ravaged countenance and a boy's eyes, terrified of rejection.

'Don't worry about it,' she replied, with more boldness than she felt, 'I'll pick it up next time. Look after it for me.' And she let herself quickly out of his house, dragging shut the heavy oak door behind her.

7

Blast. There was a hole in her tights. They were her last pair.

Kate flopped on to the bed, frowning at her reflection in the pine cheval mirror: black bra, black knickers, black tights with the knee showing through. Hmm. Attractive. The 'little black dress' she'd planned to wear would look tarty with bare legs, as it would with stockings or hold-ups. Besides, it was minus-two outside. Although, on second thoughts, it was stupid to think that ten deniers' worth of nylon and elastane could keep frost-bite at bay.

Kate considered whether her nanny might have a spare pair, although she'd never seen her in tights. Even if Paloma did own some, however, she was so tall that any tights that would stretch to fit her would sag on Kate. The Nora Batty look wasn't the stuff that dream first dates were made of.

Grumbling, Kate yanked open the wardrobe door. She was going to have to resort to trousers.

'Mummy!' Emmi strolled into the room without knocking, as usual. 'Why is your dress hanging up in the bathroom?'

'Huh? Oh – it was creased.'

'Why don't you iron it then?'

'Because you can't iron that material. The steam from the bath I had helped the creases fall out.'

Emmi's smooth, pale brow wrinkled. 'Where did they fall out to?'

Kate couldn't help smiling. 'They just sort of vanished – like magic.'

'Oh.'

Just as she was about to ask her daughter's opinion on what she should wear instead of the dress, Emmi spun on her heel and strolled out again. Kate stared after her, experiencing a tug of guilt and regret. Where had her little baby gone? When had the plump, gurgling, dimpled toddler turned into a skinny, pensive, independent young girl?

Kate looked towards her chest of drawers. There was a faded Polaroid on top, of Annabel and herself when they were about Emmi's age. Two sisters, with a Flake 99 each, on a seafront somewhere, adoring grandparents beaming behind them. Kate padded over and picked it up. She kept it on show simply for the smiles on her grandparents' faces. The frame she'd put it in was slightly too large; the picture was wonky. She stared at herself, at the girl she'd been – so like Emmi. While beside her on the cast-iron bench Annabel twinkled like a little star.

Kate knew that she'd been serious and subdued at that age because of her parents; because they didn't seem to like her; because her sister was obviously the favourite with Mummy and Daddy. But Emmi didn't have a sugar and spice sibling to compete with, and every member of her family adored her. Why then, mused Kate, was her daughter a mirror image of herself as a child? Why, in effect, did Emmi seem sad?

Half-an-hour later, Kate stood in front of the mirror in the hall, adjusting her hair over her shoulders. She paused to pick lint off her casual woollen trouser suit and frowned. Yes, she was snug, but it wasn't very feminine. On the other hand, she'd been bundled up like the Michelin Man at Tom's party and she'd still got a snog out of it. She quickly changed 'snog' (foul word) to kiss. Much better, she decided, shivering blissfully at the memory.

Trying in vain to suppress her anticipation, Kate allowed her gaze to stray beyond her appearance. She looked through the open door into the living room, recalling Tom's compliments about the decor. Her grandad had always said that she had a good eye for interior design. He had told her a couple of years ago that she'd brought the house back to life. The old-fashioned and the contemporary had been blended together to produce an airy, homely atmosphere; somewhere that looked lived-in and comfortable. Kate shrugged away from minimalism as much as she resisted clutter. It was all about a sense of balance. And now, gazing around with fresh eyes, as Tom had done, she revelled all over again in her achievement.

Divided by a beechwood dado rail, the top half of the living-room walls was painted vanilla and the bottom half pale banana. Kate liked to name colours after plants, or food and drink; it made them sound more interesting, more tangible. All around the room, like splashes from a rainbow, dried flower displays sprung up cottage-garden-style from small, large and medium-sized vases, and photographs of Emmi at various stages of her life dotted the wall above the open fireplace. Paloma and Emmi were sprawled on a clotted-cream sofa among a generous number of daffodil and saffron cushions. The little girl looked up from a TV programme about vets, long enough to give her mother a disapproving look.

'Is he late, Mummy?'

'Only a little bit,' said Kate, avoiding Paloma's eye.

The sound of an engine purring and cutting out made her swing round and face the front door. Her heart leaped as she battled with the latch. And then, moments later, there he was, standing on her doorstep holding a small bunch of flowers and a modest box of chocolates.

'I decided to be unconventional,' he grinned, stepping inside just as Kate became conscious of another presence beside her. Her daughter was staring straight up at him. Undaunted, Tom handed the chocolates to Kate. 'These are for you . . . And the flowers are for this young lady here.' He gave them to Emmi, whose eyes grew impossibly wide.

'What do you say?' Kate prompted her.

'Thank you,' whispered the little girl. But it didn't take long for her voice to return to full volume. 'Paloma, look!' she called out. 'It's that man you know. The one Mummy said wouldn't bother us again!'

Kate chewed her lip. Tom smiled sheepishly at Paloma.

'I, er, take it Kate didn't tell you exactly who she was going out with.'

'It didn't come up,' Kate muttered defensively.

Paloma was gawping. 'I – um – didn't expect to see you again.'

'I don't suppose you did. But Kate and I have run into each other a couple of times since that day and . . . well, let's just say things have been resolved to everyone's satisfaction.'

'Your brother . . . ?' Paloma left the question hanging.

'Is thoroughly enjoying his honeymoon in the Maldives, as far as I know.'

'I'm sure we can all look back and laugh now,' said Kate, rather feebly. She was desperate to make a getaway. 'Emmi, why don't you go and put those flowers in water. Paloma will help you.'

But Emmi was having none of it. 'Will you be coming home tonight, Mummy?'

'Er . . .' Kate was thrown by the question. Where did children pick up these things?

Emmi elucidated. 'Dougie at school says that sometimes his sister goes out with men at night and doesn't come home till the following morning.'

'Don't worry,' Tom interceded before Kate could wrap her head around this, 'I won't keep your mum out too long past midnight.'

Putting down the chocolates on the hall table, Kate grabbed her coat and handbag. 'Right then, we'd better be off. I suppose you've made a reservation?'

Tom nodded suavely. 'But there's plenty of time. I wanted to ask you something while Emmi was here, to see if she agreed, too. If you're both free on Sunday, I was wondering if you'd like to come over to my place for lunch?'

Kate frowned.

'I've got a dog called Tina,' Tom was saying to Emmi, who was all eyes and ears. 'And a pony.'

'A pony!' Emmi jumped up and down, tugging at her mother's sleeve. 'Can we go, Mummy? Can we?'

Kate turned to Tom. 'I didn't know you had a pony.'

'Well, er, it's not actually *mine*. It belongs to the farmer next door. But it usually comes up to my fence and hangs around with Tina. Emmi can feed it sugar lumps, if she likes.'

'What's the pony's name?' asked Emmi.

'I, um, don't actually know. Maybe you can make something up for the day.'

'Shouldn't we be going now?' asked Kate, imperious even to her own ears.

Tom blinked at her. 'You haven't said whether you want to come yet. Emmi obviously does.'

'Can we talk about it over dinner?'

'Well . . . are you going to keep Emmi and me hanging on for your answer?'

Bugger him. 'OK,' snapped Kate. 'We'll come.' And with that, she opened the front door and brushed past him, leading the way down the path until she reached the old MG which she'd admired in his 'garage' on Sunday. Tom hurried to hold the passenger door open for her. She wriggled in. Sports cars were all very well, but they made it bloody hard to be graceful.

Waving goodbye to Emmi and Paloma, they drove off in silence.

Tom was the first to speak. 'You're annoyed with me.'

'That's observant.'

'What have I done?'

She shook her head impatiently. 'You manipulated me into agreeing to come over on Sunday. You used my daughter to manoeuvre me into an impossible position.'

'I . . .' In the dim light filtering into the car, Kate could tell by his expression that he was genuinely bemused. 'I'm sorry,' he spluttered at last. 'I – I just didn't want you to think that I'm not interested in Emmi. I realise that you come as a package—'

'It's a little premature to see it like that. I wanted to keep Emmi out of it as much as possible. At least until—' Kate stopped herself, because she hadn't actually looked that far ahead. Perhaps, she realised, she hadn't dared to because she might not *see* a future. There was no denying the physical attraction that had somehow sprung up between them, but where might it lead beyond the obvious? Where did she want it to lead? Not long ago she had sat in her grandfather's flat and stated plainly that she wasn't after anything serious. What was so different now?

Her concerns about her daughter looking unhappy came to the surface again. She felt a rush of guilt over her love-life taking precedence.

Tom reached out and grabbed her hand. 'I'm sorry.' His voice was a low murmur. 'I didn't think.'

The warmth, the pressure of his fingers, reminded her of how good it had felt when he'd held her close. As he let go in order to change gear, she turned to him, relenting. 'I'm sorry too,' she sighed. 'It's just . . . I don't want to confuse Emmi. She's never known me going out with anyone, not like this . . . I don't know how she feels about it, and I don't want to confuse her into expecting something that might . . . that might never happen.'

He was silent. She must have touched a raw nerve. But then he said soberly, 'I understand. If you want to forget about Sunday—'

She grunted. 'Too late. Emmi loves anything to do with ponies.'

'So . . . ?'

'So let's just see how it goes.'

'Maybe you could tell her we're just friends? Explain to her how adult relationships work sometimes.'

'Maybe.' Kate looked unseeingly out of the window. The trouble was, she didn't know how they worked. Looking back on her relationship with Harry, she realised now that she'd been far too immature to sustain anything serious. They both had. If only there was a set of guidelines, like the Highway Code.

'Hope you like Italian,' Tom was saying. 'I should have asked before I booked really.'

'Is it that place in Addenham?'

'The one in Market Square. Do you know it?'

'I've gone past loads of times, I've just never eaten there. It's always full.'

'That's because the food's excellent. You normally have to make a reservation well in advance, but I know the owner, Luigi. He's also the chef. Try the tortellini with spinach and ricotta, it's one of his specialities.'

With a sigh, Kate endeavoured to relax in the leather bucket seat. If only for tonight, she ought to stop thinking so analytically and just enjoy the moment and Tom's company. Heathcliff and Cathy hadn't jaunted around the countryside in a racy little car, but they'd still acted as if they had. Kate had a head start on them in that respect, so why shouldn't she just accept the challenge to be young, spirited and free? Until tomorrow at least, when her alarm clock would go off at eight. So much for a long Saturday morning lie-in. She couldn't remember the last time she'd had one.

'Sorry I'm such lousy company,' apologised Tom, less than an hour later, as Kate dunked the last of her bread in the herb-riddled olive oil.

She didn't respond, mainly because she couldn't understand what had gone wrong. The plump and florid Luigi had come out to greet Tom only seconds after the waitress had shown them to their table. He'd raised his eyebrows a tad at Kate, before spreading his arms in delight at welcoming one of his favourite customers again. With a convincing Italian accent, he had taken their order himself and bounced back to the kitchen. It was around then that Kate had noticed Tom growing sullen and edgy.

'The thing is, I used to come here with Jem,' he said abruptly.

'Jem . . . ?'

'My ex.'

'Wife?' Kate felt a lump in her throat. It wasn't just the bread going down.

'Girlfriend. Partner. Live-in lover. Whatever sounds less PC, actually.' The sarcasm was directed at himself.

'How long ago did you break up?'

'It happened just before I met you,' he replied, suspiciously quickly.

'How long ago exactly?'

He considered it a moment, then muttered, 'Five weeks.'

Kate took a sip of wine and did a quick calculation of her own. 'You must have only just broken up when we first met . . .'

He hesitated. 'I suppose so.'

'Did she leave you?' Kate was beginning to feel sick and cold. 'How long did you go out for?'

'All these questions . . . It's ironic, isn't it? How much I hate the boot being on the other foot.'

'What do you mean?'

He shrugged. 'It doesn't matter. The point is that Jem and I were only together six months max, and she was only living with me for four. You might think I'm on the rebound, but I don't see it like that. If I'd met you when Jem and I were still together . . .'

'What?' she asked, hardly daring to breathe but risking a gulp of wine. Despite Tom's mood, he'd been perfectly controlled with his drinking. Just as well, considering he was driving. He was still within his meagre rations, but at the present time she didn't share his self-control.

'Who knows?' He shrugged again. 'I don't think anyone can answer that. I should have told you about Jem sooner. It's just . . . when was the right moment?

There haven't been any. We hardly know each other.'

'But why did you bring me here? Of all the places you could have picked . . .'

'Because I obviously didn't think it through properly. This is my favourite restaurant. I didn't realise I'd get so wound up being here.'

'Do you miss her? Jem?'

For a long moment, Tom stared into the tea-light candle flickering in a glass holder in the centre of the table. Then he shook his head. 'No . . . Not much . . . But when you spend time – however brief – living with someone, you're bound to miss their presence at the very least, even if you know it was doomed in the long run. More than anything I'm angry with her. And with myself.'

'Angry because she left you?'

'I shouldn't be, not really. I made it easy for her to leave. I gave her every reason to want to go.' He paused as a waitress came over with their second courses. She offered them black pepper and Parmesan before bustling off to take a drinks order from another couple.

Kate poked aimlessly at the tortellini with her fork. 'What did you do that was so bad?' she couldn't help asking.

'Nothing worthy of a Jerry Springer show. It was an accumulation of the little things that made me seem . . . dull and distant to her, I suppose. Basically, I didn't give her enough attention.'

'You said you brought her here sometimes, though.' Kate felt as if she was a marriage guidance counsellor.

'But where was I the rest of the time? I don't just mean

97

physically, but mentally, emotionally. I wasn't with her. I was in my own world.'

'Everybody has that fault, though, surely? To one extent or another. You shouldn't be so hard on yourself.'

He shook his head. 'I suppose what's bugging me about being here is that it reminds me of all the mistakes I've made . . . and all the ones I've yet to make. It's inevitable.' His voice lowered. 'I can try to learn from the past, but in the future . . . I'll just make a series of new gaffes.'

Kate was no longer feeling cold and sick. Instead, she was filled with a sudden urge to protect and nurture, which, although not exactly maternal, was springing up inside her with the same spontaneity and rawness. She suppressed the desire to lunge across the table and cradle his head against her chest. A few glasses of Pinot Grigio later and she might not have been able to resist.

As a safeguard, she tried to be detached and rational about it all. There must have been women before Jem who had been important to him too. He was in his mid-thirties, Kate guessed; he obviously had a past. It would be ridiculous for her to brood about it. Although, on the other hand, perhaps it was natural to feel jealous. Yet wasn't he implying that this time – with her – he wanted things to be different? And wasn't that why there was a warm, melting feeling in her stomach that was making her want to hug him right there and then?

The case for and against swung like a pendulum as she drank her wine and ignored her pasta.

Topping up her glass, Tom asked sharply, 'Don't you have any skeletons in *your* closet?'

She conjured up an image of a heap of old bones in her wardrobe, tangled up with her numerous shoes and handbags.

'I've always aired my skeletons in public,' she sighed. 'Much to my parents' dismay, especially Mum's. Then again, I don't think there've been that many. They caught me smoking when I was fifteen, at a cousin's birthday party. There were a few of us hiding in the gazebo. I didn't even have the decency to do it somewhere more private. Apparently, I made an exhibition of myself.' She was aware that her voice sounded perilously like her mother's.

'You don't smoke now, though.'

'I wasn't really even smoking then. It was my first time. I must have looked like Puff the Magic Dragon. It went in my mouth and shot straight out of my nose. My lungs never had a look-in.'

He smiled. 'If that's the worst thing you've ever done—'

'Oh, no!' She flapped her hand theatrically. 'Harry was the worst.'

'Harry?'

'Harry Barrett, Emmi's father. He was everything my mother dreaded. "A working class yobbo", I think she called him.' Kate described her ex-boyfriend in vivid detail, even down to the tiny silver nose-stud.

'So you went out with him to spite your family,' surmised Tom. 'And Emmi was a by-product?'

Kate would never have put it that way herself. 'Like

99

I've said before, she wasn't planned. But my parents never once suggested I should get married. Harry was the last person they wanted in the family. Yet Emmi . . . she was their first grandchild. Once she was born, once they could see her, hold her—'

'They doted on her.'

'Too much. Which meant they suffocated me. They had control, until my grandfather came to the rescue.'

Tom nodded. 'I know all about controlling influences. My mother, for instance.'

'The "old bat"?'

'I was hoping you'd forgotten,' he winced. 'It all boils down to the fact that my parents have lived separate lives for years. In fact, I can't really remember them ever being happy together. It came to a head a few years ago when Dad met someone else and finally asked for a divorce. Around the same time, he helped me buy The Croft, and with all his connections it was easy for him to get Scott a job in the City after he left university. My mother felt redundant, I suppose. That's why she was so involved in Scott's wedding.'

'Do you feel like the black sheep of the family?' Kate pressed gently.

His face clouded over. 'How did you guess?'

'Because I'm one, too,' she admitted. 'I've got a younger sister, Annabel. She never puts a foot wrong.'

'Like Scott, for the most part, although he's given Mum a few hairy moments over the years. The business with your nanny, for instance.'

Kate looked down at her plate and decided she ought

to make an attempt to eat something. She was beginning to feel light-headed.

'I don't seem to have much of an appetite myself,' said Tom. 'We should be lying on a couch; a restaurant isn't really the place.'

'Sorry?' Kate almost choked on an olive.

'A psychiatrist's couch, considering the way we're unloading ourselves.'

'Oh, right. Of course.'

Without warning, he reached across the table and hooked a strand of hair behind her ear. 'Sorry. I've been wanting to do that all evening. It, er, seemed to belong there. And that reminds me, I've forgotten your hair-clip.' He gave her an apologetic smile. 'But I've looked after it well, like you asked me to.'

She felt a crumpling sensation in her belly, and a warmth spreading outwards like shockwaves from an earthquake. *Definitely* nothing maternal about this. Her hand trembled slightly. In a clumsy gesture she dropped her fork. But she wasn't going to put it all down to lust. She'd never called it that, even though she was sure it was only a deadly sin if you acted upon it. Like pride. You couldn't help the feeling, it was only human. It was what you did about it that would count.

'I don't want to end up like my parents,' said Tom suddenly, quietly. 'Dad lives in Benidorm, with a woman half his age. Some might say he's a lucky bastard, but he didn't even come to his own son's wedding because he and my mother can't seem to cope with being in the same country any more, let alone the same room. He lives in some sort of self-imposed exile—' Tom stopped and looked down at the checked tablecloth.

'What?' asked Kate, daringly touching his arm.

'Nothing.' He snorted. 'Actually, it's only struck me now that I'm just like him.'

'How?'

'It's not worth going into.' He glanced towards the kitchen. 'Listen, I'll have to appease Luigi somehow, but as we're obviously not going to make it through the meal—'

'Do you think we could make it through a coffee somewhere?' Kate threw down the challenge with as much sparkle as she could muster.

Tom stroked the back of her hand. 'We could probably manage that much.' He smiled tiredly. 'Your place or mine?'

8

Tom sat slumped on his sofa, replaying Friday night's disastrous date in his head while toying with an unlit cigarette. He hadn't smoked in public since before his brother's wedding, and in private he'd cut right down to two or three a day. For him, it was a question of habit, the craving at its strongest immediately after a meal. But he hadn't eaten anything today yet, not even breakfast. Bloody hell, he was a mess. Shoving the cigarette determinedly back into the pack, he stood up and stretched. What he really needed in order to feel human again was a shave and a shower. Sunday mornings always affected him like this, as if his body knew it was the sabbath and refused to function properly if he didn't rest in bed until well past noon.

There was no time to laze around under the duvet with the papers today, though. As he fiddled with his Wilkinson Sword he remembered the drive back from Addenham to Beckton Lacey the other night. Kate had seemed so far away, even though she was sitting right beside him. Idiot that he was, he hadn't known what to say. The atmosphere had grown increasingly awkward. By the time they'd pulled up outside the Old Parsonage, he'd wound himself up to such an extent that her invitation to come in for coffee had caught him off guard.

'Wasn't that the plan?' She had stared at him, understandably nonplussed.

'It's just . . . you've been so quiet coming home, and I've been going on like such an arse all night—'

'No you haven't.' Her eyes were fierce and bright. 'You've just been honest. I appreciate that.'

They'd walked into the house to find Paloma still sprawled in front of the TV. She'd jumped up and made some tactful excuse about being knackered and having to go to bed. Flicking off the telly, she'd scuttled upstairs. And so he'd found himself alone again with Kate. In the glow of the lamp which stood on a small side table, her hair had rippled like a stream of gold across her shoulders. She'd stood there, in the middle of the room, small and sweet and silent, like a bride on her wedding night . . . And he'd felt privileged, and desperate to just scoop her up and do all those things he'd never thought twice about with women in the past. But in spite of the fact that he had a Durex Elite in his back pocket, he hadn't.

They'd made coffee, and sat on the sofa drinking it, without touching or looking at each other, or even sustaining a proper conversation. And then, when he had got up to leave, she had jumped to her feet, turning her face up to his, and he had pecked her chastely on the cheek and promised her the best Sunday roast ever.

Daft sod, thought Tom now, nicking himself with the razor in agitation. Who the bloody hell had he thought he was? Jamie Oliver?

*

'The roast potatoes were a bit mushy . . .'

Kate shook her head adamantly. 'They were fine.'

'And the mint sauce had too much vinegar—'

'Tom, stop it, you did a great job. I always feel I need three pairs of hands to get everything ready when I do a roast.'

'At least Emmi's enjoying herself . . .' They both looked out of the window into the back yard where the little girl was romping with Tina. 'Although I'm damned if I know where that pony's got to today. I couldn't even get *that* right.'

Kate was laughing. She sounded so like her daughter, Tom grinned and relaxed.

'Do you have a dishwasher?' she asked, glancing around.

He did indeed. A souvenir of another failed relationship, Tom realised. Alice – an aspiring actress and model – had insisted that he get one. Although he didn't mind doing the washing-up himself, there were occasions when he wasn't around, and it seemed that Alice's hands couldn't be immersed in water (not even with rubber gloves on) or her nails cracked or something. Very odd considering how long she'd used to spend in the bath.

'I'll help you load up,' Kate insisted.

They worked side by side, smiling at Emmi out of the window.

'Listen,' said Tom at last, knowing he had to broach the subject while he had the chance. 'What happened the other night – or rather, what didn't happen . . . I don't want you to think that I'm not . . . *interested.*'

'It was all wrong,' she said quickly. 'With Emmi in the house and everything.'

'I don't think we should rush into' – he paused – 'that aspect of things.'

'No. You're right.'

'I – I really like you.' He could have kicked himself for sounding as if they were fifteen-year-old school kids sheltering behind the proverbial bikeshed.

She slid the vegetable dish into the last slot on the rack. 'I really like you too,' she mumbled.

So it's best if we take things slow and see what happens?'

'Probably best, yes.'

They straightened up. He shut the machine without taking his eyes off her. 'You look relieved.'

'Only because, after Friday, I didn't know what to think.'

'Did I fancy you or not, you mean?'

Her cheeks were acquiring a pink tinge. 'It's just lately I seem to have been getting conflicting signals from all over the shop. Not just you . . .'

'You mean Dick?'

'Well, yes,' she murmured. 'Since your party he's just gone back to being impeccably boss-like. Not gruff, but not overfriendly.'

'His loss is my gain then.'

No sooner were the words out of his mouth than Tom realised how corny they sounded. But Kate didn't seem to mind. Her face was turned upwards invitingly again. Pressing down the button for eco-wash, Tom leaned in for the long-awaited kiss. Kate's lips were soft, parting easily beneath his as the dishwasher churned into life against his leg.

'I didn't see you put any powder in there,' said a sing-song child's voice from over by the door. 'Mummy always puts it in last.'

Tom sprang back. 'Shit,' he muttered.

'Bugger,' said Kate.

'Do you have any sugar lumps?' Emmi asked excitedly. 'The pony's here at last and I'm going to call it Ronan.'

Paloma stood gazing listlessly around the lounge of the Old Parsonage. Funny how the house didn't seem this empty on a weekday when Kate was at work and Emmi at school. Perhaps it was because today was Sunday and Paloma wished she was down the pub having a quiet drink with Lottie as usual. But Lottie had gone up north for the weekend to visit her gran, and even though Paloma was feeling more and more like a local at the White Hart, just a short stroll away on the other side of the green, she still didn't like the idea of going across there on her own.

She'd expected last night to be boring too, she acknowledged now, but oddly enough it hadn't been. Kate had suggested they rent a video, and once Emmi was tucked up in bed they'd settled down on the sofa with the necessary provisions. Working through the popcorn, Paloma had tried to extract gossip about Kate's date with Thomas Llewellyn, apologising for being so gobsmacked about it.

Kate had looked up from a tub of Belgian chocolate ice cream. 'I don't blame you for being surprised,' she'd sighed, going on to explain that she couldn't fathom men out lately. To Paloma's amazement, she had opened up about her boss, Dick Anthony, and about how Tom seemed to be blowing hot and cold now too. Come to think of it, Paloma couldn't remember much about the video at all. It had been some tense psychological thriller that had required far too much brain-power for a Saturday night in.

'Men like the chase,' she had pointed out, feeling very worldly-wise, even though she was a couple of years younger than Kate. 'Maybe you should play hard to get.'

'Is that what you'd do?'

'It would depend on how much I liked the bloke,' Paloma could recall admitting. 'If I really felt there was a connection between us, I probably wouldn't risk playing games.'

Paloma sighed now, lifting back the voile curtains an inch or so to look outside. A car had pulled up in front of the house. A BMW, she noted, in a gorgeous metallic denim colour. She couldn't make out the driver properly, sunlight was glinting against the side window. The car rolled forwards a few feet behind next door's hedge, until all she could make out was the boot. Someone climbed out. A young man, broad-shouldered with a sandy-coloured crop and dark sunglasses. He crossed the road, hands tucked casually into the pockets of his slacks. Standing in front of the low church wall, he seemed to be looking directly at the Old Parsonage. Paloma moved back a little. The stranger, who seemed quite attractive at this distance and might be even more so at close proximity, turned to stare at St Mary Magdalene's before glancing all around and then crossing the road again. He disappeared from view. A minute later, the car drove off.

Paloma twiddled a spiral of hair around her finger. Perhaps, she speculated, the mystery man had knocked at the cottage next door and no one had been in. Perhaps he was lost. Perhaps he was planning a wedding and was looking for a picturesque church. Perhaps, perhaps, perhaps . . . She pouted wistfully, wishing he had knocked on *her* door, or rather Kate's. He looked like the kind of bloke a girl could happily take under her wing.

Giggling, she flopped on to the sofa, feeling a smidgen more cheerful as she reached for the TV remote.

Although the nights were now closing in with that characteristic, relentless November gloom, Kate couldn't remember ever being happier. Even the fact that she had her period wasn't blighting the exuberance bubbling up inside her. So it actually came as a surprise when, sitting in Dick's office on a Tuesday afternoon, he suggested she leave work early because she didn't look well.

'Don't I?' She put a hand to her face.

'Are you coming down with something? You're terribly pale.'

She was about to mumble discreetly that it was only the time of the month when she realised that tomorrow was the dreaded Golf Day.

'Actually,' she said, rubbing her brow, 'I've been feeling rotten since lunchtime.'

Dick was perched on the edge of his desk, skimming over correspondence she had typed and printed out for him. He looked down at her again. 'Is it something you ate, maybe?'

'I don't think so. It's probably more likely some bug Emmi's brought back from school.'

'Maybe you shouldn't come on the Golf Day tomorrow.'

She struggled not to smile. 'Oh, I'm sure I'll be fine.'

Dick regarded her intently. 'If you want my opinion, Kate, I think you should go home now, and if you're still feeling off colour tonight you should just stay home for a couple of days. I know you've been looking forward to tomorrow, but we can cope without you. And it won't do you any good to hang around outside in the cold.'

'Well, if you think you can spare me . . .'

'We'll manage somehow.' He waved the letters at her. 'Leave these with me, they're not that urgent. I'll get Nat to deal with any corrections on Thursday.'

'Oh,' Kate pulled her most concerned face, 'I don't want to add to Natalia's workload—'

'It's part of her job to help cover for you. Don't fret about it. If you're ill you're ill, you can't help it.'

Kate couldn't get out of the office soon enough. Downstairs in the lobby she picked up even more speed and almost charged outside into the descending darkness. It was only ten to four. She hated this time of year; it always felt as if she was working late even when she wasn't. The Underground sign loomed like a beacon on the other side of the road. She hit the button on the pedestrian crossing and waited impatiently.

Ten minutes later, she was collapsing into a seat as her train pulled out of Liverpool Street. She'd made it with seconds to spare. As soon as she got her breath back, she rummaged in her bag and drew out her phone. The number she wanted was now stored in the memory. It was answered after three rings.

'Llewellyn Limos.'

'Tom, it's me. I got out early. How about meeting at the pub at six instead of eight? We could have dinner—'

'I'll be there.'

Neither of them wanted to hang up. They made small-talk; ridiculous, considering they were going to see each other in less than two hours. By the time Kate pressed the button to end the call, she was already a third of the way home. With a sigh, she gazed out of the window into the inky blackness beyond her reflection.

'Mummy, are we still going to Tom's again on Sunday?'

Kate looked up from the mirror where she was applying her make-up. Emmi was dangling her legs over the bed and wielding a crimson lipstick dangerously close to the pristine white duvet. Kate winced. 'Yes, darling. Why? You still want to go, don't you?'

Her daughter nodded. 'I want to see Tina and Ronan.'

'And you like Tom, too, don't you?'

'He's funny. Do you love him?'

Kate almost prodded herself in the eye with the mascara wand. 'What?'

'It's Friday now, and you've seen him nearly every

night this week. Melanie at school says you *must* be in love.'

'We've only gone out twice so far this week,' Kate pointed out hastily, sweeping the lipstick out of Emmi's hand. 'And I've only known him for a short while.'

'So?'

'So it's far too soon to be talking about love.'

Kate looked at herself in the mirror. She was twenty-seven in a few months' time, and she'd never experienced that exalted surge of emotion, never been hooked on it, never let it control her . . . not with a man at least. The only time she could claim to have fallen in love had been during that week-long stay in hospital with her new-born baby lying in a plastic cot by her bedside.

'Can I do your make-up, Mummy?' Emmi was asking.

'Um . . . not tonight, sweetie. Another time, for fun.'

'I'm getting good at it, though.'

'Of course you are,' Kate assured her. On the last occasion that Emmi had done her make-up, she'd looked like a cheap tart. Not the best time for her mother to have called round.

'It's been nice having you home when I get back from school,' said the little girl.

'I know it has, but I've got to go back to work on Monday.'

'Can't you stay off longer?'

'No, darling. I'm much better now.' Kate was feeling guilty for having skived off this long.

'Have a holiday then.'

'I can't, or I won't have any days left to take between Christmas and New Year.'

Emmi folded her arms over her chest. Kate put down the make-up mirror. 'How about if I try to get home earlier every night.'

'You always say that, but then you hardly ever *are*.'

Kate stared thoughtfully at a tiny stain on the ecru twist carpet. Since spending last Sunday at Tom's, Emmi had been noticeably more bouncy and giggly and . . . childlike. Now she seemed forlorn, and Kate's first instinct was to cheer her up. She looked at her watch. There was still time. But would Tom agree?

'Emmi,' she said, 'why don't you go and see what Paloma's doing? I've just got to make a quick call. Please, darling, it's important.'

Reluctantly, the little girl shuffled out. Kate picked up the phone from the bedside table.

'T–*om*,' she began tentatively, once he'd answered, 'I know you've probably got a perfect romantic evening planned, but you know that new Disney film that's just started showing at the Odeon . . .'

9

Heart in her mouth, Kate watched as her sister wobbled precariously into the kitchen. Annabel's sequinned basque – or was it a boob-tube? – glittered under the harsh fluorescent lights. Kate had gone for more subtle illumination at the Old Parsonage; then again, her kitchen was only half the size of this one. She blinked, still trying to work out how to classify her sister's top. It had been puzzling her all evening.

'Coffee?' asked Annabel. 'Tea?'

'Coffee,' said Kate, 'and I'll make it. We'll have instant, it's less palaver. You just sit down.'

Annabel swayed towards the breakfast bar. She gave a futile tug on her microscopic skirt, but the tops of her hold-ups were still visible. 'Suddenly,' she sighed, 'I feel really very tired.'

Kate frowned. She had never seen Annabel drunk. Tipsy, yes, but not hammered. 'You've changed where you keep the coffee.'

'It's in the cupboard by the window. I was bored one day so I rearranged everything.'

'I thought Sam and Suzy would keep you busy.'

'Jeanette takes care of all that mostly.'

'I suppose that's what you employ a nanny for,' shrugged Kate.

'*I* don't employ her, do I? It's Oliver who pays her wages.'

'But if you don't want her . . .'

'It's not a case of wanting. Oliver says we need one. Practically everyone in his department has one.'

'But maybe the wives work. Like I do. If you're home all day—'

'I do go shopping quite a bit.'

Kate shook her head in exasperation. 'Are you still taking sweeteners?' Since giving birth to the twins, Annabel's figure had gone from stick-insect to Barbie doll. She looked fantastic, but moaned unoriginally that her bum was too big.

'Sweeteners? Mmm.' Annabel seemed miles away.

Kate ran through the evening in her head as she waited for the kettle to boil. She had driven over to her sister's, which was a good forty minutes away on the other side of Addenham. From there, they'd caught a taxi into Addenham itself, descending on a pub first to 'warm up'. Annabel's idea of warming up had been to knock back as many Archers and lemonades as possible in the least amount of time. The club they had gone on to was the only place locally with a DJ and a dance-floor. Ibiza – as it was called, tongue firmly in cheek – was also quite small, and now that the terrace was closed off for the winter . . . Kate shuddered at the recollection and was glad that she hadn't been born a sardine.

In vain, she'd suggested to Annabel that they pace

themselves, and by the time they'd got to Ibiza she was already on the lime and sodas herself. She hadn't been able to keep up. She hadn't wanted to, not if she ended up acting as weirdly as her sister. Annabel was a different person. But maybe, Kate realised, as she carefully poured hot water over the Carte Noire granules, they spent so little time together that they simply didn't know each other any more.

'It was a shame no one else could come,' lamented Annabel for the umpteenth time, twirling a strand of waist-length, highlighted hair around her finger.

Kate bit her lip guiltily, also for the umpteenth time. On her part, she hadn't asked anyone. None of the few people she could claim to call friends were particularly close to Annabel. Besides, they lived miles away and she hadn't seen them in ages.

'Never mind,' she said reassuringly. 'Life's not the same as it used to be. Everyone's so busy these days. At least Mum organised your party on Sunday well in advance.'

'Huh,' Annabel grunted.

'Bella' – reverting to the childhood moniker, Kate joined her sister at the breakfast bar – 'is everything OK with you?'

'What d'you mean?' Annabel frowned into the milk jug as if it was empty rather than full.

'Well, you don't normally . . . *drink* so much. Not in the space of one evening.'

'I just felt like it.'

'But—'

'You don't realise how lucky you are, Kate,' Annabel

stated vehemently. 'You've got Emmi, but you've got your career too.'

'I'd hardly call it that,' Kate snorted.

'But you do,' said Annabel. 'I've heard you. What else is it?'

Annabel was right. Kate did refer to her secretarial work as a career, but it wasn't what she wanted to do long-term. She'd applied for a job at Anthony & Gray to be nearer to her first love – art and design. Yet it was frustrating to be so close when she was employed as a PA and not an art director. One day, though, she might come up with an idea that would make Dick and Charles take notice of her talent. This small glimmer of hope was really the only career path she could afford. But she hadn't come up with anything extraordinary enough yet, so she'd kept her ideas to herself. In her opinion, there was no point sharing them if they weren't going to set the world – or Anthony & Gray at least – on fire.

'I wish *I* did something,' Annabel was saying, 'even if it was just being a wife and mum.'

'You are a wife and mum.'

'Then why don't I feel like one?'

There was a depth and an edge to her sister that Kate hadn't come across before. She sensed that Annabel already knew the answer to her own question.

Just then, they heard a thump above them, followed by a succession of thuds as someone came down the stairs. A moment later, Oliver Bartholomew Redwood made his entrance, hands on hips, just below the burgundy cord of his dressing gown. Paisley pyjamas peeked out around his ankles. In a histrionic gesture, he swept his hair off his brow and stared at the kitchen clock for longer than was necessary before turning to them and saying calmly, 'Good *morning*, ladies.'

'Good morning, Oliver,' they tinkled back with uncanny synchronisation.

'I take it you had a pleasant evening?'

Kate flicked her gaze over his paunch. As if he were pregnant, his waistline seemed to have expanded every time she saw him.

'We had a brilliant time,' effused Annabel.

'So the disco met your expectations then?' continued her husband.

'They're not called discos any more, darling.'

'Whatever.'

'Would you like to join us for coffee?' She smiled sweetly.

He shook his head, pushing back his hair again. The Heseltine look wasn't quite so dashing on him any more, noted Kate. Not with all that extra weight. 'I just came down to see what all the commotion was about,' he said. 'Fortunately, you haven't woken the twins. They're fine, by the way.'

'Why shouldn't they be?' asked Annabel ingenuously. 'They're in far better hands than they'd be with me. Jeanette has qualifications, after all.'

'Well,' grumbled Oliver, 'I'm pleased you enjoyed yourself. I take it you'll be coming to bed soon?'

'Of course,' said Annabel. 'In a while.'

'Jeanette made up the futon in the guest room.' He smiled at Kate, if a little tensely. 'I hope you'll be comfortable.'

He sounded so much like a hotelier that she nodded politely and assured him that she would be. Without another word, he pivoted on his burgundy-slippered heel and left. There was a thud, thud, thud as he climbed the stairs. When Kate was sure that he was out of earshot, she turned to Annabel.

'Doesn't he mind you dressing like that?' She gestured to Annabel's get-up.

'Do you think he noticed?'

Kate frowned. Had her sister really been as drunk as she'd made out, or had the caffeine already blasted into her system? 'I'm sure he did. He couldn't *not* have earlier this evening, the way you were parading around the living room.'

'Well then, why didn't he say anything?' Annabel smiled, displaying perfect, albeit orthodontically corrected, teeth. 'Maybe I'll go upstairs now and play the blonde bimbo to his sugar daddy. He can be quite kinky when he wants.'

'I didn't need to know that.'

'We are married, you know. But then you always were a bit prudish about the facts of life. I never could work out how you got pregnant with Emmi.'

Kate felt her spine stiffen. 'Just because I don't bed-hop—'

'Don't jump down my throat! I didn't mean it to sound disparaging. I've never bed-hopped either, what's to boast about that? It's just that you were always the shy one around boys. And when there was the slightest reference to sex on TV or somewhere, you used to blush like a beetroot.'

How the hell did wimpish, whiny, empty-headed Annabel know what 'disparaging' meant? And how dare she say all these things that were so . . . so . . . *true*, sniffed Kate, clenching a fist under the breakfast bar as if gearing up to throw a punch.

Annabel drained the last of her coffee and put down her Denby mug very gingerly and precisely. 'Speaking of sex, have you heard from Harry lately?'

'Of course not!' Tom had asked her the same question only the other day, and now Kate gave the same standard reply: 'I'll get a card at Christmas, as usual, or maybe a phone call, if I'm lucky.'

'Well Cape Town isn't exactly round the corner.'

'No,' she mumbled. 'S'pose not.'

'At least you do hear from him. He hasn't just dropped off the face of the earth.'

'For all the good it does. Anyway,' Kate heard herself say, although she'd vowed she wasn't going to mention it, 'Harry's in the past. The present's much more interesting . . .' She tailed off, kicking herself.

'Really?' Annabel leaned towards her.

'Yes, um, I wasn't going to say anything, it was meant to be a surprise, but I'm – er – bringing someone along to your party on Sunday. Hope you don't mind?'

'Mind?' Annabel looked genuinely delighted. 'Steal my thunder, *please*, it'll give me a breather. Who is he? Where did you meet him? What's he look like?'

Kate couldn't help smiling at the bombardment. It suddenly felt very right to be sitting in a warm kitchen with her sister, discussing love, life and men. The fact that she was exhausted because it was nearly three o'clock in the morning rather than three in the afternoon was the only downside, but perhaps, in a way, that felt right too . . .

'Katie's got a boyfriend,' chanted Annabel gleefully.

It was going to be a long night. The futon would just have to wait.

Kate sincerely hoped that she'd been supplied with a guardian angel. Her grandmother had believed in them, and Kate had seen no harm in telling Emmi that they existed, as long as you didn't take it to mean that you could be as foolhardy and irresponsible as you liked because you knew you'd be safe. Kate was being foolhardy and irresponsible right now, so on second thoughts her angel had probably crossed his wings and was standing well back in order to teach her a lesson – that she shouldn't be driving. Not right now. She was far too tired after the night before.

She'd had less than three hours sleep in the end, because even after Annabel had finally let her go to bed, she'd lain awake for ages staring up at the shadows on the ceiling, thinking about Tom as if talking about him hadn't been enough.

'Mummy, why are we going so slowly?' piped up Emmi, glancing round at the queue of traffic building up behind them as they left Addenham.

'There's, um, something wrong with the car,' lied Kate.

'Really? What?'

'Er . . . the clutch. The clutch is wrong.'

'Are we going to break down?'

Kate shook her head. Sod it, her brain hurt. 'No, no, we'll make it home, no problem.' Just so long as she kept the speed down. 'I'll, er, get Tom to take a look at it.'

She really would have to provide Paloma with a mobile phone, she decided, for 'emergencies' such as this. She'd tried ringing home before setting off from her sister's, but Paloma hadn't been in. Maybe she'd gone shopping after dropping Emmi off at ballet class. Anyway, the arrangement today had been that Kate – who usually dropped her daughter off at the class and picked her up too – would simply be in charge of collecting her on the way back from Annabel's. It had seemed a good plan at the time. Kate hadn't counted on feeling so knackered.

'Are you going out with Tom tonight, Mummy?'

In spite of her general state of grottiness, Kate began to drool just picturing him. But so much more important than his firm biceps, thick dark hair, penetrating eyes – when she was snuggled against him the world seemed a much kinder place.

'Uh-huh,' she nodded dreamily.

'When do you think we'll go to the cinema again?'

So that was it. 'Definitely not tonight, young lady.'

Grumpily, Emmi folded her arms over her chest.

'I'm sorry, darling,' Kate added, 'but I haven't seen Tom in days. You know better than anyone that I've had to work late.'

'I *knew* you'd have to. You said you'd try to get home earlier, but you never do.'

Lost for words, Kate glowered into the rear-view mirror. The old man in the car behind didn't look happy. Tough. People drove too fast anyway.

'Mummy, is Tom still coming to Aunty Annabel's party tomorrow?'

'Yes. So you'll see lots of him there. Tonight we wanted to go out for a quiet dinner, just the two of us.'

'OK then,' said Emmi, as if granting permission. 'Do you think I can still have some nachos later anyway, like at the cinema?'

'Hmm. Maybe if you ask Paloma nicely . . .'

'I think Paloma's great.'

'Yes, she is,' agreed Kate. Ironically, she was beginning to find her indispensable. So what if she still hadn't learned where the fabric softener went in the washing machine? She could cook a mean shepherd's pie, and she'd perfected her sewing skills so that Kate was only too willing to hand over any new clothes that needed altering. It was liberating not to have to buy petite any more.

The hedge-flanked lane they were trundling down was now widening into Main Street, Beckton Lacey. The hedgerow disappeared, replaced initially by a row of stone cottages and then by newer houses and bungalows. St Mary Magdalene's distinctive pale steeple rose ahead. As Kate prepared to pull up in her usual spot in front of the Old Parsonage, she frowned as she realised there was already a car parked there. A BMW, behind Paloma's ancient Beetle.

Whose was it?

'Is Tom here, Mummy?' asked Emmi excitedly. 'He was talking about getting a new car!'

He *had* been thinking about it. Something bigger than the MG, he'd said, and newer than any of the beauties in his 'harem', as he'd jokingly called the collection in his barn. Kate hadn't actually thought he meant a Beamer, though. And he'd got hold of it rather sharpish. It looked brand new. Weren't there waiting lists for cars like this? Could he actually have afforded it?

She parked with her bumper encroaching an inch or two over next door's drive. Emmi clambered out first and skipped across to the shiny blue car, circling it as if she were a *Top Gear* fanatic rather than a six-year-old girl. Suddenly, out of the corner of her eye, Kate saw a flash of grey and black. Paloma was rushing down the garden path towards them, glossy curls bouncing over her skin-tight tracksuit. The nanny looked askance at Emmi, who was still examining the Beamer, then hurried over to Kate.

'He's here,' she said urgently, keeping her voice low. 'I'd been out jogging – I've gained five bloody pounds this week – and when I came back, there he was, on the doorstep.'

'So?'

'So maybe I should take Emmi out to lunch somewhere while you talk.'

'Why?'

'He said you weren't expecting him.'

'Not this morning,' said Kate. 'We're supposed to be having dinner later, though.'

Paloma looked puzzled, then realisation dawned. 'Not *Tom*. It's not Tom who's here.'

Kate wrinkled her brow. 'Then who . . . ?'

'It's Harry,' muttered Paloma. 'Harry Barrett!'

10

'Hello, Kate. You haven't changed.'

She came to a halt in the doorway between the kitchen and the living room. On the other side of the table, with a cup of tea in front of him, right beside his car keys, wallet and minuscule mobile phone, was the most divine man she had ever seen. And there wasn't a nose-stud in sight.

'I – I can't say the same about you,' she croaked, unable to tear her gaze away. This was Harry, yes, but the Harry she'd known at university had been a scrawny boy compared to this magnificently toned male before her. His hair, once an overbleached fuzz barely covering his scalp, was now a smart, slightly longer crop. He'd let it grow out to its natural colour, enviably sun-kissed around the temples.

He grinned. 'I have changed a little.' How long *was* it since they'd last spoken on the phone? His voice had acquired a trace of an accent. Anyone who didn't know him could take a calculated guess that he had been living in South Africa. 'I hope it's a change for the better,' he added.

Lost for words, and feeling five times more exhausted than before, Kate collapsed into the nearest chair.

'Your nanny was very hospitable,' Harry continued. 'If a little on edge. She kept leaping up to look out of the window. Waiting for you to come home, I presumed, so she could warn you I was here.'

'Paloma's very loyal.'

'Hardly Mary Poppins, though.'

'Emmi adores her and she adores Emmi. That's what counts.'

He nodded. 'I suppose. How *is* Emmeline?'

Kate wanted to blurt out that their little girl was wonderful, stupendous, a miraculous human being – as if to make him feel guilty. But on the other hand, she reminded herself, where exactly did his guilt lie?

'Emmi's fine,' she said.

'I'm glad to hear it.'

'Paloma's taken her out to lunch.'

'I guessed it was something like that.'

'It isn't that I don't want you to see her—'

'We've a lot to discuss on our own first, I know.'

She managed to prise her gaze away. There were crumbs scattered over the table. Paloma had evidently forgotten to clear up after breakfast, but Kate couldn't care less at the moment.

She lifted her eyes to his again. 'Harry . . . what exactly are you doing here?'

'I'm sorry,' he sighed. 'I shouldn't have turned up like this. The thing is, I came round once before, a couple of weeks ago, but I chickened out. I couldn't bring myself to knock on your door.'

'Why didn't you just phone me?'

'I suppose I didn't want to give you time to prepare.

To rehearse what you were going to say, how you were going to react. I wanted this meeting to be spontaneous.'

'But it isn't,' she pointed out. 'It's bloody unfair. You had plenty of time to "rehearse", so why couldn't I?'

In a nervous gesture he crooked a forefinger and scratched his jaw. Kate felt a surge of familiarity, as if they were sitting in the cruddy communal kitchen back in Halls, sipping tea out of cracked mugs and moaning that they were practically skint.

'This isn't easy for me,' he said softly.

'Oh, but it's a doddle for me, is it?'

'My own daughter doesn't even know me. Have you ever wondered how I feel about that?'

'She knows *of* you,' Kate volleyed back defensively. 'The first time she asked why she didn't have a daddy, I didn't know what to say. All the explanations I'd thought of just flew out of the window.'

'So what exactly—'

'I've tried to make her believe that you didn't abandon her.'

'I didn't, Kate. You broke up with me.'

He wasn't, *wasn't* going to make her feel bad about that. 'Kids don't see things like adults do. I've steered her off the subject as much as possible. She understands that you live a long way away. I've explained how we wouldn't have been happy together, and that we couldn't have made her happy, either. It's a sign of the times that she's accepted it so easily. She isn't the only child at school from a one-parent family.'

Harry was staring at her, rapt. 'I was wrong, Kate. You have changed. Not physically, you were always pretty. But you're tougher, more clued-up.'

He'd often called her pretty, Kate remembered, but usually when he was up to his eyeballs in cheap vodka, not PG Tips. As the realisation hit home that this was the first man who'd ever touched, kissed or held her intimately, a hot rush flooded through her.

'It looks like we've both been working hard since uni,' Harry continued smoothly.

'I've had to,' said Kate, adding, for want of something more original, 'Money doesn't grow on trees.'

'Why didn't you accept any of my offers to help? These last few years, I haven't been doing too badly.'

'Yes, well, I can see that now.' She'd thought he had just been bragging, typical of the Harry she'd known – full of pipe-dreams, but not the dedication he'd need to achieve them. 'Is the car yours?'

He nodded. 'I've only had it three weeks. I ordered it when I knew I was coming back to the UK.'

'How long have you been back exactly?'

'A month. Perfect timing, really. With the car, I mean.'

A month. Longer than she'd been going out with Tom. None of this was perfect timing as far as she was concerned. 'How – How long are you planning on staying for? Are you taking the car back with you? Surely they have Beamers out there?'

For a few seconds, he didn't reply. She frowned at him. His eyes were cornflower blue. She recollected that she'd always been envious of them. To the uninitiated he might appear cool and confident, but Kate knew otherwise. He was staring at her intently again, even as he fiddled with his high-tech diver's watch, betraying how he really felt: he'd always been a fidgeter when cornered.

'What would you say if I told you I'm not going back to South Africa? Not to live, at least.'

Apparently, she wouldn't say anything. She was speechless again.

'I'm back in the UK for good,' he said. 'And I'd like to get to know my daughter.'

The shock was beginning to wear off, replaced by an anger that stemmed both from her exhaustion and the fact that this had all been sprung on her without warning. Kate tried to untangle the diverse strands of her thoughts, but they were intractably knotted. She wanted Harry to leave, to give her time and space to get to grips with his news. Her gaze swung between him and the clock.

'You want me out of here, don't you?' He sounded resigned.

'I need to think clearly, and to prepare Emmi.'

'Does she know what I look like? Or rather, what I used to look like.'

'I showed her a picture of us at Glastonbury. It was the only decent one I had.'

'Basically, I don't look like too much of a tosser in it.'

'You looked relatively normal that weekend, compared to everyone else.'

A chuckle rose in his throat. 'Neither of us struck out on our own very originally or convincingly, did we? Look at me now; in some ways I used to despise the kind of person I've become.' He picked up his tiny mobile phone. 'You see this. It's top of the range, state of the art—'

'Not cheap,' she interjected.

'No. But I've slogged my guts out for it all, Kate. And maybe, somewhere along the line, I've lost something important. I've sacrificed my personal life. I've lost touch with the real me. Maybe the problem is that I don't know who I am any more.'

She wanted to snap, 'Bullshit', but he looked so earnest and attractive that she crumbled and muttered, 'Really?'

'After university, I drifted into IT – software design to be precise – simply because it was there, and I was so broke I couldn't even afford shoelaces, let alone shoes. No one was more surprised than me to find out I was actually good at it. Then, when I got the contract in South Africa, that was that. I had faith in myself, in what I could do. The money I was on would have supported a small third world nation.'

'If it was so great, why come back?'

'Because life as an expat, as a contractor, couldn't go on forever. Not for me. I needed a new challenge.'

'Of course,' said Kate, a tad insincerely, 'you're trying to find yourself again.'

'I'm starting my own company,' he announced quietly. 'Eventually I'll have people working for me, not the other way around. I've already negotiated some premises, close to Watford. Excellent access to the M25, and London, of course. And for now I'm renting a flat, too, but I'll be looking to buy my own place in the next couple of months, as an investment, if nothing else.'

Kate felt like the nodding dog in Paloma's car. 'Wow,' she murmured. 'You've got it all planned out.'

'You have to these days. Do you want to know what I'm calling the firm?'

'Do I?'

'Aztek.' He spelled it out for her, then waited, as if for her approval.

'You've spelt it wrong. Or is it supposed to mean something, other than the ancient civilisation?'

'I took the initials from all the important people in my life, past and present, and jumbled them together. I couldn't believe my luck when I came up with that. Especially with the "tek" on the end.'

'It has a certain . . . something.' She paused. 'Who are these important people exactly?'

'Adam, after my brother; Zak, after Dad; Tess, for my mum . . . E, for Emmeline, and lastly, K – for Kate.'

'Me?'

'Why not you? You're the mother of my only child. I think that makes you fairly important.'

'Yes,' she spluttered, 'but . . .'

'But what? You were special, Kate. You still are. What we had, our relationship . . . It may not have meant much to you, but I've never come close to anything like it since.'

How was she supposed to respond to that? What was wrong with her? This man was Emmi's father, and yet she hadn't held him in her heart with any kind of reverence. These last few years, she'd come to look on the situation as a simple fact of life. Yes, she'd had a baby, quite unintentionally, and Harry – also unintentionally – had provided the sperm, but that was where his role as a father had come to an end. Neither of them had wanted it to go further . . . had they?

Kate tried to cobble together some sort of reply. 'Harry, when I split up with you, it was because I knew, deep down, that you didn't want to be saddled with the responsibility of a family. We were both so young, and we weren't . . . We weren't right for each other.'

'That's such a cliché, Kate. Besides, I know why you went out with me in the first place. To get back at your parents. I was the last person they wanted you to shack up with. It's OK, don't look at me like that. Did you think I hadn't realised? The only reason I put up with it was because I loved you.'

Bloody hell, she didn't need this. Bombshell after bombshell, and meanwhile the kitchen clock ticked on relentlessly.

'You never said any of this seven years ago,' Kate retorted belligerently. 'You looked relieved when I broke it off between us. I absolved you of all responsibility when it came to our unborn child, and you didn't argue about it. Now you waltz in here after all these years—'

'Please, Kate, don't be dramatic.'

'*Me?* Dramatic?' He was the one turning it into a soap opera.

'Haven't you heard the saying, "If you love something, set it free . . ."'

133

'"If it comes back, it's yours."' sighed Kate. '"If it doesn't, it never was."' This was more like the old Harry: full of philosophical twaddle, although he'd usually reserved it for four in the morning, after several hours on the aforementioned vodka.

'It took me a long time to realise you were never going to be mine, Kate. But you can't "absolve" me from my responsibility when it comes to Emmi. No one can. I'm her father. It's as straightforward as that.'

Kate wanted to put her hands over her ears and sing, even though she was tone deaf. Anything to drown out Harry's voice, his words, and the ominous sense that her life was being invaded by an unwanted presence bent on wreaking havoc.

'Why now?' she demanded instead. 'After all these years. I can't believe you haven't come to the UK before.'

A shadow crossed his face. 'I have. Flying visits, though. There was no point telling you. I didn't want Emmi getting confused, which is all those trips would have amounted to.'

Kate couldn't pick holes in that.

'Can I ask you something?' he went on.

'What?'

'Are you seeing anyone at the moment?'

'What difference does that make?'

'You're right, it shouldn't. But if Emmi's life is already being disrupted—'

'Emmi thinks the world of Tom!'

'So how long have you been going out with this . . . Tom?'

Kate frowned. 'Not long. A few weeks.'

'So it's not serious then?'

'No,' she said, 'I suppose not. It's too soon, and I don't think—'

Harry leaned forwards. 'What?'

'Well, I wasn't looking for anything long-term.'

'But you introduced him to Emmi?'

'Yes, but . . .' Kate felt as if Harry had her trapped. 'It's complicated.'

'So I see.'

'I think it's time you left,' she muttered stroppily.

He glanced at his watch and sighed. 'You're right. I wouldn't want to outstay my welcome.' Gathering up his belongings, he scraped back his chair and stood up.

'I'll see you out,' said Kate, barely concealing her relief.

Once in the hall, though, she hovered by the pedestal table, glancing at the jotter pad next to the phone. Her mature, reasonable self took over, and she found herself scribbling down her e-mail address and work number.

He nodded gratefully as she handed them to him. 'I appreciate this, Kate. I'll be in touch in a couple of days, when you've had time to think things through.'

'Goodbye, Harry.'

She watched him walk down the path towards the car. Next door, her pernickety middle-aged neighbour was attempting to back his Nissan Micra into the road, his wife directing him out, as usual. They didn't seem pleased that her car was encroaching over their drive, even though a JCB could have passed through the gap Kate had left them.

Feeling as if the whole world was conspiring against her, Kate slammed the front door before Harry had even driven away.

11

'Here they come,' murmured Kate, 'brace your-self . . .'

Tom wet his lips, preparing to form a wide, disarming smile. He knew exactly how to handle people like the man and woman making a bee-line towards them. One mention of his mother's name usually did the trick. He tugged at the sleeves of his jacket, knowing Kate appre-ciated the trouble he'd gone to. He'd even scrubbed under his nails and clipped them into neat squares, drawing the line at buffing them, though; he wasn't *that* much of a New Man.

Kate's mother was wearing a long, floaty, yellow and orange number, more suited to a summer wedding and someone who was taller and thinner, but she had a startlingly attractive face, with golden hair layered all around it and remarkably few wrinkles for her age. Kate's father was an inch or two shorter than his wife, and more than an inch or two wider around the middle. His grey hair was thinning, his face was deeply lined and his neck flaccid. It was hard to imagine what he would have looked like in his youth, or why a stunner like Kate's mother would have fallen for him when she'd probably had her pick of suitors.

'So pleased to meet you.' Mrs Finlay shuddered to a stop in front of Tom and held out her hand.

'Mum,' said Kate, 'this is Tom Llewellyn.'

'Llewellyn. Would I know your mother?'

'Perhaps . . . Eloise Llewellyn, her maiden name was Hamilton?' Tom knew precisely what to say next. 'She's from these parts, but now lives in London. Richmond, to be precise. Her garden overlooks the river.'

Glynis Finlay's eyes sparkled at the thrill of it. 'Didn't she head the WI in Addenham?'

'So you do know her?' said Tom, injecting pleasure into his voice. 'I'll have to pass on your regards next time I speak to her . . .'

'He's perfect.'

'Do you think so?' Kate looked askance at her sister, then back across the room towards Tom, who was helping himself to the buffet.

Annabel licked her lips salaciously.

'Oi,' said Kate, 'you're married.'

'And you're not. Which is perfect too. Imagine being besotted with him if you weren't single.'

'Don't be silly! I'm not besotted with him.'

'Oh no, I forgot. You just like talking about him till four-thirty in the morning.'

'If you hadn't kept asking me all those questions . . .'

'Keep your hair on.' Annabel flicked back her own poker-straight tresses. 'You've done OK, Katie. Just don't go and blow it.'

'There's nothing to blow,' snapped Kate, then turned pink. 'And don't call me Katie.'

'Tom Llewellyn,' Annabel was repeating, over and over. 'He sounds familiar. The name struck a chord the other day, but now that I've actually seen him it's bugging me even more. Has he ever done any acting?'

Kate sighed, keeping an eye on Emmi, who was pushing one of her baby cousins around the conservatory in a toy coupé. 'Not as far as I know.'

'No, not acting' – the cogs in Annabel's brain seemed to be working overtime – '*writing!* Has he ever done any writing? I remember now, I used to love a daily newspaper column by a Tom J. Llewellyn. Can't remember which paper, it was one of the tabloids. Oliver'd tut at me for reading it. Anyhow, Tom looks familiar too, and there used to be this fuzzy little photo—'

Kate had only ever seen her sister flicking through *OK* or *Hello!* magazines. 'Tom doesn't write,' she scoffed. 'And his middle name's . . . Oh.' She frowned. 'His middle name's James. But that doesn't mean anything. He can't be the only Tom J. Llewellyn.'

'S'pose not.' Annabel picked at her lilac nail varnish.

Kate remembered Tom's study. Her frown deepened. 'What were these columns about, anyway?'

'Nothing specific. He used to make these funny observations about life. But I'm talking a couple of years back, maybe longer. As I recall, the column just stopped one day and they ran something else in its place, but it wasn't half as good. Would you like me to ask Tom about it? See if it was him?'

Kate shook her head vehemently. 'Of course not. He must have been sick of people asking him that. Besides, he would have told me if he'd been a writer, it's nothing to be ashamed of. Now, are you going to rescue Sammy before Emmi steers him into that yucca plant, or shall I?'

'So,' said Oliver, 'these cars of yours – how many have you got?'

Tom watched as Annabel's husband tucked voraciously into a mushroom vol-au-vent. An image of Henry VIII ripping at a chicken leg with his bare teeth flashed across Tom's mind. 'Er,' he replied distractedly, 'around twelve at the last count. But that's including the MG for my personal use.'

'When did this fad start then?'

Tom took a sip of the poncy European lager Kate's dad had proudly poured out for him. It tasted revolting, but Tom hadn't been in the mood for wine. 'It's, um, not technically a fad. I've been collecting them for over ten years. My father got me into it. I was always hanging out at auctions and rallies with him. He owned five vintage motors, true beauties. When he moved to Spain, he left them to me. That really boosted my collection.'

'So you add to it as and when you can afford to?'

Tom felt as if he was being interviewed by his bank manager. 'Er, I suppose so. The thing is, I get attached to cars. I've never been able to part with one, even when they're well and truly knackered in.' Oliver seemed to be choking on his vol-au-vent. Tom paused a second, to give him a chance to recover, then went on, 'Only about seventy per cent of the motors in my garage actually run, and I use about four or five on a regular basis.'

'An expensive hobby you've got there.'

Tom frowned slightly. 'Yes, it *used* to be a hobby. But when I decided to try to make money out of it—'

'So it is profitable then?'

'Anything concerning weddings usually is. That's what I use them for mostly. Although I do get the occasional birthday. And the other day, someone proposed to his girlfriend in my Armstrong Whitworth.'

'Really?' Oliver didn't look impressed. 'So, how long has Llewellyn Limos been in existence?'

Tom's awkwardness increased as Kate drifted over to join them. She was holding a plate laden with sandwiches, salad and some quiche, but didn't seem to be eating any of it. 'I started Llewellyn Limos about five years ago,' he explained to her brother-in-law. 'After I moved to The Croft and converted the barn into a garage. But it was only on a casual part-time basis then. Almost for fun, really. An old university friend dared me into it.'

'I see.' Oliver nodded. Tom half-expected him to whip out a form and start filling it in, like a mortgage application. 'What did you read at university?' was the next question.

'English,' muttered Tom, taking a gulp of the foul-tasting lager.

'I didn't know that,' said Kate.

'I suppose you never asked. It was at Edinburgh.'

'Right,' said Oliver. 'Edinburgh. So what did you actually do once you left?'

'Do?' echoed Tom, the familiar knot tightening in his stomach.

'Annabel's got it into her head that you used to write a newspaper column,' said Kate.

'Oh.' Tom recalled the dream he sometimes had when he found himself naked in the middle of a crowded room. 'That.'

He sensed Kate stiffen. Her eyes narrowed slightly. 'Is it true?'

'Well' – Tom swallowed hard – 'partly.'

'Partly?'

'I was freelance as well. I used to write features and articles and . . . stuff.'

'But you don't any more?' Oliver looked perplexed.

'No,' said Tom. 'I don't.'

'Kate . . .' It was her mother, bearing down upon them like a giant sunflower and bursting imperiously into the conversation. 'Emmi's fallen over outside and grazed her knee. I think you ought to come. Annabel's trying to deal with it on her own.'

'OK,' sighed Kate. 'Here, take this.' And Tom found himself holding her plate in one hand and his lager in the other.

'So,' broached Oliver, 'you were a writer—'

'Yes,' snapped Tom flippantly, 'but then I found salvation teaching golf.'

'Golf?' Oliver was looking more bewildered by the second.

'Didn't Kate tell you I'm a professional?' Tom felt perversely defiant now. 'I give lessons in my spare time for a bit of extra cash.' He winked. 'But don't tell the tax man.' And he laughed in a brittle manner, while Oliver stared at him dumbfounded over another mushroom vol-au-vent.

'Kate . . .'

She looked up from the empty dishes she'd just carried to the kitchen at her mother's behest. 'Hi, Grandad.'

He smiled at her gently, adjusting his tie. Kate knew he'd only worn it because it was a special occasion. Unlike many of his peers, he detested ties and cravats, and the one suit he owned only came out of retirement three or four times a year. 'I haven't had the opportunity of telling you this before,' he confided, 'but I like him. I like him a great deal.'

'You mean Tom?'

'I spoke to him for quite a while. He approached *me*, I might add, not the other way around, in case you were about to accuse me of not minding my own business.'

'It is your business, though.'

'Not really. What matters most is that you like him.'

'I don't even know him, Grandad. I thought I did, but . . .' She sighed in frustration. 'I've just found out today that he used to be a writer. It was embarrassing, really. He'd never told me. He always spoke about his cars and golf as if they were the only things he'd ever done. I suppose I just assumed . . .'

'It's easy to assume a lot of things when you first start courting someone. Unless you ask them to fill out a detailed questionnaire,' her grandfather continued wryly, 'much of what you learn is in fragments. As you piece them together, you need guesswork to fill in the gaps. It's early days, Kate.'

'But something that major,' she hissed, glancing over her shoulder as her mother bustled into the kitchen. 'I would have expected him to have told me by now.'

'It seems to me that your pride's been wounded. I'm sure that once you talk to him about it you'll calm down and realise it wasn't worth getting het up over.'

'Kate, darling,' said her mother impatiently, 'don't just leave those plates on the table. Stack them up by the others.'

'Yes, Mum.' Kate itched to just let go and watch them fall to their fate. It would have been intensely gratifying, if only for a millisecond. Instead, she put them carefully by the sink.

Her grandfather waited until Glynis had left the room before speaking again. 'Remember,' he said sagely, 'that people change occupations all the time, for a variety of reasons. Don't give Tom a hard time. I'm sure he would have told you when he was ready.'

Kate was about to grumble that she was fed up of platitudes, when she spotted Tom in the doorway. Flustered, she picked up a tea-towel and then dropped it. An image of Harry filled her mind. The new, undeniably attractive Harry. When was she going to tell Tom about him? It wasn't as if she hadn't had enough of an opportunity when they'd gone out to dinner yesterday. But, on the other hand, *what* was she going to tell him? It was so bloody complicated.

Her grandfather followed her gaze. 'I've just remembered,' he said, 'I really need a word with Oliver about my investment portfolio.' And he patted Tom's shoulder as the younger man moved aside to let him pass.

Kate grabbed the tea-towel again. 'Hello.'

'What are you doing in here?' Tom asked hesitantly.

'Er – drying plates.'

'But they all look dirty.'

'Do they?' Kate glanced around desperately. He was right. 'Well, I just wanted to help out.'

'I've a hunch that you're avoiding me.'

'Avoiding you? Why should I?'

'You haven't been yourself all afternoon. And I thought you were rather quiet yesterday. I just put it down to the fact that you were tired after your night out with your sister. But now—'

'Nothing's wrong,' she said quickly, feeling guilty. A moment later, on a note of anger, she turned the guilt on him. 'Why didn't you tell me, Tom? Something like that . . .'

'The writing?' He shrugged. 'It isn't important. It was just something I used to do. I suppose I would have told you eventually.'

'But why don't you do it any more? Did you just stop one day and throw yourself into Llewellyn Limos the next?'

He shook his head, coming closer. 'It wasn't like that. And this isn't the time or place to go into it. In fact, I don't think there's anything more I can say. I used to be a journalist, and then I wasn't. It's as simple as that.'

'But . . .' She faltered as his hand rested lightly against her hair.

'I didn't think I was any good at it,' frowned Tom. 'If a writer loses his confidence, that's it. The end.'

Kate bowed her head. She'd been petty and unfair. Tom lifted her chin, his lips advancing towards hers.

'I'm sorry,' she whispered.

But he didn't reply. Not verbally. His arms slid around her waist, pulling her close, and she forgot she was in her parents' kitchen and that her mother might burst in on them at any moment. Which was exactly what happened.

'Oh, gracious me!' cried Glynis Finlay, then spun around and went out again.

The bath was beginning to feel cold. Kate stretched across and turned the brass-coloured tap. As an afterthought she added more of the Royal Jelly bath salts Paloma had bought. When the temperature was comfortable again, she turned off the hot water and leaned her head back against a towelling heart-shaped pillow, suctioned to the other end of the bath. The water lapped up to her chin now, her hair floating against her neck and shoulders, like seaweed in a rock pool.

Thinking time. That was all she had wanted. An hour to herself to try to work out what would be the right thing to do. She felt as if she hadn't had a moment's peace since Harry had left yesterday. It had been one thing after another. Emmi and Paloma coming home . . . The date with Tom . . . Going over to Pagelton this morning to help her mother prepare for the party . . . But now, at last, total *aloneness*.

In some ways it was worse. There was no running away. No hiding. No choice but to face what was going on . . .

Harry had changed so much, she acknowledged, closing her eyes and confronting that fact first. In her mind, all these years, he hadn't altered. He'd still been bumming around in his scruffy T-shirts and ripped jeans, although the jeans had become shorts when he'd gone to South Africa. But she'd never once envisioned that he would turn out to be the kind of man he was now – the kind she'd found herself attracted to since she'd started working in London. Smart, successful, and therefore sexy.

Had he been sexy when she'd first met him? Kate wrinkled her nose. Not really. But he'd had a pleasant, cocky smile, and she'd been charmed by his attention. Most of all, she'd come to realise that becoming his girl-friend had been a sure-fire way of alarming her parents and taking the focus off Annabel for once.

What about Tom, though? Why exactly was she *his* girlfriend? Sometimes he could be smart and urbane, but quite often it was impossible to pigeon-hole him. This bothered her. For so many reasons, she was tired of rebelling. It was much easier to conform. And it made things run more smoothly for Emmi.

Opening her eyes, Kate looked heavenwards plead-ingly, somewhere beyond the small patch of mildew on the ceiling. What was she supposed to do? How was she going to deal with this?

12

'So' – Tom reached for a bottle from the wine-rack – 'what was it you wanted to talk about?'

'I won't have wine, thanks,' Kate demurred. 'Coffee or tea will be fine. In fact, on second thoughts, don't bother. I don't really want anything.'

He slid the bottle back into the rack and came over to where she stood. 'What's wrong?' His hands rested on her shoulders, gently massaging, but she pulled away. How could something so sensual jar on her nerves? Was it some sort of in-built self-defence mechanism: if she didn't feel his touch, his warmth, it would make it easier to say what she had to say?

'Kate, is this still to do with my not telling you I was a journo?'

She shook her head and wrapped her cardigan tighter around her, another form of defence perhaps. 'Can we go into the lounge and sit down or something?'

'Sure.' Tom knit his brow and led her through. 'I'll put the fire on.'

Kate watched him crouch down by the hearth, the flexed muscles of his back stretching the fabric of his shirt, which was riding up, revealing a patch of glistening flesh above the waistband of his jeans. She averted her gaze, looking at the threadbare Persian rug, then up at the long, heavy drapes over the window. Once the curtains would have been plum red, Kate guessed. Now they were faded and patchy. The sofa she was perched on made her feel like a shrunken Alice in Wonderland. It was the vibrant colour of ruby port, and so immense and soft and squashy she had loved it the minute she'd set eyes on it a few weeks ago. Tom had bought it from a second-hand furniture shop when he'd first moved in. Apparently a couple of former girlfriends had tried to cover it up with cream throws and tasselled cushions, but throws, cushions and ex-girlfriends had all been firmly relegated to the past. Kate had assured him it was best left plain, as a focal point for the room, but she'd concealed her other ideas for it, such as sinking into it with him, entwined in a long, luxurious smooch.

She shivered now at the vision of what-might-have-been. Her blood seemed to be running hot and cold with startling uncertainty. It would be so easy to reach out to him now. There was no Emmi around to interrupt them. But she tightened her resolve and struck back stoically at lust, because what else could she call it? What else was it but her inexperienced libido demanding satisfaction while the opportunity was there?

Tom rocked back on to his haunches, looking at her over his shoulder. 'Are you OK?'

Behind him, the fire sprung to life, radiating an instant heat.

'Do you remember when I told you about Emmi's dad?' Kate launched in, knowing her courage would desert her if she didn't get this over with quickly.

'Harry something-or-other.'

'Barrett. Harry Barrett.'

Tom hoisted himself up on to the sofa beside her, attempting to hold her hand. But she wouldn't let him. 'Kate, has something happened? Something to do with Harry?'

'You know I told you he was working in South Africa?'

'On contract.' Comprehension flitted across Tom's face. 'Is he back? Is that what you're trying to tell me?'

Kate nodded. 'He turned up on Saturday, out of the blue, no phone call or anything.'

'Bloody hell. He could have given you some warning.'

'It was a bit of a shock,' she admitted – an understatement. 'He's back in the UK now, starting up his own business. He's done really well for himself, better than I'd realised. And he's changed. He's so much more . . .' she could hardly say he was gorgeous '. . . mature.'

'Is he now?' said Tom dryly. 'You didn't mention any of this at your sister's party. Or when we went out to dinner even.'

'I needed time to think about it.'

'And what exactly does Harry want?'

'To get to know Emmi. I – I actually think he's ready for fatherhood now.'

'What about Emmi? Is she ready for him?'

Kate stared down at her nails. Her cuticles were in a state, as usual. 'I haven't told her yet,' she said. 'We're supposed to be seeing him this weekend. He wants to take us to lunch.'

'I see.' Tom raked a hand through his hair. 'And is Emmi the only one he wants to get close to?'

She felt her nostrils flare. 'What do you mean?'

'Oh, come on. It's all a bit cosy, isn't it? Am I supposed to just stand back and let him worm his way into your life again?'

'He's not worming into anything. Why are you acting so possessively?'

'Why?' Tom spluttered. 'Why?' His face froze for a moment, and then crumpled into something resembling defeat. 'What is it you're afraid to tell me, Kate?'

'It's just . . .' She knew what she ought to say, but the words stubbornly refused to leave her mouth.

'You think we should end this?' Tom prompted. 'Clear the way for Harry to reclaim his rightful position?'

'Now you're being silly.'

'Sorry.' He raised his hand in apology. 'I was forgetting how much more mature Harry is now. How old is he, after all? Twenty-six, twenty-seven?'

'Twenty-seven. And age has nothing to do with it.'

'Maybe not, but I'm well past my prime. Almost forty – in a little over five years.'

'My heart bleeds,' snapped Kate. What was wrong with him? Why couldn't he act like the adult he was claiming to be? 'I've got to put Emmi first,' she continued. 'And right now it would only confuse matters if we carried on seeing each other. She needs time to adjust to her dad coming back. That's more than enough for a six-year-old to take on board without having to worry about you and me as well.'

'Does she worry? I thought we all got along fine.'

'Nobody knows what's going on in her head. Not even me. It's hard for children to express themselves sometimes. They feel things so intensely, their emotions are so much a part of them . . . It's hard to explain. I just know that I've got to concentrate on Emmi. I can't afford to stress out about us, or where this is going.'

Tom was silent for a moment. 'And where *do* you think this is going?'

'I – I don't know.' She looked away again. There were tears stinging behind her eyes. Bloody ridiculous. At this early stage in their relationship all she could possibly feel for him was physical attraction. She had only known him a short while, it couldn't be anything else. And there was so much that she still didn't know, such as that business with his writing. Who could tell what might have happened given time?

'If you like,' he was saying slowly, 'we could just cool things for a while. Let Emmi come to terms with what's going on.'

She hesitated. He was being quite serious. 'But that's not fair. On you, I mean. I can't keep you hanging on like that.' She didn't sound convincing even to her own ears.

'What if I want to be kept hanging on?' His hand crept over hers on her lap. 'What if I don't mind sitting around waiting and hoping . . .' His other hand was inching under her chin, tipping her face upwards, his breath covering her mouth. How the hell had he got this close to her on the sofa without her noticing?

Suddenly, she felt her body straining towards his as if there were magnets in their lips and arms, irresistibly pulling them together. As their embrace grew more passionate, her cardigan seemed to glide off her shoulders. The buttons of his shirt popped open as if of their own accord. But just as Kate came into contact with the light scattering of hairs on his chest, his body stiffened, as if in shock. Instinctively, her gaze followed his own.

'Bugger!' She frantically tugged the cardigan back on.

Tom leapt to his feet, shirt flapping open, face like thunder. 'What the . . . ?'

The woman in the doorway at least had the decency to blush. She could easily have been six feet tall, thought Kate, eyeing her in alarm. She looked like Miss Brazil in a beauty pageant, except that she wasn't wearing a swimsuit or evening gown. Her hair was tied back loosely in a white scarf and fell almost to her waist in shiny brown ripples. Her short polo-neck jumper clung to her like a second skin, as did her suede pants. Kate trailed the pants all the way down to tan leather ankle boots, reminded of one of those miniature dolls she'd made as a child out of old-fashioned wooden clothes pegs following *Blue Peter* instructions. Lift the skirt, and the legs went all the way up to the doll's chest.

'I'm sorry,' said Miss Brazil, regaining her composure. 'I didn't mean to interrupt.'

'Bollocks,' said Tom.

'You should have told me you were entertaining, Tom.'

'I did,' he hissed.

Miss Brazil ventured closer and held out her hand to Kate, looming over her as she came around the sofa.

'I'm Jemma Whitelace. Or just plain Jem, if you like. You must be . . . ?'

'On my way out,' muttered Kate, looking around for her bag and coat. But she'd left them in the hall.

Tom grabbed her with one hand while trying to do up his shirt with the other. 'No, you don't.'

'Of course not,' said Miss Brazil. 'I'm sorry I barged in at such an . . . inopportune moment, but now that I'm here we may as well be civilised about it. Do you have any wine open?' She glanced around. 'No? I'll just go fetch a bottle then.'

'Jem—'

'Don't worry.' She smiled ravishingly at Tom, even though he'd practically bitten her head off. 'I know where you keep your corkscrew.' She looked at Kate again, arching an eyebrow. 'Don't we all?'

Acute embarrassment and the heat from the fire were making Kate feel dizzy. Her hair was sticking to her neck and hanging in sweaty fronds over her face. She swept it back and tried to take deep breaths, realising that Tom had left the lounge too. She could hear his raised voice from the direction of the kitchen.

'What the bloody hell do you think you're playing at, Jem?'

But her reply was inaudible.

'I told you I had plans tonight,' Tom railed on. 'I told you it was inconvenient.'

There was another pause.

'I don't have to justify myself to you any more,' he boomed. 'And I'm not on the bloody rebound. Kate's . . .' But either his sentence stopped there or he'd remembered to turn the volume down. Either way, Kate felt two inches tall.

A few seconds later, Jem sailed back into the lounge carrying a bottle of Chardonnay and three glasses, casually dangling the stems from her long, French-manicured fingers. Tom was hot on her heels. Behind him was Tina, who had been asleep in her basket in the kitchen when Kate had first arrived. The little dog started yapping and jumping around Jem's ankles with what seemed to be ecstasy, but Jem just ignored her and concentrated on uncorking the wine.

Tom sank down on to a small footstool, head in his hands. All the fight appeared to have left him.

'I don't want a drink,' murmured Kate, as Jem settled beside her. 'I'm driving.'

'One won't hurt.' Jem slid a full glass along the coffee table. 'I drove down here myself. I suppose I'll have to stay over. In the spare room, of course. Why aren't you staying over, Kate? I'm surprised Tom hasn't asked you.'

'I haven't asked *you*, either,' he said, looking exhausted, 'but that isn't going to stop you, is it?'

'I left my toothbrush here when I went,' Jem chattered on. 'Isn't that handy?'

'I threw it out,' Tom informed her.

'Oh well. I'll have to borrow yours.' She smiled at him pointedly, then turned to Kate. 'Mind if I smoke?' Without waiting for a response, she started hunting amongst the paraphernalia on the coffee table.

'You won't find any there,' said Tom. 'I gave up.'

'Again?' Jem sighed despairingly. 'They're probably still in the bin.'

'I doubt it. I chucked out my last pack a couple of weeks ago.'

She faltered. 'Oh. What about your emergency supply?'

'That *was* the emergency supply.'

'You mean you haven't *any* cigarettes in the house?' Jem looked across at him in astonishment. For the first time, Kate realised that Miss Brazil was a human being.

'Not unless you brought some with you.' Tom seemed to have mustered up some of his former spirit.

Jem sprang to her feet and moved quickly towards the door. Tina bounced back to life and started yapping around her ankles again. Before Kate or Tom could speak, Jem returned with a tiny red handbag. She scowled down at the dog. 'She still hasn't got any manners, has she?'

'On the contrary, she's just selective about when to use them. Listen, Jem—'

'We can talk later, can't we, Tom? There's plenty of time.' Jem had lit one of her cigarettes and was wafting smoke about with nervous, jerky movements. Kate didn't feel quite so intimidated any more, even when Jem fixed chocolate brown eyes on her and asked, 'So how long have you known Tom?'

'Not long . . .' Despite the other woman's faultless looks, there was a vulnerability about her that was propelling Kate to rally back. '. . . But long enough.'

'Please drink some wine,' insisted Jem. 'Otherwise Tom and I will have to finish the whole bottle on our own. You know what it's like when you get blotto with a man, it can lead to all sorts of things.'

'And sometimes you don't even need to get blotto,' added Tom with a flourish.

'I really do have to go.' Kate rose to her feet, determined no one would stop her this time.

'Shame,' said Jem. 'Still, it was nice meeting you. Sorry I interrupted before. I didn't think Tom would mind me using my old key.'

Kate shrugged, as if she didn't give a toss. 'At least we weren't down to our underwear. You know what Tom's boxers can be like.' She waved a hand in front of her nose, as if there was something whiffy in the air all of a sudden.

The cigarette almost fell out of Jem's mouth.

Kate turned on her heel. Behind her, Tom barely stifled a snort of laughter. She could hear him scrambling up and following her, but she didn't look round until she'd retrieved her coat and bag from a chair in the hall. Tom had closed the lounge door.

'Goodbye,' she said, endeavouring to sound calm.

He stood over her, his hand cradling the side of her face. 'I'm sorry about Jem. She rang me the other day, told me she missed me, wanted to talk things over. She suggested tonight, but I said I was busy.'

'I assume she came to see exactly how busy.'

'I said I was cooking dinner for a friend,' Tom admitted.

'A lie on one count then. You didn't cook me dinner.'

Tom looked at her quizzically, his hand dropping to his side. 'You're also more than just a friend.'

Kate wasn't going to crumble a second time. 'When you think about it, Jem saved us from making a stupid mistake. And I can't keep you hanging on indefinitely. I don't know how long Emmi's going to need to come to terms with meeting Harry.'

'I told you, I'd wait. This business with Jem . . . It's coming up to Christmas, she's lonely. It's easy for her to imagine we can make a go of it again.'

'Maybe you should. I remember how upset you were when you first told me about her.'

'I also told you why I was upset. Anyway, I don't know what I saw in her in the first place.'

'You're deluding yourself. She's beautiful.'

He smoothed back Kate's hair. 'So are you.'

She almost laughed derisively, but her throat was too choked up.

Tom went on, 'Jem's amazing to look at, but scratch the surface . . .'

'She's just a woman,' said Kate, trying to keep the croak out of her voice. 'And I think she's in love with you. She deserves a chance. You said yourself that you were to blame for her leaving. Now that you realise where you went wrong, you might get it right if you tried again.'

He didn't reply, which probably meant he was considering it. And if he was considering it, then he wasn't excluding the possibility of a reconciliation. However remote this possibility, Kate didn't want to be around to witness it. Jem had known Tom for far longer than her, even lived with him, merging into his existence, creating day-to-day memories alongside him, learning where his weak spots were.

'I'm sorry,' said Kate. 'If Jem wasn't around . . .'

'She isn't "around".'

'At this moment in time she's sitting in your living room. I've got to make a clean break of it, for all our sakes, so that everyone can think clearly.'

'Crap,' he spat. 'You're running away.'

'I'm putting my daughter first,' Kate retaliated. 'There's no negotiating when it comes to Emmi. Until you're a parent, you won't understand.'

There was a pause, punctuated at the end with a frustrated sigh. 'The problem is, I do,' he said crabbily. 'That doesn't mean I have to agree, or accept it with any form of grace. Basically you're dumping me. I'm sorry I can't be a good sport about it.'

The lump in her throat seemed to double in size. She opened the front door. Outside in the courtyard was a newish Audi TT. Jem's, of course. It gleamed in the moonlight, making it look as if her battered little car hadn't been waxed in years.

Kate just wanted to get home and hide under the duvet, blocking it all out, the whole ill-timed mess. But she knew, even before she turned her back on Tom and started hurrying away, rummaging in her bag for her keys, that nothing could shut it out. No fifteen-tog-worth of eiderdown, no amount of tea, or wine, or Bach Rescue Remedy, or even cuddles from Emmi, could suppress the gloom rushing up inside her. As if, like drilling for oil, she'd tapped into some hidden supply of misery that would last her all through Christmas and indefinitely into the new year.

13

'But, Mummy, *why* can't we go and see Tom today? It's Sunday. We always see Tom on Sundays.'

Emmi looked up at her mum, who was in front of the bathroom mirror splodging fleshy coloured make-up under her eyes and then trying to blend it in. She looked as if she'd been crying, but it was only ten o'clock in the morning and they'd been up for almost an hour having breakfast and getting washed. Could people cry in their sleep? Emmi had heard that they could walk and talk, so maybe crying was the same.

'Darling, we've only seen Tom three Sundays, including your aunt's birthday party.'

'Yes,' said Emmi, 'but why aren't we seeing him *today*?'

'Because . . .'

'Have you and Tom split up? Melanie says her cousin split up with her husband last month, but they went to someone at the council or something, and he patched everything up.'

With a sigh, her mum plonked down on the edge of the bath. Emmi started to feel the same way she did when she was car-sick on long journeys.

'*Have* you and Tom split up?' she asked, her voice

barely above a whisper, as if saying it quietly would make it less likely to be true. When her mum didn't reply, she hurried on, louder, 'Maybe you could go to the same person at the council and he could patch it up for you.'

'I think you mean a counsellor, darling. Someone who listens to other people's problems and tries to help. But Tom and I don't need to go to one of those.'

'So you're still together?'

Her mum sighed again. 'It's not that simple. We still like each other, but . . . we decided that we needed to stop going out for a while.'

'Why?'

'Because – because I've got lots of things muddling through my head at the moment.'

'Did you have a row?'

'No, nothing like that. It's just . . . maybe when things sort themselves out, we'll start going out again.'

'What things?'

'Emmi, you know I said we were going out to lunch today, but not with Tom? Well, that doesn't mean it's just you and me. We're going with someone else. Someone who wants to meet you very much.'

Emmi cocked her head to one side. She felt sicker, yet excited too, as if her tummy was full of bubbles trying to pop out. 'Who, Mummy?'

'Do you remember I told you that your daddy lived abroad, very far away?'

'Yes.'

'Well, he's back in England again, and he came to talk to me a week ago, to tell me that he wants to see you. It was the day that Paloma took you to McDonald's. I said an old friend had visited me.'

'You wouldn't tell me much. Did that big BMW car belong to him?'

Her mother nodded.

Emmi pictured the photograph she'd seen of her father. His name was Harry, and he was wearing a black T-shirt with the name of a band scribbled across the chest in white. 'Is he coming to live with us?' she asked, wondering if he would sleep in the same room as her mother. The junk room was too full of junk, and Paloma was in the other one.

Her mum shook her head. 'No, darling. But he's back in England for good now, and he's not going to be too far away. He wants to get to know you.' There was a pause. 'How do you feel about that?'

'Will he take me to the zoo and buy me ice cream?'

Mummy was pale; she looked like she didn't know what to say.

'Melanie's dad takes her to the zoo sometimes,' Emmi went on. 'Or the cinema, or just shopping, but he always buys her ice cream.'

'I suppose he will, if you ask him to . . .'

'I'll remember to say "please".' She reached out and took her mother's hand. It felt cold, yet sweaty. 'Are you sad, Mummy?'

'No.' Her eyes looked watery. 'I'm perfectly fine. I just want you to be happy.'

'But I don't like it when you're sad.'

'I'm not.' Her mum wrapped her up in a big cuddle. 'I'm just a bit tired.'

'Maybe Daddy can give you some money so you don't have to work so hard,' suggested Emmi.

But her mum didn't say anything. She just hugged her tighter.

The whole damn world was full of Christmas trees.

For the majority of her life, Kate had dreaded fairy lights, tinsel and plastic angels with gauze or paper wings. What was the point of it all? Beyond the religious aspect, the whole event was manufactured for happy children whose parents showered them with affection as well as presents. Annabel had adored it, of course, but Kate had gone through the motions like an intricately programmed robot.

And then there were those other memories, too. Such as doing that pregnancy test at her parents' house on Christmas Eve, after which she'd blamed her dicky tummy on too many mince pies. She'd kept the performance up until New Year, when she'd trekked up to Edinburgh with Harry and some of his friends and blurted out her secret in a crowded pub. She'd got herself drunk, hoping it would bring on an early miscarriage, but the subsequent guilt had been worse than any hangover.

Such a contrast, Kate recalled, to the following Christmas. She'd filled an entire album with photographs of Emmi . . . in a bouncy chair under the Christmas tree . . . on Santa's knee . . . asleep in her buggy at Carol Service . . . on Christmas morning, surrounded by toys and clothes and a tricycle she wouldn't be able to ride for ages. There was even a photograph of Emmi having her first ever spoonful of baby rice while everyone else sat around eating turkey.

Seeing Christmas through her daughter's eyes had transformed it, enriching it with a texture and wonder that had been missing from her own childhood. And this year, because of Tom, she had felt it would be even more special. Yet now . . .

Bugger it, she thought, as an innocuous-looking fir snagged her angora sweater. Even the upmarket restaurant Harry had brought them to, with all its Feng Shui-ness, had enough Christmas trees to constitute a small forest.

Emmi sat primly on a low, hard chair, the table at chest height, her eyes like a startled rabbit's. The waiter had spread a napkin on her lap. Kate noticed how she didn't dare touch it, as if someone would rebuke her if it moved a centimetre out of place.

'I think I'll have oysters followed by the Dover sole,' declared Harry, closing the menu with a satisfied grin.

'Mummy, do they do fishfingers?'

Kate pored over the menu herself, trying to find something her daughter would enjoy.

Harry rubbed his hands together in anticipation. 'Have you ever tried oysters, Emmi?'

'She's had cockles at the seaside,' Kate answered for her.

'I'm al – allergic to them,' faltered Emmi, a frown criss-crossing her brow.

'According to the doctor, she can't have shellfish,' explained Kate. 'Or snails.'

'I see. Did the cockles make you ill, Emmi?'

The little girl nodded. 'I threw up a lot.'

'I'm sorry about that.' Harry ran a finger around the inside of his collar.

'I threw up over Granny's lap and in Grandpa's car.'

Kate pretended to cough while stifling a smile. Harry didn't appear to be looking forward to his oysters and Dover sole quite as much now.

'Mummy, can I have chips?'

'Hmm. I think you'll like the salmon fishcakes with mashed potato.'

'You can have chips, if you want,' said Harry magnanimously.

Kate frowned. She knew he was only acting on instinct, but that didn't make it any easier to put up with. In his desperation for his daughter to like him, he was ingratiating himself the only way he knew how – by pandering to her. All Kate could do was bite her tongue. It wouldn't be wise or considerate to argue in front of Emmi.

'Oh!' said Harry, in that patronising voice adults sometimes use to beguile children. 'What have I got here?' He patted his breast-pocket, then pulled out a small, square box wrapped in red and gold paper. 'It looks like an early Christmas present. I wonder who it's for? Let me see . . . there's a tag . . . Oh, my! It says here it's for Emmeline Finlay.'

Emmi's eyes sparkled. 'For me?'

Kate ground her teeth in exasperation.

'Go on,' urged Harry, 'open it.'

Emmi did as she was told. Inside the box was a small,

gold pendant. It was shaped like a ballerina. 'Mummy, look!'

'It's lovely,' Kate forced herself to agree. 'Would you like me to help you put it on?'

Emmi nodded. 'Yes, please.'

'Don't forget to say thank you to your . . . to Harry.' Kate couldn't say 'father', it seemed to catch in her throat.

'Thank you,' said Emmi.

'There's no need,' beamed Harry. 'Your mother used to write to me now and again, telling me all about you. She said in her last letter that you loved ballet, so . . .'

'Mummy,' said Emmi, 'can I have some more bread?'

Harry looked disconcerted by the change of subject. He clearly hadn't spent much time around children. Kate turned to her daughter and shook her head.

'No, darling, or you won't eat the rest of your lunch.'

But Harry was already summoning over a waiter. 'Let her have more bread if she wants,' he contested. 'Where's the harm in it?'

It was one of those clear winter days when a stroll in the park seems a good idea. But the light was already fading by the time they left the restaurant and drove back to Beckton Lacey. Emmi, however, who often went with Paloma to the park opposite the primary school, wasn't about to be deterred. Kate realised this all too well. She also decided that it would be preferable to hang around in the cold dusk with Harry rather than in her lounge maintaining a polite front over a pot of tea and biscuits.

'I want to go to the playground!' stated Emmi, as soon as they'd parked the car and climbed out, 'I want to go on the swings!'

Harry assumed a brave face. 'OK.'

Kate noticed that his jacket, although expensive and fashionable, wasn't particularly warm. Feeling smug, she huddled into her coat and tucked her hands into her pockets.

Emmi ran ahead, out of earshot. It was Harry who spoke first.

'So,' he said, 'what about Tim?'

'Tim?' asked Kate.

'Sorry. It was *Tom*, wasn't it? Tom was the guy you were seeing.'

Kate was sure Harry had known it was Tom all along. 'What about him?'

'Are you still seeing him?'

'Why shouldn't I be?'

'No reason. I just thought, considering it wasn't serious, that you . . . Well, considering how much else is going on . . .'

If he said 'considering' one more time, she was going to scream. 'If you must know, I'm *not* seeing him any more.'

'Oh.' Harry twiddled his watch. 'What went wrong?'

Kate turned her head sharply. Tears were threatening to well up. It was so pathetic that she couldn't be an adult about it. 'Nothing went wrong. And it's not your concern. Just—'

'What?'

'I tried to let Emmi down gently. I didn't tell her that

167

Tom and I had split up for good, I said we were just having a break from each other.'

'*Have* you split up for good?'

A vision of Jem flashed across her mind's eye. Kate nodded.

'Don't worry.' Harry looked sympathetic as he rubbed her arm. 'I won't mention him when Emmi's around.'

'There's no need to mention him at all any more,' sniffed Kate. 'Oh sod it, I hate the cold, it always makes my nose run.'

'Here, take my hankie. It's clean.'

'Mummy!' called Emmi. 'Will you push me on the swings?'

'I'll do it,' said Harry, bounding over, looking so handsome and debonair that even Beckton Lacey's militant feminist, out walking her wolfhound, swivelled her head in his direction. 'Isn't that what dads are for?'

14

It was almost three-thirty. Sitting at her desk at work, Kate noticed that she had a new e-mail. From Dick Anthony, '*Re: Tonight*'. She opened it and read, '*Are you coming downstairs later? It won't be the same without you. And you know I'm off as from tomorrow, so this is your last chance for a Christmas drink with your fabulous employer.*'

Groaning inwardly, she typed back, '*I can't. I'm busy.*'

A minute later, Dick mailed her again. '*Nothing's that urgent. You can have the night off!*'

'*I meant, at home,*' Kate replied.

'*Emmi won't mind.*'

Kate buried her head in her hands. Harry was supposed to be coming over for dinner. She wasn't looking forward to it. In fact, she could have used the excuse that it was her work's Christmas do to wriggle out of it. Except that she hadn't fancied an evening at the Cork and Cheese either, watching everyone get steadily drunk and listening to Natalia and her cronies taking over the karaoke machine. She'd felt as if she were hovering between the frying pan and the fire.

Sitting upright again, she typed, '*Sorry, I have other plans I can't get out of.*'

Another reply came speeding back. '*Everyone else will be there. You're letting the side down.*'

Damn. It was hard enough trying to fit in at Anthony & Gray without alienating herself further. Would it seem snooty of her if she didn't turn up?

'*Perhaps one drink won't hurt,*' she conceded.

'*Great,*' wrote Dick. '*I'll swing by your desk at five-thirty to make certain you don't escape.*'

What was it with the man? wondered Kate, un-wittingly flattered. He had been boss-like for ages, yet out of the blue he was practically flirting with her again. Someone had said to her once that women were more complex than men. At the time she'd been inclined to agree, but now . . . Well, now she wasn't so sure.

Every firm in the building seemed to be celebrating downstairs tonight. The Cork and Cheese's usual decor was a hotchpotch of whirling ceiling fans, exotic potted palms, wicker chairs and tables and tartan soft furnishings. Kate had found it all rather bizarre, until she'd learned that the owners were a married couple, the wife hailing from Singapore and the husband from Inverness. *Chalk* and Cheese would have been a more suitable name. And it was even worse now that it was December – a case of Raffles Hotel meets Santa's Highland Grotto.

Kate perched precariously on a stool at the wicker and brass bar, blinking around her like a dazzled child. Also like a child she'd murmured, 'Lemonade,' when Dick had asked her what she was drinking.

He'd raised his eyebrows in mock horror. 'I'm not sure that's allowed at your age.'

'Sorry?'

'No,' he continued, 'it's definitely going to have to be something like this White Grenache here. Or do you prefer dry? I'm not clued-up on wines much. If I like the taste, I like it. If I don't, I don't. I can't see the point in being a snob about it.'

'White Grenache?' Kate had echoed, watching Natalia swirling a cocktail stick in a huge jug of sangria.

'It's this Californian rosé.'

'Oh – OK. Just a glass, though.'

'I'll get a bottle for starters and we'll see how we go from there.'

And so here she was, on her second glass, only half listening to Dick raving on about the latest contract they'd landed, when he broke off abruptly and asked, 'Is everything all right, Kate?'

'Huh?'

'You don't seem particularly with it.'

She glanced at her watch. It was six-fifteen already. The wine had relaxed her, left her feeling mellow. Perhaps she wasn't being very attentive to Dick, but she was enjoying just sitting there, chilling out while all around her the first signs of mass intoxication were being exhibited.

'Will you excuse me a moment?' she said. 'I need to make a quick call.'

Finding a quiet-ish spot in the corridor outside the Ladies', she took her mobile out of her pocket and rang home. Paloma answered, sounding flustered. 'Yes?'

'Is something wrong?'

'No . . . No, Emmi's fine. She's watching TV at the moment.'

'The thing is, I'm running a bit late,' said Kate, without going into detail. 'Harry will probably arrive before I do.'

'Um, he's already here.'

Kate checked her watch again. 'I thought he was coming round at seven.'

'He, er, wanted to spend more time with Emmi.'

'Oh . . . I see. Fair enough. Can you tell him I'll be back before eight. In fact, if you all want to start eating without me, go ahead. What are you cooking?'

'Only bangers and mash.'

'That used to be one of Harry's favourites.'

'It still is. I mean,' said Paloma hastily, 'he's just told me it is. Just now.'

'Good. Well, like I said, go ahead without me, I won't mind. I'll see you all later. Give Emmi my love.'

'I will.'

Kate ended the call. Thank the Lord for Paloma. She sounded particularly scatty this evening, but at least Emmi wasn't facing Harry on her own. It would have to happen sooner or later, though; Kate couldn't act as a perpetual buffer between them. It wasn't fair to Harry, and perhaps her own attitude towards him wasn't helping Emmi with the bonding process.

As she returned to the bar, Kate realised that it was probably best if she stayed away a little longer than she'd said, to give father and daughter a chance to talk. Paloma was more impartial than Kate. She would blend into the background and simply keep a watchful eye on Emmi to make sure she didn't get overly upset. All things considered, thought Kate, it didn't matter that Dick had poured her another glass of wine.

'I'm glad you changed your mind and came along tonight,' he confided, helping her back up on to the bar stool. 'I know what Charles and Henry are like when they've had one too many. And the rest of them are even worse. If you weren't here to keep me sane . . .'

'I can't stay long,' Kate insisted, as the introduction to 'Wannabe' crackled out from the overhead speakers. She turned towards the small platform where the karaoke machine stood. Natalia and three other 'Spice Girls' were strutting around in high heels and mini-skirts, with enough make-up on to send Boots' profits soaring, and larger false lashes than Emmi's Furby.

'Bring back Geri Halliwell,' muttered Dick.

Kate couldn't help smirking.

'Last Christmas was hellish,' he went on. 'The PA we had back then had a face like an old shoe-box.'

'Sorry?'

'Oh, it's an expression my father uses. Don't ask me what it means. Well, apart from ugly. But I was so relieved when she said she was quitting. And when the agency sent you along, I thought to myself, here's a nice, intelligent, straightfoward sort of girl. Bored working in financial circles, and who could blame her? Not glamorous, but not plain. Good track record. Different from Nat and co., and supporting a young daughter. You may have noticed that this is a mainly female firm,' Dick added sardonically. 'Apart from the upper echelons. But

Charles always seems to go for the same *type* of female. I fancied a change so I overrode his decision. He wanted to hire an ex-model with a 36D bust and lips like Mick Jagger's. Enough was enough.'

Kate stared at Dick, wondering what she ought to be feeling. Flattered again? Insulted? For the moment, she was just taken aback. 'What about your previous secretary – the one with a face like an old shoe-box? Wasn't she different from Nat and the others, too?'

'Drastically. But she only got the job because her mother's like *that* with Charles's aunt.' Dick crossed two fingers to illustrate his point. 'As I said, I much prefer you.' And he topped up her glass again. 'Another bottle, I think. Unless you feel daring enough to risk the sangria? Nat poured me a glass while you were making your phone call. It wasn't too bad.'

Kate shook her head. She was only sipping at the White Grenache, but the level in her glass seemed to go down surprisingly quickly.

'So what have you got Emmi for Christmas?' asked Dick, sounding genuinely interested.

She shrugged. 'Just some new outfits for her Barbies. And a couple of CDs.'

'What music does she like?'

'Anything her friends are into. I'm hoping she'll develop her own tastes as she gets older.'

Dick chuckled. Kate relaxed again, the music pulsing through her, carried along by the wine. It struck her that the depression she'd been floundering in this last couple of weeks had lifted slightly. Whether that was due to Dick's company, the alcohol, or the sheer mindlessness of the revelry going on around her, she didn't know. Maybe it was a combination of the three. All she knew was that another hour had passed by the time she looked at her watch again. If she was to make the seven-fifty-four train, she'd have to put her skates on.

'I really, really do have to go,' she said with regret, easing herself off the stool and finding that the floor was further down than she'd calculated. She wobbled slightly.

'We haven't even danced yet.' Dick looked disappointed.

She glanced towards the stage, which had been turned into an impromptu dance-floor. It was jam-packed with dishevelled, inebriated creatures writhing to the strains of Lionel Richie and 'All Night Long'.

Kate shook her head. 'I don't think we'd fit,' she said. 'There's going to be an accident any minute. Besides, I haven't got time.'

Her legs still felt rather more unsteady than she'd hoped. She stood swaying on the spot, and then, on impulse, leaned across and kissed Dick's cheek. 'I feel as if I've been monopolising you,' she giggled, as he reached out to stabilise her.

'On the contrary. Tom's a lucky man.'

At the mention of his name, Kate felt her chest tighten. 'I've, er, got to dash upstairs to fetch my bag and coat. Sorry I'm rushing off, but I'll miss my train otherwise.'

Dick waved his hand in an expansive, theatrical gesture. 'Abandon me if you must. Leave me to the mercies of this debauched rabble. I'm sure I'll be fine.'

Kate felt as if her heart would explode with the unfairness of life. Even the knowledge that the world was full of people less fortunate than herself didn't help.

'Have a good Christmas.' She couldn't even meet Dick's eye. 'See you in the new year.' And before he could reply, she turned and tottered towards the door which gave directly on to the lobby.

Once in the lift, she leaned against the side and closed her eyes. Instantly everything started to whirl. Sod it. Why hadn't she eaten some crisps or peanuts? Why had she drunk so much wine? *Why* was missing Tom such a physical torment, as if every part of her was involved rather than simply her emotions?

As she walked through the Marie Celeste-like office towards her cubicle, she knew she wasn't going to make the seven-fifty-four. Collapsing into her chair, she folded her arms on her desk and lowered her head. So this was what it felt like to be that spinning top Emmi had loved to play with as a toddler. Or maybe it was as if someone had put her brain on spin cycle in a washing machine. Round and round and—

'Kate . . .'

She leapt in shock. Dick was looming over the desk. Shadows gathered around him and made him seem even taller and more swarthy. 'Oh, damn,' she muttered, 'you scared me.'

'I'm sorry.' His voice was like velvet. 'I didn't mean to.'

'What are you doing here?'

'I followed you up.'

'Oh . . . Why?'

He sat on her desk, and seemed to bring the shadows closer, as if he wanted to envelop her in them. 'After you left, I sat there for a minute or two, thinking.'

'Really?' She shivered, but didn't know why. It wasn't as if she was cold.

'And then it struck me.'

'What did?'

'That if I came up and found you were still here, I'd know for sure.'

Kate picked up a pen, twiddled it for a moment and then dropped it again. 'Know what for sure?'

'That you weren't really in a rush to catch your train. That what you wanted was to test me.'

As he leaned closer, she caught a whiff of the alcohol on his breath. A bolt of trepidation shot through her.

'You're a clever girl,' he murmured. 'But I'm a clever boy, and even if I can't stay one step ahead, at least I can keep up.'

'Er, Dick, I'm not certain I know what you mean.'

'There's no need to pretend. The game's over now. Have I passed? Do I get my prize?'

As he made a lunge for her, Kate pushed her chair back on its castors as far as it would go. When she hit the back of the cubicle, she sprang to her feet and grabbed her bag and coat, holding them in front of her chest like a shield. She couldn't believe this was happening. Right now she would give anything for Natalia to turn up in all her smug glory.

Dick was staring at her, a smile teasing his lips. 'I see,' he said. 'The game's still on. I suppose it's more fun this way. A little fantasy never did any harm.'

Kate backed away from him. 'This isn't a game,' she stressed, her heart hammering. 'The only reason I decided not to rush off was because I wasn't going to make my train, *not* because I expected you to come up and find me. You're my employer, Dick, that's all.'

'I understand. You're into role-play.' He advanced towards her. 'That's fine by me . . .'

Role-play? What was he on about? He really *was* her employer. Oh, God, help! Kate turned to flee, but found that she'd reversed into a corner. Dick was coming closer. Automatically, she took another step back but found herself sandwiched between a pair of high filing cabinets. Now she was well and truly trapped. Of course, she could scream, but who was around to hear her? The security guard that normally wandered around the building was probably downstairs getting plastered, too.

'I only want a kiss,' Dick was saying. 'It *is* Christmas.'

There was something farcical about all this, like a *Carry On* film, yet the fear inside Kate was real, strangling her sense of humour.

'It's tantamount to sexual harassment,' she heard herself utter primly, as she flicked at something tickling her ear – a bloody spider plant, she realised.

'Hardly mistletoe,' Dick was chuckling, moving straggling green leaves out of the way. 'But we can improvise.'

'Dick, please,' said Kate, her voice finding strength again and rising in volume. 'This isn't a good idea.'

'Just one little kiss . . .'

'I'll tell Tom,' she said firmly. 'I'll tell Tom you made a pass at me.'

Instantly, Dick seemed to freeze, eyebrows curved in alarm. Kate took her opportunity. Without even needing to stoop, she dodged under his outstretched arm.

'I'm – I'm sorry,' he mumbled.

Still clutching her bag and coat, Kate hesitated and looked back at him over her shoulder. Her legs were even more jelly-like than before, but she knew she had to rely on them to get her out of there. She just wanted to get home now. This was her punishment for trying to avoid Harry.

'Please,' Dick was saying, without making any move to follow her. 'I'm sorry . . . I wasn't going to hurt you . . .'

A part of her seemed to register that information and accept it; so readily, it was as if she had always suspected but had been waiting for him to say it. Was that the real reason why she hadn't screamed? Why she hadn't panicked as much as she'd thought she would? After all, a rapist wasn't necessarily a stranger. Admittedly, with Dick there was a time, not that long ago, when she'd wanted him to get amorous with her. Too much had happened since then, though. Resistance had sprung up inside her without a second thought.

'Don't tell Tom,' Dick was begging.

Kate frowned. 'I won't,' she promised. And then she hurried away, through reception to the lifts, her gait steadier than she'd expected. One set of lift doors opened almost as soon as she'd pressed the button. She went in and hit 'G'. The doors hummed closed, cocooning her inside. She hadn't thought Dick would come after her. He'd looked so pathetic, leaning against the filing cabinet with a lock of dark hair drooping over his brow. Kate sighed and threw back her head, blinking at the tiny lights on the ceiling, scattered randomly to resemble stars.

Thankfully, he was off now until the new year. She wouldn't have to face him during the last few days before the Christmas holidays. If they each had any sense, they would try to forget what had happened, but that was easier said than done. In all honesty, Kate didn't know how she would react when she next saw him. It was one of those things she would push to the back of her mind, like so much else lately. A tight squeeze, but she could probably manage it.

She lowered her bag to the floor and shrugged into her coat. As the doors hummed open again, she jerked the strap of the bag into its usual position over her shoulder and narrowed her eyes against the bright domed lights of the vast lobby. Charging past the Cork and Cheese, she exited through the revolving main door into the street.

The outside world was a dark, bitter place punctuated by glaring headlamps and coloured lights strung incongruously in office windows. As Kate headed for the Underground, her breath formed plumes in the frosty air. If she was to break down and cry right now, it seemed that the tears might freeze on her cheeks. She felt sick and alone. Her only consolation would be arriving home to find that Emmi was still up.

*

'I'm going to bed,' said Emmi, standing in the kitchen doorway looking in at Paloma and her dad. They were sitting at the table, where they'd remained even after tea was over. Emmi had gone into the lounge to watch the end of the video Paloma had rented for her as a surprise. She hadn't minded watching it on her own. In fact, she'd preferred it. When her dad had first got there, he'd tried to talk to her, asking her things about school and her friends, but he hadn't really sounded interested in her answers, so what was the point?

The video had been funny, but Emmi hadn't felt like laughing. She'd been looking forward to seeing her mum tonight, but she'd got her hopes up too much. Even though her dad had come for tea, her mum still hadn't made it home.

Emmi had poked at her food, even though it was bangers and mash, one of her favourites. She hadn't felt hungry, and she'd excused herself as soon as she could. Paloma and her dad had lots to talk about, even if it was just silly things like whether her dad preferred Joop – whatever that was – to Polo, or whether Paloma preferred red roses to white ones. Stuff like that.

Emmi had wondered if Paloma fancied her dad, because he *was* quite handsome, like the prince in her *Sleeping Beauty* book, but she'd decided that this wasn't so. Emmi had noticed that Paloma avoided touching her dad, and if he moved his chair nearer to her, she moved hers away slightly. In fact, once he'd even reached across the table and squeezed her hand, but she'd jumped and pulled away, frowning at him crossly. Her dad probably fancied Paloma, Emmi realised, because Melanie at school had said that a man could fancy loads of different women at the same time. Whether he was married or not didn't seem to matter. They couldn't help it, Melanie had said, it was in their jeans. But Emmi hadn't asked what this meant, in case everyone laughed at her.

Climbing the stairs, she heard Paloma giggling quietly in the kitchen. Maybe her dad had told one of his stupid jokes, scowled Emmi. They weren't funny, not like Tom's . . .

She went into the bathroom to brush her teeth, swallowing the lump in her throat. Somehow, she didn't think she was going to be having a bath tonight. Not that she had one every night. But anyway, Paloma seemed to have forgotten to come upstairs.

Once in her bedroom, Emmi took off her daytime clothes and wriggled into her pyjamas, tucking herself up in bed and reaching for the book she'd brought home from the library. As she turned the pages, her eyelids started growing heavy. The last thing she was aware of before drifting off to sleep was the sound of a key turning in the front door.

15

Jem was wearing the same short, gold dress that had caught Tom's eyes when he'd first met her, at a mutual acquaintance's birthday party. It was slightly stretchy, which meant it clung provocatively, leaving very little to the imagination. Tom knew from experience that she probably only had a thong on underneath. She closed the front door behind him and instantly snaked her arms around his waist, kissing him with open lips and an ardent tongue. Caught off guard, he dropped his overnight bag and reacted as most single, red-blooded men would when assailed by a beautiful woman. But when she suggested an early Christmas present was waiting for him in the bedroom, he extracted himself promptly from her embrace.

'We've got time before the others get here,' Jem murmured seductively.

'And we agreed to take it slow this time,' Tom reminded her. He fished out the champagne bottle he'd brought. 'This really needs chilling.'

The mass of dark hair piled high on her head seemed to tremble indignantly as she went ahead into the kitchen. 'Just put your bag in the bedroom, Tom,' she called back over her shoulder. 'Out of the way, so no one trips over it.'

He did as he was asked, then followed her into the kitchen. 'Don't get into a strop, Jem. Remember what happened last time. We both leapt in with our eyes shut and it was a disaster.'

'Of course it was! I'm not going to go and live in that shack of yours again. This time you can bloody well move yourself up here.'

Tom stood blinking at her as she opened her fridge and jammed in the champagne. Eventually he said, 'It was your idea to move in with me. You wanted to give the country a try.'

'And I did. The country and I don't gel.'

'How about if I lived in an eight-bed place with an en-suite Jacuzzi to the master bedroom?'

'I'm not that fussy, Tom. But central heating would have been nice.' She shrugged. 'Listen, I'm a city girl, darling. This is where I belong. And it's not as if I don't have enough room here.' She gestured around her flat. 'You're welcome to my study, and you can bring as many books as you like with you. Even that mutt of yours can come.'

'Jem—'

'Cigarette?' She picked up a packet from the breakfast bar and held it out to him challengingly. 'Or are you still abstaining?'

He was tempted, but shook his head.

'My, you've turned into a well-behaved boy.' Jem lit one for herself and puffed at it greedily. 'That little blonde must have been a positive influence.'

'Her name's Kate,' said Tom, his stomach knotting.

'Well, she was obviously very good for you in some ways, but I hope she didn't turn you into even more of a bore than you already were.' Jem smiled archly, and stroked a gold-varnished nail across his cheek. 'Only time will tell.'

Tom felt a sudden burning desire to lash out, but he'd never been violent with a woman and wasn't about to start now. It would be easy, he realised, to push her up against the wall and vent his frustration in other ways, but that was exactly what she wanted. If he played into her hands, if he transferred pain and anger into relieving his sexual energy on Jem's terms, he would add guilt to his list of woes and only aggravate the situation.

'Are you going to offer me a drink?' he muttered grittily.

She stared at him for a moment, obviously realising that he'd won the first round. 'Wine?'

'Whatever.'

'I've discovered this divine little vintage . . .' She set about uncorking a bottle, then led the way into the lounge where she hit play on her hi-fi. The strains of 'Yesterday' filled the high-ceilinged room. 'Your favourite – see? I remembered!' She held a glass out to him. 'Shall we make a toast?'

In spite of his reservations, Tom replied, 'To us?'

Jem glowed, in more ways than one. The bronzing powder she'd smoothed over her bare shoulders shimmered in the light of the numerous candles dotted around the room. The only other illumination came from the discreet little fairy lights on the tree. 'To us,' she echoed.

They clinked glasses. Tom thought about the bracelet he'd bought for her last minute in the antique shop off Addenham's Market Square. It was silver, inlaid with those yellow stones he couldn't remember the name of. He hadn't known what to get her. She probably wouldn't even *pretend* to like it when she opened it tomorrow morning.

Reaching down under the tree, she picked up a small box and handed it to him. 'I want you to open this now,' she said.

Tom obliged. Inside the box was a Yale key attached to a heart-shaped key ring.

'I was being tacky,' she giggled. 'The key to my heart, and all that. Isn't it the most marvellous tat?'

'I take it it's real?'

'For the flat.' She picked up another key off the mantelpiece. 'And this opens the door downstairs. If I'd put them both on the key ring it wouldn't have had quite the same effect. As if I've got two hearts, or something.' She laughed nervously.

'Jem—'

'Oh shit, that's the buzzer. They're arriving, and I haven't even got the salad done.' She put down her wine and hurried into the hall, calling back, 'Darling, be a good host and see to their drinks, won't you?'

With a sigh, Tom flicked lint off his silk shirt, which was one of the ones Jem had bought him when they'd started going out the first time round. He wondered if she'd even noticed. It wasn't his style, but he'd made the effort. Even his trousers were new. What was he doing? Why was he here? If his intention was to obliterate Katharine Rose Finlay from his memory, why hadn't he slept with Jem at the earliest opportunity? Why was he dawdling? In the hope that he'd get a call on his mobile in the middle of dinner? 'Tom, it's Kate. I'm sorry. I want you back. Harry's a scumbag. Emmi loves you best. Blah, blah, blah.' *Who the hell was he kidding?*

'How are you doing?' A broad Irish accent jolted him brusquely back to Jem's flat. 'I'm Aidan Patricks. Delighted to meet you.'

On automatic pilot, Tom stuck out his hand and allowed it to be pumped in a zealous handshake. Details filtered slowly into his brain. The man who'd just arrived was of medium build and could only have been around twenty-five. He had a shock of auburn hair and a trim goatee, and his eyes – his most striking feature, elevating him to handsomeness – were a vibrant green. Of course, realised Tom, that might just be down to coloured contact lenses; in which case Aidan Patricks would merely be—

Oh bollocks. The name finally sank in. Was this the same Aidan Patricks who was currently being fêted by the literary world for what Tom could only describe as pretentious, depressing crap? He'd picked up a copy of *The Irish Rover* in Addenham Library, and read it from cover to cover, if only to see if he could find a plot. Or a character he liked.

'I used to read your column when I was at college,'

Aidan was saying. 'Being a writer myself, it's great to actually meet you. Jem tells me you're going to start writing again. Although, I'm not kidding, I don't know why you gave up. Have you ever tried fiction, or isn't that your thing?'

Tom suddenly felt very old and tired. Jem had simply said she was inviting a few friends over. 'Then we can be on our own Christmas Day.' But she could have given him some warning about who these 'friends' would be. Then again, he obviously hadn't been interested enough to ask her.

'Aid,' she scolded, popping her head around the door, 'don't give Tom a hard time so early on. Save a *few* questions for later.'

'Sure enough.' Aidan slapped Tom on the back. 'You're a lucky man.' He lowered his voice. 'Jem's a babe.'

'Don't I know it,' he replied blandly, remembering his role as host before Jem could get around to admonishing him, too. 'I'm sorry, it's very remiss of me not to ask – would you like a drink?'

'I'll have a glass of whatever you're having.'

The intercom buzzer sounded again. 'Let the festivities commence!' Tom couldn't suppress his sarcasm any longer.

Aidan frowned slightly. 'Did someone forget to tell you? It's Christmas!' And then he laughed at his own joke, while Tom debated – in true Cluedo fashion – whether to bash him over the head with the nearest candlestick.

★

Apart from Aidan Patricks, Jem had invited one female friend and two other male friends, none of whom Tom had met before. He had always thought that she collected new members for her entourage with unnerving ease, and discarded them with even less fuss. Hardly anyone had visited her when she'd lived at The Croft – not even her father. Since taking early retirement, he lived with his second wife somewhere in Devon. Jem had said that he rarely ventured as far as London any more, so Tom hadn't been surprised. Jem had two step-sisters but no blood siblings, her mother having died when she was just a baby. She'd been sent to boarding school when she was only eight for causing too much friction amongst her new step-family.

'We could go down to Devon together on Boxing Day,' Jem had suggested. 'Daddy would love to meet you, and Briony and Belinda will have left by then.'

It was like Cinderella and the Ugly Sisters, Tom had mused, except that Jem had never been dressed in rags and forced to clean out grates. Far from it. Even now, her extravagent lifestyle was still subsidised by her father.

'I said to Scott and Vie that I'd go to theirs on Boxing Day,' he'd told her. 'They're looking after Tina. But you're welcome to join me.'

'You know I can't,' she'd snapped. 'I promised Daddy.'

So that was that. He wondered if she was getting back at him now by throwing the sort of 'intimate' dinner party she knew he hated. Or maybe she was just showing him off. The only saving grace was the food – as impressive as ever. But then, amazingly enough, Jem excelled in the kitchen, almost as much as in the bedroom.

As the meal progressed, Tom cottoned on to two things. Even though he hadn't replied to her earlier question, she was taking it for granted that he was moving in with her in the new year. Secondly, according to Jem, he was going to start writing his column again. As if it was that easy.

'What about Llewellyn Limos?' he asked, when he got a word in edgeways. 'And the golf lessons?'

'What about them?' Her fork, loaded with the last of the stuffed squid in a tomato and basil sauce, came to a halt in mid-air.

'I have enough trouble finding a parking space for the MG in this road, let alone my whole fleet.'

'You make it sound like an Armada!' piped up Lawrence, who was one of the campest men Tom had met in real life. 'Isn't it exciting!'

'Seriously, Jem,' Tom ploughed on, 'have you considered what I'm supposed to do with the limo business?'

'You don't have to do anything just yet, you can put it on hold.'

'What about all the bookings I've got? I've taken deposits . . .'

'Then hire someone to take care of it. They could live at The Croft for now, like a sort of housesitter, until you decide if you're going to sell.'

'Sell?'

'There's no point keeping that shack if you're living in London, is there? Unless you finally finish doing it up and rent it out or something.'

Tom was rapidly losing his appetite. Jem had the future mapped out, while he couldn't bear to look further than the day after tomorrow.

'For dessert, there's *mille feuille* of white chocolate with strawberry mousse,' she announced, rising to her feet.

Aidan leaned across and patted her bottom. 'Ah, you know the way to a man's heart, that you do.'

Tom waited for the outraged slap, but Jem just giggled and sashayed towards the kitchen, asking Lawrence and Fiona (a vampish redhead who ran a boutique on the King's Road) to collect together the dirty dishes and bring them through.

Tom was left at the table with Aidan and the editor of a new men's magazine which had recently been launched on an already saturated market.

'So, Tom,' Ed, the editor, began, 'this column of yours, it had a comic edge, did it?'

'Always had me creased up,' Aidan chipped in.

'It had a serious side, too,' Tom said flatly.

'Serious and yet comic . . .' Ed looked interested. 'I like it.'

'I think people have been doing it for years,' Tom added. 'It's nothing new.'

'I might be looking for something along those lines for the magazine.'

'Really?' said Tom, without making it sound like a question.

'You should give it a go.' Aidan was hugely enthusiastic, as if he'd been put up to it – by Jem, Tom conjectured.

'Of course, I presume this column of yours used to appeal to the masses,' continued Ed. 'And *Bonding*, as in male bonding' – he paused (for applause? wondered Tom) – 'is predominantly targeting men, so anyone who writes for us would have to adhere to a few simple criteria—'

'You mean, you'd want me to be sexist?' said Tom.

Ed laughed weakly. 'You can't put it like that, not these days.'

Tom folded and unfolded his napkin, as if giving the matter of writing for *Bonding* due consideration. 'But, basically, you'd like me to call a tit a tit?'

Ed was about to reply when Jem reappeared, Lawrence and Fiona in tow. The subject was dropped, to Tom's perverse dismay. He'd enjoyed the pretence of being interested.

'So, Tom, will you tell us now why you gave up the writing?' Aidan wasn't going to quit asking. 'Don't tell me you had writer's block? Did the lovely Jem here inspire you to start again?' He smiled at her appreciatively. 'You'd make a great muse, Jemma Whitelace.'

'I was bored,' said Tom. 'And if I've learned anything, it isn't so much a case of writing about what you know, but what you care about.' He suspected that Aidan had done neither with *The Irish Rover*.

Ed waved a dessert spoon at him. 'Do you mean to say, Tom, that you ran out of things to care about?'

Blimey. This was the first question directed at him all evening – from someone other than himself – that had made him think, not just on a superficial level but deeper, where it counted. What if this 'not caring' business was part of the reason he hadn't written anything since . . . since a few years back? Would things have been different if he and Kate had stayed together?

He felt Jem prod him. 'Are you going to answer that, darling?'

It took every shred of integrity he had left in him to say, 'Actually . . . I'm not sure I can.'

The guests had left. Tom and Jem were alone with the CD player and the rapidly waning candles. Past midnight, it was officially Christmas Day. Tom sat hunched on the black leather sofa, remembering when he and Scott were kids, creeping downstairs to see if the presents were out around the tree yet, only to be sent straight back up to bed by Dad. Tom had tried the excuse of 'But it's five-past-twelve. It's Christmas now!' only to be amicably cuffed round the ear for his impudence.

He wondered if he'd ever feel like that about Christmas again.

'You look tired, darling.' Jem strolled out of the kitchen, a hand on one hip, the other tweaking at her hair, which had defied gravity for the entire evening but which Tom guessed was about to come down with the removal of a few strategically positioned pins. It was a trick she often used to precipitate sex.

She sank beside him on the sofa, and sure enough, down tumbled her hair, wave after glorious wave. 'You haven't drunk much,' she commented. 'One-and-a-half glasses.'

'You'd be great on *Crimewatch*.'

'Then again,' she went on, ignoring his remark, 'with alcohol there's always the risk that it might hamper your performance, and I want our first official reconciliation to be perfect.'

'I think we need to talk, Jem.'

Her hand squeezed his knee. 'Not now, surely?'

With effort, he removed her hand as it crept upwards, and placed it back in her lap. 'Yes, Jem. Now.'

'Then let me have a cigarette. *Pre*-coitally.'

He watched as she lit one, then asked, 'How many reconciliations do you envisage us having?'

'Sorry?'

'Just a moment ago, you said it was our "first". Do you see us having many? Is that the kind of relationship you want? The sort of couple you expect us to be?'

'What's wrong with falling out and making up again? It stops things becoming stale.'

'What about simply getting along?'

'That's boring.'

Tom shook his head. 'It's what I want, Jem. Something . . . comfortable.'

She stared at him for a long moment, then shrugged. 'I can do comfortable.'

'I don't think you can. I'm not sure you know how to. But that isn't your fault, it's who you are. We're all products of our pasts.'

There was a rasp in her voice as she said, 'Without someone like me behind you, Tom, you're going to waste your talent. You need me to kick you up the arse when all you want to do is sit on it. There's nothing I despise more than a gift like yours being thrown away.'

'Fair enough. But I'm not just someone who used to write. I'm *someone*, full stop. I'm an ordinary bloke who'd like an ordinary life.'

'And you don't think writing can be ordinary? It sounds a damn sight more normal than dressing up in that chauffeur's uniform and ferrying strangers around in those bloody cars of yours.'

'You used to like me dressing up in that uniform,' Tom couldn't resist reminding her.

'I used to like a lot of things.'

'But now?' He sighed, frustrated. 'The way I see it, Jem, you want to change me. Not in a small way, but completely. You want to install me in your study and your bedroom and your life here in London, and you want me to perform on cue. Being your friend is way down the list of things you expect from me. I'm an appendage to you, an acquisition, something to show off about.'

Now that the words were starting to flow, he felt an utter bastard for doing this to her tonight of all nights. She was sitting in a mist of cigarette smoke, her face unnaturally pale, her eyes red-rimmed and slightly bloodshot. Yes, she was a product of her past, but allowing her to continue to believe in something that was never going to happen wouldn't change that fact; nor would it alter his decision that he wasn't part of her future. When it came down to it, he was a bastard whatever he did.

'So what are you saying?' she asked, resorting to the cliché that people use when they know what's going on but prefer to deny it.

'I'm not coming to live with you, Jem.'

'I see. Not now – or not ever?'

'Not ever. It isn't going to work. For various reasons.'

'So when I lived with you, it didn't matter that I was *your* appendage, *your* acquisition . . .'

'I never tried to change you,' he defended himself honestly. 'Maybe you tried to change yourself, but it didn't work, so you blamed me. I'll own up to the fact that I neglected you, yes. Perhaps I'm not ready to be in a healthy adult relationship yet.'

'Not with me, at least.'

Tom hesitated. How did you tell someone that you never loved them? Surely you couldn't? Surely you could only lie?

'What we had, Jem . . . it was great for a time.' He was resorting to clichés himself now. 'But something like that . . . something that *intense*, it never lasts. It ran its course. We both have to accept that and move on.'

'So I've got memories, and you've got – what? Her?'

'Her?' Tom frowned.

'Kate,' said Jem, without malice.

Tom shook his head. 'No. I haven't got Kate. That ran its course, too.'

'Short but sweet.' Jem stubbed out her cigarette. 'The worst kind.' She stood up briskly. 'Are you still staying over? I don't think the couch is too uncomfortable. I've probably got a blanket or a throw somewhere you can have.'

Tom stood up too. 'I'll make a move, Jem. If I stay, I'll only be prolonging—'

'My agony?' She laughed falsely, her arms folded over

her chest, as if she was cold. 'All this is my fault for missing you too much and giving into it. I should have just kept away, saved us both this pathetic farting about.'

He shuffled around on the spot, feeling cruddy. 'I'm sorry—'

She raised a hand. 'Stop it. Please. There's no need. I'm a big girl, I can make my own mistakes without your help. So if you're leaving, just get on with it. I'd like to be a big girl on my own, if that's all right?' She led the way into the hall, disappearing into the bedroom for a moment to retrieve his overnight bag. 'Are you going straight home?' she asked matter-of-factly.

Taking his bag, he shook his head. 'I've got a key to my mother's place. It's only ten or fifteen minutes from here. She's away with friends till after the New Year. I'll kip there tonight and drive down to Scott's in the morning.'

'Good idea.'

'I'll probably raid Mother's Burt Bacharach collection or something,' he said faintly, wondering why a simple 'goodbye' seemed insufficient at times like this.

'You can have your Beatles CDs back, if you want.'

'It doesn't matter . . . Keep them.' He still had her bracelet, the one he'd intended to give her as a Christmas present. Perhaps the shop would take it back . . .

Bugger, this was a nightmare. He took a deep breath. 'Goodbye, Jem.'

'Goodbye, Tom.' She leaned across, brushing her lips against his cheek. 'Be ordinary, in your own unique way.' And she closed the door behind him, the stabbing of her heels on the wood floor rapidly dying away as he stood listening outside on the dimly lit landing.

'Merry Christmas,' he murmured, and then turned and walked slowly down the flight of stairs, out of the front door and half-way up the road to where he'd eventually managed to park his MG only a few hours before.

16

Scott and Vie lived on the outskirts of Addenham in a red-brick house that belonged to Tom and Scott's mother. Although it couldn't be called large, it stood imposingly in a half-acre of land at the end of a long, straight drive. A few years ago it had been used in a TV adaptation of a Jane Austen novel. Well, at least the front of it had, recalled Tom, as he parked his MG. Round the back there was a whopping uPVC double-glazed conservatory.

Their mother, who was much happier living in Richmond, had been renting it out to Scott for a couple of years now. That was better than parting with a house that had been in her family for generations, although when Scott had been living the bachelor life she'd kept regular checks on him, rooting out empty beer cans behind armchairs with a sniffer dog's expertise.

The house was ideal for a young couple like Scott and Vie. Among other handy features, there was a study, which was perfect for their two desks and two laptops; a guest room, for when friends came to stay at weekends; a nursery (for any future arrivals), complete with antique rocking horse; and a main bedroom adjacent to a large bathroom with a free-standing bath taking pride of place in the centre.

It was Vie who answered the door to Tom that cold, crisp morning.

'Hello, Viennetta,' he greeted her sheepishly. 'Merry Christmas.'

Her surprised smile quickly turned to one of delight. She hugged him effusively, explaining, 'You're my brother now, so it's allowed.'

'And you've been drinking already, haven't you?'

'Just a sherry or two,' she retorted playfully. 'Well, why not? It's Christmas Day! Tina's playing in the garden, by the way. She's been no trouble. I'd rather like a dog of my own, you know, but Scott's not so easily convinced.' Vie frowned slightly. 'Aren't you supposed to be up in town?'

'I was. Last night, I mean. At Jem's.'

'But you aren't there now. I thought—'

'It's over this time – for good. My decision, for a change. Do you know, I'd never dumped anyone before. I've always been dumped first. I'd rather it hadn't happened at Christmas . . .'

Vie sighed. 'I'm sure you wouldn't have done it if you hadn't had to.'

Tom regarded his sister-in-law appreciatively. She had the kind of hair that fluctuated in colour between red and blonde. It fell straight past her shoulders and then flicked upwards and outwards, whether naturally or otherwise, Tom didn't know. It was just always like that. She never wore an Alice band, though, just a diamanté clip on special occasions. Today, for a change, she was sporting a clump of green plastic holly with berries covered in red glitter.

Scott poked his head around a door along the hall. 'Tom! What the hell are you doing here?'

Tom smiled ruefully. 'I know your invitation was for tomorrow . . .'

'You're never normally this early for anything. Damn, now I'll have to peel more spuds. What went wrong, mate? I thought you had it all sorted with Jem?'

'So did she.' Tom took off his coat. Vie hung it on a peg, then nudged him along the hall.

'Come on,' she fussed, 'have a sherry or whisky or something. You'll stay over tonight, of course?'

'If it's no trouble . . .'

'There's always a fresh duvet on the guest bed. And you're certainly not going to drink if you're planning to drive.'

'No, ma'am.'

'Less of that, thank you,' Vie grinned.

Tom couldn't help but grin back, admiring her most for her sense of humour. She refused to take herself, or anyone else, too seriously. Scott would never get overly big for his boots if she had anything to do with it.

They went through into the conservatory, which was adequately warm thanks to a small portable heater positioned in one corner. A modest Christmas tree stood in the centre, flanked by a heap of torn and scrunched up wrapping paper and a jumble of opened presents.

'Yours are under there somewhere,' Vie sighed. 'I don't think we unwrapped them accidentally. Feel free to burrow around.'

Tom grew increasingly sheepish. 'I – er – forgot to bring yours.'

Vie flapped her hand dismissively. 'Sod the gifts. I'd much rather have you here.'

''Course we would.' Scott slapped his back. 'We've sorted out the photos from the wedding and honeymoon—'

'—so prepare to be bored silly later,' warned Vie.

Tom turned away to look at the tree, raking a hand through his unkempt hair. In the midst of all this Yuletide spirit, how on earth could he feel lonelier than ever?

'I shouldn't be here,' he muttered. 'You wanted to be on your own Christmas Day. You're newlyweds, for pity's sake.'

'Too right,' nodded Vie. 'So now that you've acknowledged that fact, you can get on with quaffing our booze and scoffing our food and generally ruining our day. Unless of course you agree to cheer up, in which case you can stop feeling guilty and start having fun. It's very simple, really.'

Another smile spread irresistibly across his countenance. Caught up in the moment, he turned and enveloped his sister-in-law in a fond and grateful bear-hug.

'Oh, cripes,' she squealed. 'You're a one-man rugby scrum!'

'Why couldn't I have got involved with someone uncomplicated like you?' demanded Tom, releasing her. She stood swaying dazedly in front of him, festive hair-clip askew. 'And that was meant to be a compliment.'

Scott slapped his back again. 'Jem's not worth it, mate.'

'I'm not talking about Jem,' said Tom after a pause. He groaned. 'That's the point. It would be so bloody easy if I were.'

'Don't you think a turkey looks like a lump of cellulite?' asked Annabel.

Kate blinked down at the roasting dish.

'Not so much now. It's far more noticeable when it's raw,' continued her sister. 'And chickens are much the same. Shouldn't Mum and Dad be here with Grandad by now?'

'Er, any minute.'

'What's cellulite?' asked Emmi.

'A dimply sort of fat on a woman's thighs,' answered Annabel. 'But don't fret, sweetheart, you won't have to worry about it for a good few years.'

Kate sighed.

Paloma clattered into the kitchen with a tray full of the empty mugs that were always left dotted around the house. 'I've managed to track down all but one.'

'I think I left it by the bath this morning,' Kate owned up.

Annabel turned to Paloma. 'Do *you* think a turkey looks like a lump of cellulite?'

Paloma patted her bum. 'Wouldn't know!'

Annabel laughed and got up off her own bum to help load the dishwasher.

Kate gently slapped Emmi's hand, which was inching towards a prawn. 'No, darling. They're your Grandad's favourites. And they might upset your tummy, anyway.'

'Is she allergic to crustaceans as well as molluscs?' asked Annabel.

Kate frowned. 'I'm not sure.'

'They look funny when they've still got their coats on.' Emmi poked at them with a cocktail stick. 'Could I have one as a pet if you bought it alive?'

'No, darling. Prawns aren't pets.'

'Does my dad like them, too?'

Silence descended on the kitchen. Neither Annabel nor Paloma were looking at Kate directly, but she could sense that their ears were trained for her answer.

'Probably,' she said. 'Why don't you go and ask him?'

Emmi scratched her nose. 'But I want to help in here.'

'Well then, you can actually help by running upstairs and fetching the mug I left by the bath. Please, darling. We need to put it in the dishwasher.'

'Why are you washing things up *before* we eat?' Emmi looked puzzled.

'Because we've used lots of pots and pans and things for cooking,' said Annabel, 'and after we eat, we'll have loads of dirty dishes and we'll have to fill up the dish-washer all over again.'

'Oh.' Emmi thought about it a second, then skipped out of the kitchen using the door leading directly into the hall.

Annabel peeked through a gap in the other door. 'They're getting on like a house on fire out there,' she murmured over her shoulder.

Kate had tried to block out the voices coming from

the lounge – Oliver and Harry, discussing business. She gnashed her teeth in irritation.

Annabel came back to the table. 'The banker and the wanker,' she whispered. 'Always guaranteed to be best of pals.'

'Ssshhh!'

'Sorry.' Annabel kept her voice low. 'But I'm not keen on your Mr Barrett. I never have been. I can't believe you chucked Tom.'

Kate took a deep breath. 'Don't let Emmi hear you slagging off Harry.'

'I don't think she likes him either, though.'

'Of course she does. He's her father.'

'So?'

'So—'

'Here's the mug, Mummy.' The little girl ran back into the kitchen. 'Aunty Annabel,' she said breathlessly, 'Sam and Suzy are waking up. Do you think they're hungry?'

'Probably, sweetheart.'

'Would they like a prawn each?'

'I don't think so.' Annabel took her hand. 'Come on, let's go and see if their nappies need changing.'

Kate glanced around the kitchen, trying to work out what had to be done next. She ought to have made a list. Cooking wasn't one of her strengths. When she'd suggested last Christmas that everyone come round to hers next time, it had seemed a good idea to get away from the stuffy rituals of her parents' celebrations or Annabel's over-the-top festivities. She'd decided well in advance on an understated Victorian theme, but by the time it had come around she hadn't been in the mood. Emmi and Paloma had taken over the decorations and Kate had just concentrated on the food side of things. Now, catching sight of her reflection in the oven door, she screwed up her face in agitation. Her cheeks were flushed from the heat generated by the cooking and the stress of playing hostess when all she really wanted was to flee upstairs and bury her head under a pillow.

Harry swanned into the kitchen, magnificent in a mottled grey polo-neck and black trousers by Maine. 'Hello girls!' He grinned at Kate and Paloma, and draped his arms over their shoulders. 'How are things coming along in here then?'

'OK,' mumbled Kate, sweeping her hair off her face. One day, surely, her fringe would have grown out completely and ought to be long enough to stay in a scrunchie for an entire five minutes. 'Bugger,' she spat, 'these parsnips aren't properly cooked.'

'Calm down,' soothed Harry. 'Have some wine.'

She shrugged his arm off her shoulder, a dozen expletives on the tip of her tongue, but by some miracle she managed to keep them in.

'Talking of wine,' went on Harry, 'do you happen to have another bottle of the red? It was rather good.'

Kate scowled at him. 'You haven't finished a whole bottle already? It's only you and Oliver drinking it.'

Harry stood staring at her, his arm still draped over Paloma's shoulder. Kate noticed that her nanny looked a little abashed, although as stunning as ever: black curls loose and shiny around her made-up face, a purple sweater clinging over her ample bust and skimming the hips of her tight, dark trousers. Whereas Kate had made hardly any effort. She'd just thrown on a long, red, woollen dress and left her face stripped bare apart from a touch of mascara. The dress was a classic, but beginning to sag and show its age. Emmi had made her wear earrings shaped like Christmas wreaths which had tiny lights that flashed red and green. When Kate had answered the door to Harry an hour ago, he'd snorted and said she looked like one of Santa's Little Helpers.

Unamused, she'd replied, 'An elf, you mean?'

'Er – a very feminine one.'

'I thought women liked being called elfin?' Oliver had chortled, shaking Harry's hand and striking up an instant camaraderie.

'Would you like help laying the table, Kate?' Paloma asked now, taking a step forward so that Harry's arm slid off her shoulder.

'I'd be grateful.' Kate fished out another bottle of red wine from a box on the floor and thrust it at Harry. 'Here, I think the corkscrew's still on the coffee table.'

He nodded, returning to the lounge full of boozy bonhomie, performing an impression of the late Oliver Reed, whereupon the other Oliver guffawed.

Kate wanted to cry, but suddenly there was a loud rapping on the front door. Her spirits rose a little at the thought of seeing her grandfather, but sank again when she remembered she'd have to be nice to her parents for the rest of the day. They already knew Harry was going to be there, but how would they react when they saw for themselves how much he'd changed?

'Oliver, can you answer that?' she yelled.

She felt a hand tugging on her dress. It was Emmi, looking concerned.

'Are you all right, Mummy?'

'Yes – er – it's just a bit hot in here.'

'Should we open a window?'

Annabel came into the kitchen, a twin lodged firmly in the crook of each arm. 'I didn't realise before, but it's like the tropics in here compared to upstairs!'

Paloma was already stretching up over the sink, releasing the window latch. She didn't even need to stand on a chair, the way Kate would have had to.

'That's better,' sighed Annabel. 'Now, is any of the turkey carved yet? I'd like to make a purée with some vegetables for the twins' lunch. I think it's about time they didn't have something straight out of a jar, à la Jeanette.'

Vie sat opposite Tom in the kitchen. His brother leaned against the Welsh dresser. Tom could feel both sets of eyes on him, anxious and intent. He sat slumped in a hard, wooden chair, grinding his fist into the table. 'I'm such a stupid arse,' he moaned.

'You're the strangest looking arse *I've* ever seen,' Vie replied grimly. 'But I'll reserve judgement on the stupid part.'

Tom lifted his head. 'Thank you.'

'So,' proceeded Vie, her voice softening, 'now that you've filled us in on some of what we missed while we were away, perhaps you ought to tell us when it started going pear-shaped.'

A timer sounded. Scott leapt into action, looking dapper in his oven gloves. 'Sorry! Carry on, spill the beans. I'm still listening. I've just got to rescue the turkey.'

Vie obviously felt more gentle, feminine coaxing was required. 'Ignore him, Tom. When did you realise how you felt about Kate?'

He threw back his head and stared bleakly at the ceiling. 'I think I knew for certain the same instant I also knew she was intending to dump me. If that makes sense.'

'It's common enough,' said Scott. 'We rarely appreciate what we have until faced with the prospect of losing it.'

Tom realised that his brother was speaking from experience. After all, he'd almost lost Vie.

There was a puzzled look on her face. 'So let me get this straight, Tom. Since that day at your house, you haven't made contact with her? You haven't tried to . . . win her back?'

'It's not that easy. Not with a child involved. I'd hardly get into Kate's good books if I complicated things further.' He explained the reasons behind the break-up in more detail.

'But you don't actually know how she feels about *you*?'

'I know she liked me. We were attracted to each other.' Tom shrugged. 'It was just a few dates. We never slept together.' He grimaced, adding, 'I did meet her parents, but that's another story.'

Vie stared distractedly at the cauliflower and sprouts

cooking in the electric steamer. 'She doesn't sound like your usual type anyway.'

'She isn't.' He was pensive for a moment. 'The second time I met her, at the driving range, most of her hair was scraped back off her face in this tight, black band. I had to resist the urge to yank it out. The first time I'd seen her she was so fresh and pretty, her hair fluffy and loose around her shoulders. So . . . sweet.'

Scott raised his eyebrows at his wife. 'You could never say that about any of his other girlfriends.'

'No,' agreed Vie. 'From what I've heard, a few of them were fluffy and most of them were loose, but *sweet* . . .' She shook her head emphatically.

Tom snorted. 'Stop taking the piss.' But he only half meant it.

Vie reached over and patted his hand. 'Sorry. Tell us more about Kate.'

He could picture her vividly, wrapped in that over-sized cardigan, face flushed, hair bedraggled.

'She has amazing eyes,' he said. 'An undiluted shade of grey, without a hint of blue or green. And her daughter's are just the same.'

'Didn't the kid get in the way at all?' asked Scott.

'Emmi isn't a snotty-nosed brat, if that's what you're thinking. She didn't seem to resent me going out with her mum. She's bright for her age, and she could be a hell of a chatterbox once she got started.'

'It sounds as if you're missing her too,' said Vie.

Tom stared into space. 'I suppose I am. I never told Kate this, but sometimes I'd pretend that Emmi was mine. There was this one time, when we went to the cinema, I grabbed her hand as we crossed the road, and it felt . . . right. I was naturally protective of her. I liked that.'

'See!' Vie turned to Scott. 'Tom's living proof that you both haven't been scarred for life by your parents.'

Tom looked from his brother to his sister-in-law. 'I sense an "issue" going on here.'

Vie shrugged, adjusting her hair-clip. 'He's agonising that he'll make a lousy father because he didn't have a very good role model.'

Tom's eyebrows shot up. 'You're not—'

'Pregnant? No,' sighed Vie. 'But I'd like to be. I just wish Scott could be more enthusiastic. I want us both to be young enough to race about after our children until they're well past toddlerhood, so I don't see the point in hanging around.'

'It's not that I'm afraid to lose my independence or anything,' Scott put in defensively. 'I know some men have trouble with that. You probably think I'm too much of a kid myself still, that I'll miss going for drinks every night after work, that kind of thing. But I've cut down on all that already. I'm not really bothered about it. And Vie's happy to work part-time, or whatever. Money's not a problem. It's just – well, what kind of a dad would I make? Look at the "family unit" we grew up in, Tom. I wouldn't know where to start.'

'You start with wiping bottoms and take it from there,' said Vie.

'She's right.' Tom smiled thinly at Scott, experiencing a powerful tug on the brotherly bond between them. 'Our parents hated each other, not *us*. There doesn't have to be a recurring pattern, generation after generation. And Dad tries his best, on the rare occasions we see him. He could have been a hell of a lot worse.'

'I know.' Scott prodded the turkey, which was well and truly done. 'But it still scares the shit out of me.'

'So did marriage,' Tom reminded him. 'Then Vie came along. Listen, I reckon we'd both make decent dads. I might never get the chance to test that out, but you've got the opportunity right here, with a gorgeous woman who you happen to love and who'd make a wonderful mother.'

'Stop it,' said Vie, 'I'm blushing!'

'So you should. You deserve every accolade going.'

'Are you chatting up my wife?' Scott demanded archly.

'Please let him carry on,' begged Vie. 'I'm actually really enjoying it.'

17

Kate sat at the table with her elbows pinned to her sides, which wasn't the best way to use cutlery effectively, but she'd ended up with Harry on the left and her mother on the right, both of them encroaching on her meagre space. The kitchen at the Old Parsonage, which Kate had always regarded as a fair size (although not by comparison to Oliver and Annabel's), felt tiny with eight adults, one child and two babies packed into it, along with one turkey, twelve crackers, two large Christmas puddings and the rest of the paraphernalia that accompanied the occasion. Harry and Oliver sat on folding garden chairs that Kate had dusted down and brought in from the shed. They hadn't seemed pleased about it, but tough. She herself was making do with the spindly antique stool that usually stood in a corner with a dried herb display in a basket on top.

'Such a shame this house doesn't have a separate dining room,' bemoaned Kate's mother, who had Paloma seated on her other side.

'It did have,' said Grandad, 'but it was so small we couldn't fit a large enough table in it. That was when Joyce and I turned it into the study. I thought you were aware of that.'

'Mum,' said Kate, trying to change the subject, 'could you pass the cranberry sauce, please?'

'Of course, dear. It's a little watery, isn't it?'

Kate had a sour taste in her mouth that had nothing to do with the chewy sage and onion stuffing. She began counting to ten in her head, but only got as far as four before Harry interrupted.

'Mrs Finlay, will you pull your cracker with me?' He flashed her his most winning smile.

Kate's mother dissolved under his cornflower blue gaze. 'I'd be delighted. And, please, *do* call me Glynis.'

When he'd been Harry the Student, even 'Mrs Finlay' hadn't been good enough. Now that he was Harry the Dashing and Successful Businessman, things were radically different.

Minutes later, after a flurry of snapping crackers and a lusty chorus of disapproval from the twins in their portable highchairs, everyone was wearing a paper crown, apart from Sam and Suzy who had tried to eat theirs (although they hadn't technically pulled a cracker). Kate had ripped hers deliberately as she'd put it on, but Emmi innocently pointed out that there was a spare cracker and insisted on pulling it with her great-grandfather in order to procure a new hat for her mum.

'I'll pull it with you, Emmi,' volunteered Harry, who was sitting closer to her.

Emmi looked at him, tight-lipped. Kate frowned, remembering Annabel's earlier remark, although she couldn't understand it. How could a child not like his or her father? Wasn't it biologically ingrained at conception? Kate regarded her own dad, sitting like a beached whale at the far end of the table, and suddenly comprehended that 'like' was an entirely different concept to 'love'.

'I haven't pulled one with you yet, Emmi,' she said quickly, attempting to diffuse the situation. 'Do you mind, Harry?'

He stared at her for a second, then shook his head. 'Be my guest.'

Actually, you're *mine*, Kate wanted to huff. But she hadn't been catty to him in public yet, and she wasn't about to start now. When she'd issued the invitation for him to join them today, she'd also made the comment that she expected he was spending it with his own family. But then he'd pointed out that Emmi *was* his family and that he ought to be with her as much as possible, especially at Christmas.

In the last few weeks since he'd turned up, Kate had tried searching for a resemblance between him and Emmi, as if by stumbling across a characteristic, a look, a sign that they were related, she might warm to him again. She often reminded herself that without him she wouldn't have her daughter, but even that didn't melt the frost blanketing her heart. With each day, the resentment seemed to grow. Before long, she wouldn't know how to handle it, and then what?

As if Annabel had read her mind, she turned to Harry and asked, 'Does Emmi remind you of anyone – apart from Kate? Your mother or grandmother, perhaps? I can't see anything of you in her.'

'Er,' Harry looked thrown, 'I suppose she's like my mother was in some ways. I mean, she looks like Kate,

215

no one could dispute that, but her character . . .'

Perturbed, Kate found herself crumpling the napkin in her lap. Didn't they realise that Emmi was present, hanging on to every word? They were talking about a grandmother she would never meet, delving into the history of a family even Kate knew very little about. Harry's mother had died when he was a boy, and he had never taken Kate home to Leicester to meet his father or younger brother. She'd only ever seen a handful of faded Polaroids. Harry had spoken about them fondly enough, but he'd rarely made a trip up to visit them. In the holidays, he'd usually hung out with friends. Even when Emmi was born, his father and brother hadn't made any effort to come and see her, and Harry had never suggested to Kate that they should. Sometimes she wondered if he'd even told them he had a daughter.

'Do you think we could put the travel cot in the lounge?' Annabel was saying now, directing the question at Kate. 'The twins are getting a bit fretful being strapped in, but I can't let them roam around loose or they'll get up to all sorts.'

Kate nodded, grateful for the diversion.

'It makes a wonderful playpen, all that mesh to bounce off of.' Annabel smiled, then nudged Oliver. 'Go on, darling, be a hunk, fetch it down for me, please. It's in Kate's room. You'll have to fold it up or you'll never make it down the stairs.'

Oliver grumbled melodramatically, but did as he was asked.

*

'Shall we make egg nogs?' said Vie. 'Or snowballs?'

Tom opened one eyelid and looked across at her. She was curled up beside Scott on the sofa. There was a *Coronation Street* special on, but no one was paying much attention. The remote control was out of reach and they couldn't be bothered to get up to switch the television off, even though Vie had insisted they ought to be playing 'parlour games'.

'We're like something out of *The Royle Family*,' she said. 'Sitting around on our backsides watching TV.'

Her husband moaned, lifting his gold paper crown to look at her. 'I'm not watching TV, I'm having a kip.' He pulled the crown down over his eyes again.

'So we're not having egg nogs, then?'

'How d'you make them?' asked Tom. 'I've forgotten.'

'Well,' said Vie slowly, 'you need eggs.'

'We've run out,' Scott reminded her.

'Oh. That puts a damper on breakfast tomorrow, too.'

Tom picked up his can of lager from the floor and gave Tina a perfunctory pat on the head. She barely twitched. Clearly, she'd also had too much Christmas dinner. 'I'd rather stick to beer anyway, thanks, Vie.'

'Boring!' She pouted sulkily. 'I still think we should play a game.'

'Not charades,' pleaded Scott.

'Something like Truth or Dare.'

'Oh hell.' Tom pulled his own paper crown over his eyes and wished he was in the Rover's Return, sitting alone in one of those booths with a packet of pork scratchings.

'Tom,' began Vie.

'Yes?'

'What's your life's ambition?'

'Huh?'

'Well, is there anything you really want to do?'

Tom pretended he was thick. 'Don't understand. Sorry.'

'It's quite simple,' frowned Vie. 'In my case, I want to learn to fly. And once I've got my licence, I want to go to Australia and circle Ayers Rock. All on my own. At sunset.'

'That's nice. Are you flying yourself all the way there, or relying on Quantas to do the bulk for you?'

She prodded his leg with her foot. 'Patronising sod!'

'I want to go to Las Vegas,' Scott announced groggily. 'And I want to win a million at roulette.'

'Dollars or sterling?' asked Tom.

'Can't you be serious?' snapped Vie.

'Of course I can. When I grow up, I want to write a novel.'

She groaned. 'There's always one person who says that. Can't you be more original?'

'Nope.' Tom shook his head. 'I really do.'

'Always has,' said Scott, lifting his hat. 'Since as far back as I can remember.'

Vie looked at Tom with interest now. 'So why haven't you done it then?'

'I can't write any more.'

'Can't or won't?'

'Both.'

Scott squeezed his wife's knee. 'Best not to go into it, my love.'

But Vie's countenance flooded with curiosity. 'Why not? I know you're not into journalism any more, Tom, but why can't you tackle fiction? What sort of novel would you want to write?'

'A Booker Prize winner.'

'Oh, something simple then.'

'Tom couldn't settle for anything less than a great literary classic,' said Scott. 'He'd be the Charles Dickens of the twenty-first century if he could.'

'Or the Hemingway,' added Tom.

Vie looked at him in a motherly, caring way. 'Don't you think you're setting your sights rather high? Maybe that's why you haven't actually written it yet, because you're afraid of failing.'

Tom took a swig of lager. 'I have written something. I just never finished it.'

'Oh?' Scott raised an eyebrow. 'When did you start?'

'When I was at uni.'

'Bloody hell, mate, that was fifteen years ago. What kind of story was it?'

'A love story, with the background of a thriller, and a bit of comedy thrown in.'

'Very Booker Prize,' said Vie.

'Why haven't you finished it?' asked Scott.

'Because it was rubbish. And I didn't know anything about love, except shagging.'

'Lovely,' Vie sniffed, with good-natured contempt. 'Can't you carry on with it now? Update it or something. You've got the maturity, the experience—'

'A larger vocabulary,' chipped in Scott.

Tom pulled a face. 'What the hell do I know about

love *now*? I'm still crap at it. The non-shagging part, that is.'

Vie shook her head in frustration. 'Maybe you could write down how you feel about losing Kate. You don't have to be profound, just honest. Let it all flow out and see what happens. At the very least, it might make you feel better. You can always think up a plot later.'

Tom stared at his lager can, his fingers aching to crush it into a jagged metal ball. But just as he realised it still contained liquid and that he'd probably get rather wet, he felt Vie's hand on his shoulder, her hair grazing his cheek as she leaned over him, sighing.

'See, Tom darling? I've even made the effort to get up. I'm sorry for being so pushy. Everything's going to be fine, you know. Scott and I are living proof that things work out one way or another.'

Tom nodded, but couldn't trust himself to speak.

Having just saved the twins from being electrocuted by the fairy lights they'd managed to pull off the tree, Kate was positioning the travel cot out of harm's reach when her mother sidled up to her.

'Next year, Kate dear, I think we should definitely have Christmas in Pagelton or at your sister's,' she said quietly. 'It's all very well for you to say it was your turn, but it is rather cramped here.'

Kate bit her lip. 'I think everyone enjoyed themselves, though. Isn't Christmas about families getting together? Does it matter where it takes place?'

'Exactly.'

Kate realised she'd fallen into a trap of her own

making. 'Well,' she said obstinately, 'it was about time I did my bit.'

'Whatever, dear.' With a sigh, Glynis Finlay tossed back the strand of tinsel around her neck. Emmi had insisted that all the women wear one, like feather boas.

She'd wanted Suzy to have one too, but Annabel had patiently explained that Sam would probably strangle her with it.

'Mum, why didn't you go to the pub with the men?' asked Kate, wishing everyone could have gone and left her in peace.'

'Me? A pub! I wouldn't dream of it.'

'Oh, that's right,' said Kate. 'They're common.'

'Darling, what's the matter with you? You'll never get anywhere with Harry if you carry on being waspish like this. You were positively frigid around him, and just look at you – you've made hardly any effort. You used to at least *attempt* to be well-groomed.'

Kate opened and closed her mouth, but no sound came out. Indignation gushed up inside her.

'I'm not sure Kate wants to get anywhere with Harry, Mum,' said Annabel, joining the conversation at an opportune moment.

'He happens to be Emmi's father,' said Kate, finding strength in numbers. 'That's as far as it goes.'

'Just because he's so fit he makes George Clooney look like Quasimodo, it doesn't necessarily follow that he's relationship material.' Annabel folded her arms over her chest and blinked at her mother challengingly.

'Really, I don't know what's got into you both. Too much feminism, probably.'

Kate noticed Paloma in the hallway, staring in at them. How long had she been listening, and why was she blushing? It wasn't like her to be embarrassed about anything. 'What's wrong?' Kate asked.

'Nothing,' Paloma was quick to assure her. 'I just checked upstairs and Emmi's crashed out on her bed. She must be whacked – she didn't even make it under the duvet.'

'I wish the twins would go to sleep that easily,' said Annabel.

'You didn't see Emmi last night,' Kate told her. 'She was still awake at two, desperate for a glimpse of Santa.'

Their mother heaved a shuddering sigh. 'I wish you knew how petty your current problems are, compared to those I have to contend with. Why is it that your children always cause you more heartache and worry the older they get? As if they never learn a thing you teach them.'

Kate scowled, sensing that a lecture was imminent. 'Mum—'

'I'll have my say whether you like it or not. Harry Barrett is about as eligible as a young man can be. And, as you said yourself, he's also Emmeline's father. It's her that you ought to be considering, not your own taste in men. Or lack of it, as the case may be. If you're still mooning over that Thomas Llewellyn, you should just stop and count yourself lucky that Harry came back when he did—'

'Er, I should probably go and make us all some tea,' interrupted Paloma, her blush deepening by the second.

'You've done enough already,' said Kate.

'Sorry?'

'With the cooking and clearing up. It's supposed to be your day off. I wanted you here as my guest, not my employee.' Although Kate knew that this was just something else for her mother to tut over.

'Oh.' Paloma looked relieved.

'Thomas comes from fine enough stock,' Glynis Finlay was spouting now, 'yet it doesn't seem to have done him much good.'

'He's not a stud horse,' Kate bristled, 'and I'm not some mare that needs impregnating.'

'Mum, when you first met Tom you were all over him like a rash,' Annabel reminded her.

'But after I spoke to him at length—'

'Found out he wasn't anything like his mother, you mean.' Kate could feel tears trickling over her cheeks. She hoped everyone would put them down to anger.

'Frankly, Kate, he's a wastrel. Oliver spoke to him in depth about his work, and told us afterwards that it all sounds rather shambolic. Thomas Llewellyn doesn't seem to know *what* to do with his life, which, for your sake and Emmi's, could be absolutely disastrous.'

'It doesn't matter any more, though, does it Mum?' Kate struggled to keep her voice under control. 'I won't be seeing Tom again. It's over. But just because he's out of the picture, that doesn't mean I'm going to ride off into the sunset in Harry's BMW.'

Glynis Finlay pouted, but remained silent.

'*I'll* make us some tea,' announced Annabel, flicking back her hair with a gesture that spoke volumes.

When had her sister grown up? wondered Kate

admiringly and with a trace of jealousy. And why the hell had she been left straggling behind like the squealing runt of the litter?

Their mother was making a fuss of ensconcing herself in the armchair next to the travel cot. She had an injured air about her as she picked up a teddy bear from the coffee table and waved it in the twins' faces, emitting strange cooing noises.

'I'd like a sweetener in my tea,' she called out, as Annabel stalked into the kitchen. 'I'm on a diet,' she explained. 'And if there's any Christmas cake left, I'll have a tiny sliver . . .'

18

Kate strode out of the Tube station, the din of the traffic mercifully drowning out her squeaking trainers. She felt short and frumpy in a suit and long coat without her heels to complete the ensemble, but she'd taken to wearing comfier shoes on the way to and from work, as more and more women were doing. She was carrying her office shoes in a rucksack. New Yorkers had been doing it for years, hadn't they? Workers in London had been slow catching on.

To perk herself up, she went into Starbucks for a coffee. Wondering whether to attempt drinking it as she walked – considering she'd burned her hand the last time she'd tried – she jumped in alarm when a familiar voice spoke casually over her shoulder.

'This is on me.'

She looked round. Dick Anthony was handing a twenty-pound note to the girl behind the counter.

'I'll have the same.' He smiled rakishly at the girl, then turned to Kate. 'Will you join me?'

She frowned at her watch. 'Well . . .'

'We can both be late. Nat will circulate the gossip, of course, but we're probably past caring.'

His dark eyes held hers, and she found herself being led away from the counter towards a table. She sat down without a word, swinging her rucksack on to the floor between her feet and undoing a couple of buttons on her coat.

'I've got a confession to make,' said Dick. 'I've been lying in wait for you.'

Now she was even more disconcerted. 'Look—'

'We can't avoid each other for ever. It's bloody hard having a PA who doesn't talk to you. At this rate, I'll have to hire a temp.'

'Maybe you should,' said Kate. It was strange how the encounter before Christmas had somehow left her feeling stronger, as if she had a hold over him. 'In fact, it's about time you hired someone on a more permanent basis.'

He looked nonplussed. 'Are you saying . . . ?'

'I'm not quitting. I can't afford to. But you should have taken someone else on as well as me. I do enough work most days for two people.'

'Why haven't you said anything before?'

'I should have thought it was obvious that I was busy. And I've been too naïve and too much of a coward to come out and say it. I just thought it was the way things had to be.'

'I suppose getting paid overtime comes in handy.'

'Of course, I won't deny that. Emmi has a few extra treats, but that isn't what she needs. She's in bed by the time I get home most nights. Buying her a new Barbie accessory and taking her out somewhere nice doesn't make up for the fact that we don't spend enough time together. It might have eased my guilt in the past, but it doesn't any more.'

Dick nodded thoughtfully. 'I've a mounting list of apologies to make. Not just for what happened—'

'I'd rather you didn't mention that.'

'I'd rather not either.' His mouth twisted wryly. 'But I've got to. I'm sorry, Kate, I was a bastard, and I've had a crap few weeks if that's any consolation.'

'You were drunk, and I wasn't exactly sober myself.'

'You're also the woman I'd least want to hit on. Which sounds as if I don't find you attractive, when I do. You're one of the most *natural* people I know. The thing is, out of everyone at Anthony & Gray, I probably respect you most. Which makes it unforgivable that I treated you the way I did.'

'Not unforgivable,' said Kate, surprised at what he was saying. 'Just hard to forget.'

'I understand. But I meant it – about respecting you. Although admittedly I've got a funny way of showing it. Anyway, I think that's why I turned to you when my relationship started going sour.' He pulled another face. 'Yes, that's right, Dick Anthony was having a full-blown "relationship". I know I've got a reputation as a womaniser, but I've never been that bad. People just seem to expect the worst of me.'

'Do you ever bother to put them straight?'

'No.' Dick smiled ruefully. 'Which didn't help matters when I met Laura. She was a waitress at the bistro round the corner from the office. Not my usual type, but maybe that was why it was so different. It all got intense rather quickly. We ended up crashing

227

headlong into the proverbial brick wall.'

'Brick wall?' Kate wondered if there was a proverb she hadn't heard of.

'Commitment, marriage, kids, trips to IKEA, you name it.'

'You mean, she wanted to settle down and you felt you weren't ready?'

Dick smiled again, shaking his head. 'Actually, *I* was the one who wanted to settle down.'

Kate blinked. 'Oh . . .' There was a long pause. As she sat there, virtually gawping at him, she realised that his face was one of the most symmetrical she had ever come across. It was a tidy countenance, every feature regular, the bone structure precise. Instead of looking at him from the perspective of a heterosexual female, her artistic eye followed each curve and hollow as if she were about to immortalise him in a portrait or sculpture. Tom, she remembered with a stab of pain, was ruggedly good-looking, Harry was downright handsome, but Dick, she acknowledged, was the only man she'd ever met who could literally be called beautiful. She doubted he'd thank her for saying it, though.

He sighed. 'Have you ever wondered if there's someone out there who's right for you, Kate?'

She shrugged. 'I used to believe that there was one person for everyone. One special love. Feel free to stick your fingers down your throat.'

He waved his hand dismissively. 'Now you see, according to some people, men aren't supposed to believe in monogamy. It's not part of our conditioning. We're just meant to procreate generously with the most attractive females of the species. But there has to be something else, doesn't there? I never wanted to live the whole of my life on my own, but what's the point in sharing it with one woman after another? Isn't it more meaningful to find a companion you can get along with, and then raise a family and grow old together?'

Kate was beginning to think that this Laura person needed her head examining. Then again, so did she. There were women all over the world crying out for someone like Dick, but she wasn't one of them. Once upon a time she'd fancied him; she wasn't dim enough to have forgotten. Yet since then something had changed. Perhaps some sort of chemical reaction had taken place in her brain which had made men like Dick and Harry – amazingly gorgeous men – *un*fanciable. She could understand why she *ought* to have the hots for them, but not why she didn't.

'Have you ever met someone you liked,' Dick was asking, 'someone you felt was right for you, and then tried to fall in love with them? I've seen people do it. Sometimes it works – you hear about it happening in some arranged marriages – but I've come to the conclusion that it only works because it's meant to. It doesn't matter *how* you fall in love, even if you try forcing it, because it only happens if it's supposed to.'

'I – I've never really thought of it that way.'

Dick seemed to be waking up from his introspection. He took in his surroundings as if he'd been a long way away and hadn't wanted to return. 'I guess I tried it to some extent with you,' he said gravely.

'With me?' Kate dropped the packet of sugar she'd been fiddling with.

'When things started going wrong with Laura, suddenly there you were, in the lift that day, flustered and late. And I'd always liked you. Admired you for being a single mother with a full-time job. Anyway, I asked you out. I used you, I suppose, to blot out what I was really feeling. So that's something else to apologise to you for.'

Comprehension was beginning to strike Kate with relentless clarity. 'And that's why you blew hot and cold . . .'

'Laura and I were on and off for weeks, going round in the same old circles. I think I was relieved when Tom came on the scene. It gave me an excuse to leave you alone.'

Kate stared down at the table. 'That was another bloody rebound romance.'

'Sorry?'

'Tom.' She spoke louder. 'When we met, he'd just broken up with Miss Brazil.'

'Who?'

'Well, I called her Miss Brazil. She was so stunningly beautiful and Latin-looking.'

Dick's tidy brow was now furrowed and messy. 'So you and Tom, you aren't . . . I'm sorry, I just . . .'

'It's OK. We *were* going out, but I was the one who had to end it. And that was before I'd even met Jem.'

'Jem?'

'Jemima Whitesilk, or something stupid like that. AKA Miss Brazil.'

'Jemma Whitelace?'

'That was it.' Kate bit her lip. 'Do you know her?'

'Not to speak to. She's deputy editor at Athene Aphrodite.'

'Is that some women's magazine I haven't heard of?' scoffed Kate. 'Like *Marie Claire*, only more obscure?'

'No, er' – Dick tugged uncomfortably at his tie – 'they publish erotic fiction.'

Shocked, Kate almost sent her cappuccino flying. 'Oh! I didn't have a cat in hell's chance then.'

'Pardon?'

She could already feel a characteristic blush coming on, rushing up to colour her throat and face until they would probably match the suit she was wearing. 'Against someone like her,' she mumbled. 'If she, um, reads a lot of that sort of . . . fiction, then she's bound to know a thing or two about men, and how to . . . er . . .'

'I see what you mean.' Dick's brow was still creased. 'But I'm sure she was with Aidan Patricks at that New Year's Eve party in Soho. Someone pointed her out to me. I only dropped by, I wasn't in the mood for that kind of thing, but—'

'Aidan Patricks the writer?'

'Not my cup of tea, but he's making a name for himself all the same.'

'And she was with him? Jem?'

'They seemed very . . . intimate.'

'All over each other?'

'As close as they could get in public without being obscene. Kate, are you all right?'

'Not really.' As hard as she tried, she couldn't force

her lips to straighten out again. They seemed hell-bent on smiling inanely. And what were they smiling about? The fact that Jem had probably left Tom a second time? And what was the good in that? There was still Emmi to consider. Tom was still unsuitable. Her mother had been right about that much. It had spelled disaster from the start. But somehow, in spite of all that, Kate couldn't stop herself blurting out in frustration, 'Sod Harry Barrett!'

Dick looked even more confused. 'And who's he?'

'Emmi's father.' Kate summarised the situation for Dick's benefit.

'So you're thinking of hooking up with Harry again? For Emmi's sake?'

Kate shook her head. 'He'd drive me bonkers. Even though my mother thinks it would be the sensible solution all round.'

'Does he want to get back together with you?'

'I – I don't know. He said all these things when he came back, about how he hadn't been serious about anyone else since we split up. And he didn't seem to want me seeing Tom . . .'

Dick stroked his jaw thoughtfully. 'Tom's a decent chap, you know. Everyone has their faults, but I've always forgiven him his. He didn't have the best of childhoods, with his parents at each other's throats most of the time. It affected him quite a bit while he was at school. He's extremely intelligent; he could have done even better academically. We've kept in touch on and off down the years, and I've never been surprised by anything he's done – except for giving up the writing. I can't fathom that at all, and he's yet to give me a valid reason.'

Kate stared down at an old coffee stain on the table. 'I didn't even know he was a writer at first. I had to ask him about it when my sister recognised his name.'

'Strange . . . But he has that side to him. Very secretive.'

'I'm too old for mysteries,' said Kate resolutely.

Dick twitched an eyebrow. 'I wish I were ten years younger. I'd be more or less your age, and believe me, I wouldn't think of myself as "too old".'

Kate pursed her lips. 'I've got Emmi to consider.'

'Fair enough. But I hope you don't use that as an excuse. Something to hide behind when the world gets a little too . . . uncertain.'

She started buttoning up her coat. 'Well, much as I'm enjoying this tête-à-tête, I've got work to do, even if you haven't.'

'Kate, my lovelife might be hopeless, but, however clichéd this sounds, I don't want to see that happen to you.'

She stood up, making a fuss of swinging her rucksack into position, aware that people were staring. 'Thanks for the coffee.'

She didn't look at Dick as she slalomed her way past the other tables towards the door, but she was well aware he was right behind her.

'We may as well walk together,' he said.

Kate could feel his gaze boring down on her. He could match her pace effortlessly, so there was no point trying to evade him.

'Just as long as you don't keep playing agony aunt,' she grumbled.

'How about concerned older brother?'

'I'm not fifteen, thank you, I can take care of myself.'

'OK, but I'm going to ask you one more thing. If Harry hadn't come back, do you think you'd still be with Tom?'

Dick had slowed down, but Kate wasn't about to fall into that trap. She kept going, her angry, determined gait shattered by vehement hooting as she walked straight into the path of a traffic-dodging black cab. A moment later she stood trembling on the kerb, yanked back by Dick, who had a firm hold of her arm, as if he couldn't trust her not to do it again. She opened her mouth to speak.

'Don't bother, Kate,' he said shakily. 'You've just given me all the answer I needed.'

19

So, what was it again . . . ? Kate tried to remember. Three coffees, two teas and one Evian? Or was it one coffee, three teas and two Evians? Oh bugger, she hated this part of her job. And she was dressed in a black skirt and white blouse, so she could easily have been mistaken for one of those waitresses in the tea shop that had just opened in Beckton Lacey. The clients in Dick's office were the sort to look down their noses at her; if she cocked up their order – or however else she was supposed to refer to it – she'd be even more demoralised.

'Excuse me . . . Kate.'

Damn. What did Natalia want? 'Mmm?'

'There's a call for you. Your sister. She says you're not picking up your phone.'

'Obviously, seeing as I'm not at my desk.'

'She says she doesn't want to leave a message on your voice mail. The call diverted to reception. I've got her on the line now.'

Kate realised she'd forgotten to switch the kettle on. Sod it. 'Can you ask her to call back later?'

'I would,' said Natalia testily, 'but she says it's important and can't wait.'

'OK, OK, I'll be there in a second.' Kate groaned. What did Annabel want that was so imperative? Suddenly, she felt an unwelcome prick of *déjà vu*. Her sister had called urgently once before, last year when Grandad had had his accident . . .

Kate let the teaspoon she'd been holding drop on to the work-surface and quickly followed Natalia out of the kitchenette and back to reception.

'Put the call through to my desk, please.' It would be more private.

The phone was already purring by the time Kate reached it. 'Annabel?'

'Oh, thank God I've got hold of you.' She sounded tearful. 'Something terrible's happened.'

Kate sat down heavily. 'What?'

'It's his heart . . . I didn't know he had a problem . . .'

Kate couldn't bear it. She loved her grandfather so much.

'We're at Addenham Infirmary,' her sister went on. 'I think you ought to come right away. Dad looks awful . . .'

Afterwards, Kate would remember that the colour of the walls was a pale salmon, but at the time, as she walked along the corridor, she wasn't aware of taking that detail in. The smell was the overpowering feature, the clinical antisepticky smell that pervaded everywhere, so that even when she was outside in the relatively fresh air again, it seemed to be clinging to her skin and hair and clothes, like smoke from a crowded pub.

She would remember the tubes attached to her father

as if they were some strange form of plumbing. And the greyish pallor of his face, mirrored by the woman at his bedside. Kate had never seen her mother looking so far from immaculate. Dark circles beneath lacklustre eyes, wiry blonde hair flattened into a shapeless mass . . .

And the soft, rhythmic beeping of the monitor, which fixed itself in Kate's head like a song on a radio, so that even when she was driving home later she could hear it. Even when she was lying in bed, alone in the dark, the sound was still with her.

But the overriding memory would be of Annabel. Organising plastic visitors' chairs, refilling the water jug, insisting her mother eat something, fetching tea . . . Annabel with her long, silken hair secured in a plait, her face bare, her shirt shapeless and baggy over an old pair of jeans. Annabel the Princess, bereft of her sparkle but all the more dazzling for it.

'He's sleeping now,' she said, after Kate had sat there for over five minutes, watching him. 'He was awake a while back. He spoke to us.'

'Did he?' Kate wished he would wake up now and speak again. But then, what would she say to him? What had she ever said to him? As a child, she had never run up to him and flung herself into his arms when he came home from the office. 'Daddy, look at the picture I drew today!' That had been Annabel's role: to excel, to attract and demand affection. Kate had just sat back, as she was doing now, loving her parents from a distance.

'Where's Grandad?' she asked.

'There's a garden,' said Annabel. 'Apparently he found it when a friend of his from the retirement flats was in here. He said he wanted to be on his own for a while.'

'Oh.'

'Why don't you go and find him?'

'Not if he wants to be alone.'

'He'd rather be with you,' said their mother, from the other side of the bed. 'I think you should go to him, Kate.'

'But Dad—'

'Your father's going to be fine. Like your sister said, he's sleeping now.'

Kate stood up, smoothing a hand over her skirt. 'OK,' she sighed, and picked up her coat.

Out in the corridor, she spotted a nurse and asked for directions. But the garden wasn't far. Down a flight of steps, a couple of left turns, and she was there. It was built into a courtyard. All around the edge there was a sheltered walkway lined with benches. Her grandfather sat staring into an empty flowerbed. He didn't stir as she drew nearer. Even when she was close enough to read the plaque on the back of the bench seat – 'In Memory of Emile Loxley, with love always, Lucinda Loxley' – her grandfather didn't make any acknowledgement that she was there. Without speaking, she sat down beside him.

'I suppose,' he said at last, still without looking at her, 'in a month or two, that flower bed might be full of crocuses or tulips.'

'It might be.'

'I couldn't bear to be inside,' he went on. 'I couldn't sit there . . . looking at him . . .'

'Aren't you cold, though?'

'I don't feel it. Go back in if you want, you don't have to stay here.'

'But I want to.'

'It's not the same for us,' he said quietly. 'Not like it is for your mother and Annabel. We feel . . . differently about him.'

Kate fumbled for his hand.

'We're alike, you and I,' her grandfather continued, 'because we've never crossed that divide. We love him, in our own ways, because of what he is to us. But we don't like *who* he is, the person, his . . . character. Your mother and Annabel bridged the gap; perhaps they didn't have that far to go, or perhaps he made it easier for them. They're close to him. We're not . . . Are you following any of this, or is it just the rambling of a senile old man?'

'It makes sense.'

'You're not just saying that to make me feel better?'

'No, Grandad.'

'I hope you never know how it feels to have a child you don't respect,' he said after a pause, stretching down to pick up a sweet wrapper that had blown against his shoe. 'Oh, when your father was a baby, a small boy, he was the apple of my eye. And your grandmother's. But as he grew older . . . I'd like to think Joyce and I didn't neglect him, that we were there for him when he needed us . . . We mould our children to a certain extent, but they have their own personalities, their own traits. There are times when we're completely powerless. We watch them grow up and turn into the kind of person we don't get along with . . . and there's nothing we can do about it. We still love them, but we can't – what's the term nowadays? – *connect* with them.'

Kate thought about her relationship with her daughter. If Dick really had spoken to Charles, and if they honestly *were* going to take on someone else to share her workload, then she'd be able to get home at a more reasonable hour, in time for Emmi's bath if not her tea. Anything would be better than arriving home to find Emmi in bed, asleep. Kate knew that there was so much she was missing out on, although she'd tried to deny it, to make up for it at weekends, but she couldn't go on pretending.

'To outlive a child . . .' Her grandfather groaned. 'I never thought it would happen . . .'

Kate shivered. The cold air was bitter. It felt as if it was attacking from the inside out as well as the outside in. 'But Dad's going to be all right, isn't he? Annabel said—'

'I'm talking about the possibility. I don't think I've ever faced it. And the guilt . . .' For the first time that afternoon, her grandfather made eye contact with her for more than just a fleeting second. 'If it were you or Emmi lying in that bed, I know I'd want to die. If anything happened to either of you . . . there would be nothing to go on for.'

'But Annabel . . . ? The twins . . . ?'

'They're not the reason I go on, day in, day out without Joyce. It was always you. And Emmi. And when I had the accident, when I couldn't look after Emmi any more . . .'

'Grandad—'

'But that was just as well, because she needs someone like Paloma, someone who can keep up with her when you're not there. It turned out for the best. It's just . . . What I'm trying to say is that you and Emmi mean more to me than the fact that my own son almost died today. And you would have meant as much to your grandmother. I don't want to give in to guilt over your father, though. Joyce wouldn't want me to. She used to say that most of the time guilt gets in the way of the important stuff. And in this case, perhaps she was right.'

Kate shivered again, and muttered spontaneously, 'I wish I had what you and Gran had.'

Her grandfather turned towards her. 'You don't think you still can? You're not even twenty-seven yet.'

She shrugged. 'Sometimes I think it was easier in your day.'

'So Harry Barrett still isn't The One?'

Kate snorted – a knee-jerk reaction. To cover up, she said, 'Harry's Emmi's father.' But even that didn't come out the way she'd wanted it to.

'Being a parent in a biological sense doesn't automatically make you one in practice,' said her grandfather. 'Some men aren't designed to be fathers, just as some women make terrible mothers. Harry's intentions were probably good, but I don't think he was . . . sufficiently prepared.'

'Now you're being polite.'

'I'm just saying.'

She rose to her feet, adjusting her coat. 'It's freezing out here. I'm going back inside. Are you coming?'

He nodded, clambering up. 'It's time.'

As they walked along, Kate instinctively looped her arm through his. 'I'm sorry.'

'So am I.' There was a pause. 'It's not your fault if you weren't sufficiently prepared either.'

'For motherhood?' Her eyebrows shot up.

But her grandfather shook his head. 'For needing someone, and being needed yourself. Not solely as a mother.'

Kate ground to a halt, almost dragging him back with her. 'What do you mean?'

'Exactly what I said. If you were ready, you'd have understood.'

'Grandad—'

'Not now, Katie. Not today. And don't look at me like that.'

Kate was so infuriated, she wanted to stamp her foot like a surly child. But she knew how futile clashing with her grandfather was. He always had to have the last word. And the one before that.

Two days went by with no visible improvement in her father's condition. The medical staff didn't seem discouraged, but Kate and the rest of her family were slowly worn down by it. Dick had kindly given her compassionate leave for as long as she needed, and had already rustled up a temp called Stephanie, who sounded extremely well-qualified and more than able to cope in Kate's absence.

'We might ask her to stay on as your assistant when you get back, if you feel you can get along with her,'

Dick had said. 'Apparently she's only been temping because she hasn't found anywhere she wants to settle permanently. Fingers crossed she likes it here . . .'

And so that particular problem seemed to have been solved. If only she'd plucked up the courage to mention it to Dick before now. But her previous bosses had been so stroppy; if she'd confided in them that she wasn't happy, they would have reminded her that there were plenty of girls waiting in line to fill her position. Dick Anthony was a different breed, but it had taken months for that to dawn on her. Besides, Charles Gray could be a little intimidating. Kate told herself not to get stressed out wishing she'd done something about it sooner.

'Is that you, Glynnie?'

Kate jumped, and looked down at the hospital bed. Her father's eyes were still closed, but his hand was groping around, as if searching for something.

'Dad, it's me, Kate.' She'd been sitting here for almost two hours, since visiting time began, waiting for him to stir. The day before, only Annabel and her mother had been here when he'd been awake. This afternoon, however, Annabel was spending time with the twins, and, ironically, just five minutes ago, Kate had persuaded her mother to go outside for some fresh air.

'Dad' – she took his hand – 'how are you feeling?'

'Bella?'

'It's Kate, Dad.'

'Katie?' He hadn't called her that since she'd been a child. And come to think of it, she'd never heard him call her mum Glynnie. Slowly, his eyes fluttered open. 'I haven't seen you in so long, Katie.'

243

'I've been here on and off, with Mum and Annabel. Mum's getting some air. Do you want me to try and find her?'

His fingers twisted around hers. 'No, I want to look at you. You've grown into such a pretty girl. When you were a baby, you were always crying. Whatever we did, it wasn't good enough. And you didn't smile . . .'

Kate was aware that she hadn't been an easy infant, but she'd never realised how bad.

'It was your birth,' her father continued. She wondered if he was delirious. 'It was difficult, you see. The specialist said it might have affected you. And when your mother fell pregnant with your sister, she was so depressed. It wasn't planned. That made it even harder for her to cope with you. But Bella was different. She was easy from the start. It turned things around for us as parents. Do you understand, Katie? Your grandparents managed so well with you. You seemed to have an affinity with them that you didn't have with us.'

Kate couldn't speak. Her throat was too constricted. She stared at the monitor, then back at her father. He looked ashen.

'Maybe it was a vicious circle,' he said, sighing. 'Perhaps you sensed that we treated Bella differently, and that led you to believe we didn't love you. But we did. We do. It just reached a stage where we both found it hard to show it, and you seemed happier to keep us at arm's length. You only let your grandparents in. And as you grew up, you were so clever, and independent, and—'

'Stephen?'

Kate looked up, feeling a pang of disappointment as her mother's shadow fell across the bed.

'Why didn't you fetch me?' Glynis demanded, rebuking Kate. 'How long has he been awake?'

'Not long . . . I offered to get you, but Dad wanted to talk to me.'

'Has he been coherent? Yesterday it was all nonsense. I didn't want to worry you.'

He was staring at the ceiling, as if it was perfectly fine for them to talk about him as if he wasn't there.

'He's been making sense,' was all Kate said, her emotions whirling. They whirled even more riotously when she looked up again.

Behind her mother, carrying a small bunch of daffodils and something wrapped in brown paper, stood Tom.

Glynis Finlay frowned and gestured over her shoulder. 'It's Thomas Llewellyn, Kate. I bumped into him outside. I said there was no need but he insisted on coming in.'

He took a step forward, his gaze never leaving Kate's face. 'I, er, brought these.' The daffodils trembled slightly in his hand. 'Early blooms,' he explained. 'And, um, some grapes. Incredibly unoriginal, but . . .'

'Now I suppose I'll have to ask a nurse if they've got a vase,' sighed Glynis peevishly.

As soon as her mother had wandered off, Kate stammered, 'How – How did you know about Dad?'

'From Dick.'

'Of course . . .' How else? Kate wished she'd washed

245

her hair that morning and taken time to put on make-up. A second later, she reminded herself that she wasn't going out with this man any more. There was no need to impress him. It didn't matter what she looked like.

That still didn't stop her wishing she'd washed her hair.

Diffidently, she stood up. 'Would you like my chair?' she asked, even though there were a couple of others going spare.

'Don't be naïve, girl,' snapped her father. 'He hasn't come to see *me*. Take him to the cafeteria or something. But leave the grapes here.'

'Dad?' Kate glanced at him again. He was still pale, but his eyes were shooting sparks.

'Go on, girl, what are you waiting for?'

'Er . . . when Mum gets back with the vase, can you tell her where I've gone, please.'

He made a noise like a snort.

'Are you sure you'll be OK?' Kate asked, concerned.

He made the snorting noise again. 'I'll even be coherent,' he promised.

Tom was looking guilty. 'I, um, hope you feel better soon, Mr Finlay.'

'So do I, Mr Llewellyn.'

Kate grabbed Tom's sleeve, keen to make a getaway before her mother came back.

'I feel that I'm here under false pretences,' he admitted a few minutes later, as they bought two coffees in the cafeteria. 'I never know what to say to patients in hospital. I rang your house first and Paloma told me you were here. I wouldn't have come otherwise. I'm sorry about your father . . .'

Kate led the way to a free table. 'It was a shock,' she acknowledged. 'Even though we should have seen it coming. I hate to say he brought it upon himself. The doctors are optimistic, so long as Dad changes his diet and takes up some gentle form of exercise.'

'I can recommend golf.'

'He used to play when he was younger, so maybe he'll start up again. Especially if Mum can persuade him to take early retirement. It'll be a battle, but she'll have Annabel and me on her side.'

'Well, if your father wants a refresher course in chipping and putting, he knows who to call.'

Kate smiled dryly, changing the subject. 'So you've spoken to Dick quite recently then?'

'He called me yesterday. It started off as a normal sort of chat, and then he turned the subject on to you and told me what had happened with your dad. Said he was worried about you, and would I go and make sure you were bearing up.'

'Is that all he said?'

'More or less. And also that you wouldn't be averse to seeing me.'

Words surged into Kate's mouth. *I can't believe you're here . . . I've missed you so much . . . I've been miserable since we broke up.*

'Not "averse", no. You look well. Did you have a good Christmas?'

'Er . . .'

'I had it at my place for the first time. It was mad of me.'

247

'Was, um, Harry there?'

Kate wafted her hand about nonchalantly. 'Mmm. And Annabel and the kids, and Grandad and—'

'Are you seeing Harry?'

Kate's hand stopped wafting. 'Seeing him? As in, going out?' When Tom nodded, she was rather fast in replying, 'No, of course not. You know that wasn't the reason I ended things between you and me.'

'I remember. You wanted to simplify things for Emmi. Did it work?'

'To a degree.' Things had just become more complicated in other ways.

'You haven't asked me about Jem yet.'

'What about her?' Kate didn't want to let on that she knew about the New Year's Eve party and Aidan Patricks. Maybe Tom didn't know about it himself.

'I did start seeing her again,' he admitted. 'But nothing happened. We didn't . . . you know. That was my choice, not hers, and as soon as I realised I was making a mistake, I ended it.'

'Oh.'

'So, does Harry see a lot of Emmi then?'

Could she detect jealousy in his tone? 'Quite a bit.'

'Has he come to the hospital much?'

'Why should he?'

'I thought he'd want to give you moral support.'

Kate shrugged. 'He's better off with Emmi. There's no need for him here.' She neglected to add that she preferred it that way.

They sat there for a moment, listening to the rattle of cups from behind the counter and the hiss of steam escaping from some tea or coffee machine. At last Kate added, as blithely as she could, 'You can report back to Dick now. Tell him I'm bearing up and I'll be back to work as soon as I know Dad's got the all-clear.'

Tom nodded. 'I'll phone him tonight. But, Kate, I want you to remember one thing. I'm here for you. We may not be going out any more, but that isn't going to stop me being your friend.'

'That's very . . . kind of you.'

His hand spread over hers on the table. 'I mean it. If you need someone to talk to, you know where I am.'

Kate dearly wanted to dive into his lap and snuggle up against him for solace. But it wasn't simply the fact that they were in a public place that prevented her; it was the knowledge that once she was snuggled up she wouldn't want it to stop there. He was offering her friendship, nothing more. He hadn't said anything about dating her again. Dick had had no right to involve him, and perhaps Tom had only come along today because he felt he ought to, rather than because he wanted to.

'I appreciate it,' she said faintly, wondering how many more clichés they could get through.

His fingers squeezed hers. 'Just promise you'll remember what I said.'

'I promise.'

He seemed to content himself with that, and as his hand slid away across the table, desolation rose in one huge wave to engulf her.

20

When the fire started to die out, Tom didn't bother stoking it back to life. Instead, he wrapped himself in the duvet which had been rolled up on the sofa beside him. Watching TV for a while, the consciousness started seeping in that he was hungry. When had he last had a substantial meal? He racked his brains. Today was Friday, so it had probably been the grill-up he'd had on Wednesday morning, before that wedding at Addenham Manor. He remembered eating onions and then trying to brush and gargle and Smint away the taste, in case the bride, posing for a photograph and overwhelmed by emotion, leaned into the Daimler and kissed him, which seemed to happen rather too often.

With a groan, he realised hunger wasn't going to go away unless he fed it something other than toast and Marmite or the odd banana. It would require effort, but he was going to have to heat something up in the microwave. Shoving back the duvet, thrusting his feet into tatty old flip-flops, he stood up and slouched into the kitchen. Brrr, his legs were cold. Opening the freezer didn't help. He pulled out a ready-made meal for one, and after frowning over the instructions, popped it in the microwave. While he was waiting, he made himself a coffee.

Fifteen minutes later, he was sitting in front of the TV again with a tray on his lap. Fork in one hand, remote control in the other, he flicked channels. Rubbish . . . Rubbish . . . Rubbish . . . More hopeful . . . Rubbish. He returned to Channel Four and the American sitcom, realising progress would mean he'd end up with hundreds of channels to flick through and even more crap to moan about. Scott had switched to satellite ages ago. Or was it cable? Tom chewed a mouthful of rubbery moussaka and tried to remember.

Suddenly, as one of the girls in the sitcom was about to show off her new nightie, there was a knock on Tom's front door. Bugger. Who the hell . . .? The knocking had woken Tina, who'd been asleep on the hearth rug. Leaping wildly around his feet, she followed him into the hall. As he negotiated the lock, the little dog pawed the wooden front door and added scratch marks to the multitude that were already there.

'OK, OK,' muttered Tom. 'Give me a chance, girl.' He grabbed Tina's collar, holding her back with one hand while he opened the door with the other.

In the dim pool of light shed by the lamp above their heads, stood Kate. He blinked at her. She blinked back, then her eyes grew wide. Dismayed, Tom looked down at himself, recalling far too late that he was only wearing flip-flops, an old university sweatshirt and black silk boxer shorts with red lips all over them.

'I've come at a bad time,' Kate mumbled.

'No, it's just . . . late. I wasn't expecting anyone.'

'You weren't in bed?'

Tom hadn't been to bed in days. It was easier to get off to sleep on the sofa, wrapped up like a spring roll in the duvet, watching television until it bored him senseless. 'No,' he said, 'I was just vegging out in front of the TV.'

She stepped hesitantly into the hall and started slipping her anorak off.

'I'd keep that on until I get the fire going again,' Tom warned sheepishly, motioning towards the lounge. 'You'll have to excuse the mess.' He picked up a rubber bone from the floor. 'Tina and I have been complete slobs lately.'

'That's OK.' Frowning, Kate picked her way over half-a-dozen CDs strewn on the floor.

'It's not OK,' Tom looked towards Tina, who had the remote control in her mouth. 'Sod the little minx! I buy her a new toy each week, but she'd rather play with my stuff.'

'Not too different from Emmi,' said Kate, and then stopped short, turning pink. 'Oh!'

Tom became aware of panting and moaning emanating softly from the direction of the TV. He followed Kate's gaze, and gawped at the sight of a naked couple tangled together in the throes of passion. Bloody hell. Now she'd think he'd been watching soft porn. Making a lunge for his dog, he wrestled the remote from her mouth.

'She must have changed channels. I was watching Four.' But he didn't sound convincing. 'It's true,' he said, flicking back to the sitcom he'd been watching. 'See!'

'You don't have to explain yourself to me.' Kate perched on the edge of the sofa. 'I'm not your mother.'

Tom tossed the duvet on to the floor, making room to sit down himself. But no sooner had he sat, than he stood up again. 'The fire,' he said, flustered, and set about relighting it.

'Um, was this your supper by any chance?'

He glanced back at the tray he'd dumped on the floor when he'd gone to answer the door. Tina was demolishing what was left of the moussaka. Tom grinned and lied, 'Just as well I wasn't that hungry.'

When the fire had taken hold sufficiently, he crawled back to the sofa and hauled himself up, studying Kate properly for the first time that evening. She looked pale and drawn as she took off her anorak.

'How's your father?' he asked tentatively.

She stared down at her hands. 'He was quite poorly earlier on.'

'Oh . . . I'm sorry . . .'

'A minor blip,' she added bitterly, 'according to the specialist. But Dad's over the worst now apparently. I stayed with Mum and Annabel until I knew.'

Tom sighed. 'Good.'

Kate lifted her gaze to his, her eyes misty. 'I . . . I didn't know who else to turn to. I was driving home, but I didn't want to be there . . .' Without further ado, the dam burst. Tears spilled out over her cheeks as if there was no more room for them inside her. Within seconds, she was sobbing noisily.

Tina, who had a phobia about people crying, fled from the room. Tom half-wished he could follow her.

Kate was pulling out tissue after tissue from the pocket of her cardigan. She seemed to have an entire box stuffed down there under the masses of wool. Which was just as well, thought Tom, feeling apprehensive and inadequate. All he had to offer her was bog roll.

Despite his qualms, he reached out and drew her gingerly into his arms. Her warmth against him was searing. She nestled her face into his neck, as she had in the past, yet this time it felt different. For starters, they weren't going out. Maybe that was why he was so full of trepidation about touching her. They weren't a couple any more. He'd stoically offered her his friendship, and told her he'd be there for her, but he hadn't expected *this*. What exactly did she want from him? A shoulder to cry on? Someone who wasn't family or involved with the family, to offer a detached point of view? He found himself wishing absurdly that she'd written out her expectations beforehand and handed him the DOs and DON'Ts as she'd walked through the door.

'I'm sorry,' she was blubbering, 'I'm being stupid.'

'Hey' – he held on to her as she tried to pull away – 'let me be the judge of that. I know how I'd feel if it was my dad lying in that hospital, so I don't blame you for breaking down like this. It's not a sign of weakness or anything like that.'

'But I have been stupid. Pretending I can cope. Doing everything for Emmi's sake without thinking what was actually best for her—'

'Kate, slow down.' She was gulping for air. If she wasn't careful, she'd hyperventilate. 'Listen to me. You're an amazing mother, but you're not perfect

254

because nobody ever can be. Realising your mistakes, rectifying them, that's what sets you apart, that's what will make you as close to perfect as you can get.'

Slowly, she nodded, and then, without warning, she launched herself at him, snuggling up to his chest where she could probably hear his heart galloping as if it were being ridden by Frankie Dettori. He wasn't sure if she'd been referring to Harry, with regards to Emmi, or her job at Anthony & Gray. And her signals about what she wanted him to do next were all over the place. She was still crying, although she was becoming calmer, and one of her hands had slipped – inadvertently? – beneath his sweatshirt, coming to rest on his stomach, which he was holding in so she wouldn't notice any trace of flab.

'I'm sorry,' she sniffed again.

'What for?' he muttered, feeling as if his lounge had turned into a sauna.

But she didn't answer. Instead, her lips came into close proximity with his own, her breath sweet and inviting. This particular signal couldn't be misread, and trying to analyse the reason behind it wasn't Tom's first instinct. Kissing her had become a priority. He couldn't hold out any longer.

21

Kate's nose was blocked from the crying. She could scarcely breathe. With relief, she felt Tom's lips leave her mouth and trail over her eyelids to her hair, fluttering gently, like butterflies, before trailing downwards again. As his stubble grazed her neck, she shivered. His hands fumbled hastily with the buttons of her cardigan. She helped him undo it and then wriggled out of it. Beneath the cardigan was a jumper. She cursed herself for throwing on the layers after she'd left the hospital. But the heating in her car had packed up completely. With the fire in here now crackling vigorously, Kate was keen to shed her woollens. And desire wasn't helping. Somehow her clothing seemed tangled around her.

Finally, she reached her thermal vest, which was so long and opaque that it obscured her lace bra and matching panties. Hardly the height of sex appeal, but it didn't seem to put Tom off. He knelt over her on the sofa and stripped off his sweatshirt, his chest rising and falling urgently. Within seconds, the vest, bra and panties had gone, along with the red and black boxer shorts. It had been so long since she'd experienced a man's bare skin against her own, Kate melted into the sensation, the sofa sinking beneath her, moulding itself to her form.

During her previous sexual encounters she had felt awkward, and she hadn't been entirely sober. The anticipation had never been matched by the act itself, with Harry misinterpreting everything he thought he knew about women and going through the motions in an almost mechanical fashion. In his mind he was probably as accomplished as Casanova. Once he'd reached satisfaction himself, the clumsy fumbling would come to an abrupt halt, any intimacy and romance ending there also. Yet Kate would succumb to him again and again, too shy to tell him exactly what she thought might turn her on. Each time she'd been disappointed, but Tom was a different type of partner altogether.

She had never felt as aroused as this. And she hadn't expected his touch to wipe away all trace of denial. The fullness of her feelings was rising to the surface as clearly and sharply as glass. She had resisted confronting the truth, but now she had no choice. She was madly and maddeningly in love with him. This was more than just physical attraction. It had been so much more from early on in their relationship, but admitting it to herself would have left her unprotected, with everything apparently out of her control. And now it had led to this: sleeping with him for all the wrong reasons and the right reasons, without knowing how he felt about her in return.

A shudder went through her as her need for him grew. He answered it by entering her. With a loud moan, she arched her back to receive him. They moved together, out of rhythm at first, and then slower, more gently, until they matched each other perfectly. Something deep inside her was being turned like the key in a clockwork toy. The sensation was delicious and intense and almost unbearable. As Tom's strokes became more fierce, more purposeful, she felt as if a wave was swallowing up her entire body. It crashed over her just as the pressure grew too much, bringing with it an incredible sense of release and fulfilment. Instinctively, she pulled Tom closer. The same wave seemed to be transferred to his own body. He gasped and rode it, before Kate felt his weight bear down, heavy and sated. She lay back, clinging desperately to the last vibrations of pleasure as if they were the final flickering rays of a long, hot summer.

Eventually, she felt Tom stir. He rolled off her but remained on the sofa, pressed against her side, thrusting an arm beneath her to keep his balance. She couldn't see his face, her head was buried in the region of his armpit. A second wave struck her. This time it was exhaustion. She'd found it so hard to sleep lately. Her eyelids fluttered closed, but she felt herself start to shiver, her muscles moving in little spasms as the sweat cooled on her skin. Another weight pressed down, lighter than Tom. A duvet. It tucked itself in around her.

'Are you all right?' he asked quietly, his breath warm against her ear.

'Yes,' she mumbled after a pause. 'Tired.'

'There's not much room side by side. Would you like me to get off?'

Despite her cramped position, she managed a shrug. 'Only if you want,' she lied, too timid to say, 'Don't you dare.'

He couldn't be comfortable, but to her relief he didn't peel himself away. He draped his free arm over the duvet. 'If you're tired, you might as well try to get some sleep,' he suggested.

She shrugged again, although every limb felt twice as heavy as it ought to. She was totally spent. There was no hope of summoning up the energy she would need to move. Yet her heart still functioned with a passion that had suddenly and irrevocably been set loose, reminding her that for as long as she lived, and whatever happened to her, she would never forget Tom Llewellyn or the way he had made her feel.

Her last fleeting thought, before she drifted off to sleep, was that the funny little butterflies had landed back in her hair . . .

There was a melodic beeping sound, muffled, but loud enough to creep into Kate's head and drag her back to consciousness. Lifting her eyelids to form slits, she saw that the room was grey and dark. Someone was scrambling about. The beeping stopped. She heard Tom's voice, then footsteps dying away.

A minute or two later, he was back, dropping with a thud on to the floor by the side of the sofa. Steeling herself, Kate opened her eyes fully. He was wearing his sweatshirt again, she could tell that much. He was also wrapped in a tartan blanket. As if sensing her gaze on him, he turned his head.

'You're awake.' He reached up and switched on a reading lamp.

Holding the duvet around her, she edged herself

into a sitting position. 'I heard a noise . . .'

'Your mobile. It was in the pocket of your jacket. I didn't want to wake you so I answered it. You don't mind?'

'Who was it?'

'Paloma. She fell asleep waiting up for you last night. When she woke up, she saw you weren't back. She was worried.'

'What time is it?' Kate frowned.

'Just gone six.'

'Oh hell.' She tried to run a hand through her hair, but it was a mass of knots sticking up at peculiar angles. She probably looked like Medusa the Gorgon. 'Did you tell her I'd stayed here?'

'I told her you'd slept on the couch.'

'Did she believe you?'

'Hard to say.'

'You mean she didn't?'

'Would you?'

Kate pouted. 'But it's the truth.'

'Selectively speaking.' He pushed aside the blanket, and she saw he was now wearing jeans. Then she noticed the pillow on the floor.

'Didn't you go to bed?'

'No . . . um . . . when I almost fell off the sofa, I decided it would be safer to end up on the floor voluntarily.'

'You must have been uncomfortable.'

'I was fine. I wanted to be near . . .'

'What?'

'Um, to the fire. In case a spark flew out or something. I don't like to leave it burning all night.'

Kate looked at the ashes in the grate. 'But it wasn't burning all night. It must have died out ages ago.'

'Er, it did. That's when I got a few hours' kip. I just couldn't be bothered going upstairs. Listen, do you want some breakfast?'

Musing as to why he kept a pair of jeans, a blanket and a pillow downstairs, but not curious enough to ask him, she said abstractedly, 'I don't feel hungry.'

'No? OK. Neither do I, really.'

'I ought to go home . . .' She peeked discreetly beneath the duvet, but a miracle hadn't occurred. She was still naked. Her clothes hadn't somehow materialised on to her body. Glancing around, she spotted them in a neat pile by the TV. 'I'd, er, better get dressed first.'

'Good idea.'

She waited. He didn't budge. 'Would you mind if I used your shower?' she asked, wondering if she could make it upstairs still wrapped in the duvet.

He winced. 'I wouldn't advise it. It's not working a hundred per cent. You could have a bath, though. There should be enough hot water.'

'I'll do that then.' Kate tried to stand up, but the duvet was too large. If she tried to walk in it plus carry her clothes upstairs, she'd probably trip. Allowing Tom another view of her breasts would be far more sensible than breaking her neck. It was amazing, she speculated, how lust could sweep away inhibitions as if they were flimsy, fragile things. 'On second thoughts,' she said, 'I think I'll forget about a bath. I can have a shower when I get home.'

Tom shrugged. 'Whatever's best.' He shuffled on his

knees to the TV and retrieved her clothes, bringing them over to the sofa. 'I'll, um, leave you to it then.' At last he'd got the message. 'If you need me, I'll be in the kitchen.'

He hauled himself to his feet and headed towards the door. Faltering, he turned round, scratching the back of his head. 'Kate . . .'

'Yes?'

'You're . . .'

'What?'

'You're on the pill, right?'

She felt a coldness steal over her. The consequences of what they'd done had crossed her mind, but now that Tom was putting it into words . . . Her reassuring nod was a blatant lie. What was the point in worrying him, though? He might end up phoning her at every opportunity during the next few weeks to check. That was the last thing she needed. Hearing his voice full of dread would be even worse than not hearing it at all.

He sighed, obviously relieved. 'I know it's not just a contraceptive, so I wasn't implying that you take it . . . just in case. But lots of women use it to help with their periods, don't they?'

Tom sounded embarrassed. She couldn't tear him down by informing him that she wasn't one of those women. This was *her* fault, and she wasn't going to start blaming him for any part of it. The day before yesterday he'd offered to be her friend, and she'd already abused that by throwing herself at him. He hadn't seemed to mind, but then he was a man. She was almost certain that this wasn't his first one-night stand. It would be dangerous to hope that he had only responded to her advances because he felt the same way as she did.

He left the room. Methodically, Kate unravelled her underwear, which was twisted together, and piled on the layers again. She picked up her anorak, the pockets bulging with her purse, phone and keys, and went down the hall to the kitchen. Tom was crouched over Tina's basket. Kate couldn't help thinking that he looked very paternal, like a father keeping watch over his child's cradle.

Oh God. She was feeling sick already. But that was just apprehension starting to gnaw away inside her. Of course, there was the morning-after pill. It wasn't too late to do something about it. But she knew, even as she stood there silently fearing the worst, that this wasn't an option.

The memory of that New Year's Day in Scotland had only seemed to intensify over the years . . . Harry sitting by her bedside, rubbing her back while she threw up. The hangover beating a loud tattoo in her skull, but ten times worse than that, the guilt eating away at the rest of her. She couldn't help what she believed. You didn't have to be a Catholic. Her grandmother had taught her that much.

Tom straightened up, spotting Kate in the doorway.

'Leaving already?'

'I'd better.'

'Are you sure you don't want a coffee? One for the road?'

She shook her head. 'Thanks, but I've got to get off.'

His stomach sank. Kate's attitude had cooled radically

since yesterday. Clearly, what had happened between them didn't mean their relationship was about to be resumed. Last night had been a one-off, but it was the first time he'd truly understood why they called it making love. Not that he'd ever repeat that during a blokeish conversation in a heaving pub.

Had it been worth the way he felt now, though? Disgusted with himself for taking advantage of Kate when she was obviously at her most vulnerable. It wasn't as if she hadn't been consenting, but still . . . her state of mind couldn't have been described as stable. At least she was on the pill; they didn't need to sweat over an unplanned pregnancy. He owned condoms, of course, but what bloody use were they sitting in their wrappers in the bathroom cabinet?

She was turning her back on him, walking away, out of his life again. The fact that they'd been as physically close as two adults could be, now meant that the distance between them was insurmountable. It might have been so different, if they'd both felt the same way.

He trailed after her down the hall. 'Take care of yourself,' he muttered.

'You too.'

Panic rose inside him as he followed her outside. 'Kate . . .'

She turned round. Her face was pale, her eyes darker than he'd ever seen them.

His voice seemed to catch in his throat, but he managed to get the words out. 'How about dinner this week?'

Her eyes grew even darker. 'You don't have to do this.'

'Do what?'

'Make me feel better.'

He frowned. 'I'm not. I honestly want to take you out.'

She shook her head. 'We can't start that again.'

'Why not? Because of Harry?'

'Because it's not going anywhere,' she flung back vehemently. 'Because I used to think I wanted something casual and fun, with no strings attached. But now I know I'm not made for that. I *do* want strings. I want them attached to every part of me. Pulling me down, if that's the way you want to see it. And I don't just need all that for Emmi's sake, to give her the security she deserves. I need it for myself. My grandfather made me realise that. He said I wasn't ready, because I didn't understand what he meant. But now I do. And I am ready.'

Tom was silent a moment, taking this in. 'And you don't think I can give you that?'

She seemed to be considering it, but somehow he knew she'd already made up her mind. 'No,' she said at last. 'And you don't have to pretend you want to.' She gestured up at the house. 'Just look around you. You're not the sort of man who conforms or wants to be tied down. You might have thought playing dad to Emmi was fun, but like most novelties, it would have palled. And then what? You drop us both, just like that.'

Tom couldn't believe what he was hearing. Was this the image he projected? The man people thought he was? Or was it Kate's perspective alone? Did she honestly think so little of him, or was this just the best excuse she could come up with? The questions rattled around in his head, stirring anger and pride.

'Let go of me, please,' she demanded.

It dawned on him that he'd been forcibly holding her back. He released her arm. 'I'm sorry . . .'

He was losing her, letting her go. He didn't know why she had come here last night. She probably didn't know herself. It was just one of those things. It had happened, and that was the end of it. He watched her climb into her car. She grappled with the manual choke, before revving the engine as if she was starting a race. Finally, she drove off, disappearing around a bend in the drive.

Dragging his flip-flops, he went back inside. Tina was still asleep in the kitchen, oblivious to the fact that he needed a cigarette and a stiff drink, even though he had none of the former and no way enough of the latter. When she woke up she'd expect her Pedigree Chum – he had copious amounts of that, naturally – and her usual morning frisk-about in the yard, as if nothing had happened.

In desperation, Tom reached for the handset of his phone, which was lying on the kitchen table almost out of battery, and, because the memory facility wasn't working, jabbed out a number he knew off by heart.

22

'Are you all right?' Paloma asked, the instant Kate stepped through the front door of the Old Parsonage.

'Ssshhh . . . Does Emmi know I've been out all night?'

'No, she's still in bed.'

Kate sighed with relief. 'I don't want her to find out, so you mustn't let it slip.'

'OK.' Paloma nodded. 'Tom said you went round there last night, that you slept on his sofa. I don't understand. You rang when you were leaving the hospital and said everything was fine. I thought you were coming straight home. I waited up—'

'But you dropped off. I know, Tom said.'

Paloma looked confused. 'I thought you and him weren't—'

'We're not,' said Kate, far too quickly. 'I did sleep on the sofa. I was tired and—'

'You could have rung again.'

'I know. I should have. I suppose I dropped off myself. Now I've really got to go and have a shower.'

'Kate, listen.' Paloma practically jumped into her path. 'Pretend I'm not your employee for a minute. I mean, I know you don't treat me like a skivvy or anything, but pretend I'm just your friend.'

Kate frowned, disorientated. 'Is something bothering you?' She just wanted to run upstairs and wash away all trace of Tom. The scent of him was still clinging to her. It was too tantalising.

'It's just, if I was your friend, you'd confide in me.'

Kate thought about it. Would she? Would she dare tell anyone what a fool she'd been? That she'd been weak? That her self-esteem now resembled a withered-up old flower? 'I'm fine,' she said. 'I don't know what you mean.'

'You know that Emmi misses Tom?'

'Does she?' Kate strove to balance interest with insouciance. 'Has she said anything to you?'

Paloma nodded. 'She's mentioned it.'

'She hasn't spoken about him to me in ages.'

'That's because she says you get upset.'

Why were children so astute? Surely it couldn't be good for them? 'Has she said anything else?'

Paloma hesitated, staring down at the floor a moment, chewing her lip. Her complexion was suddenly pink and blotchy. 'No. It's just . . . when I've been with her and Harry, she doesn't seem to be having a good time.'

'What about Harry?'

'What about him?' Paloma asked, almost defiantly.

'Does he have a good time?'

'He does try. He makes an effort. But it wasn't as if he was heavily involved with Emmi from her birth. It would have made bonding easier for him if he had been. Some people can't tune in to children's wavelengths. It's as if there's a mental valve they go through

268

when they grow up, and they can't ever pass backwards into childhood. They can't remember how it felt being a kid.'

'I'm sure with time . . .' Kate's shrug belied her anxieties. 'It was Harry who wanted to see her. I've got to give him a chance. You can't rush these things.' She was edging nearer the stairs, impatient to escape.

'Tom can tune in. He does it without thinking.'

At the mention of his name, Kate's heart seemed to knock painfully against her rib cage. How long was it since he'd last come up in the conversation? Half-a-minute? Less? And how long would it take for the anguish to wear off? Weeks? Months? Years?

Never?

'Tom's a natural,' Paloma was grinding on, like a pestle against a mortar. 'He knows what to do around children, what to say. And Emmi absolutely adores him—'

'Now you're exaggerating!' Kate bit back quickly.

Paloma tilted her head to one side. 'Am I?'

Tom sank a double whisky in one go and gasped with satisfaction.

'Steady on,' frowned his brother.

'I needed that.'

'You said the same thing four rounds ago. Heaven knows how many you'd had at home before we got there.'

'Not many, there was sod-all in the bottle.'

Scott shook his head. 'And I can't believe you're smoking again.'

'I can,' sighed Vie. 'I remember when George Barnes-Foster dumped me. I smoked a whole packet of those mentholy things.'

Scott looked at her, his jaw dropping. 'You never told me this.'

'What? About George Barnes-Foster? Or the fact that I used to smoke?' Vie glanced around nonchalantly, catching the eye of the Abbot Inn's resident lech, seated a few tables away. He leered at her, his white whiskers twitching with unconcealed excitement. Vie raised her eyebrows. 'However does this pub survive?' She dipped into her packet of pork scratchings. 'These are lovely,' she munched, 'but I'm not sure about the rest of this place. It always gives me the creeps.'

'That's because it's haunted.' Tom fiddled with a cheap plastic lighter, and lit a Marlboro out of the packet he'd purchased with clumsy desperation from the machine beside the men's loos.

'Haunted! Who by? Buxom Serving Wench or Ruthless Highwayman?'

'Pissed Old Fart.'

'That's you then,' snorted Scott. He turned to Vie. 'Am I supposed to know who George Barnes-Foster is?'

'I knew you wouldn't let it lie. Darling, I was only sixteen. He was the first boy I ever went out with. The first to break my heart. He taught me to kiss, drink and smoke like a trooper.'

Tom felt a chuckle rise in his throat. He let it out with a raucous cough. 'I can just imagine it.'

'You mean Georgy-Porgy?' Scott asked his wife. 'That's what you used to call him, wasn't it? You've always made it sound so innocent.'

'It was, in a way. He dumped me because I wouldn't let him take off my bra. Looking back, I suppose I was quite bold to stand up to him, considering he said it was a test of my love, or some such rubbish. And I gave up the ciggies when I was seventeen. I read in a magazine that smoking gives you wrinkles.' She shuddered. 'Put me off for life.'

Scott was looking at her in admiration. 'There's a hell of a lot I don't know about you yet, isn't there?'

Vie smiled. 'Like the dance of the seven veils, darling. I've got to keep your interest up.'

'Seven veils,' echoed Tom. 'Isn't that what you wore at your wedding? Seemed like it, at least.'

Vie poked him in the chest. 'Oi, you! Less of that.'

Tom sighed, and took a long drag on his cigarette. 'I can't believe I'm doing this. Getting pissed. Smoking again. And I can't believe I asked you to come along and watch me do it.'

'Neither can I,' said Scott. 'I was hoping to have a lie-in.'

'And I'm ovulating,' added Vie. She glanced at her watch. 'I'm probably still good for another nine hours, though, so that gives us plenty of time.' She smiled suggestively at her husband, then turned to Tom. 'What *I* can't believe is that they actually let us in here at eight-thirty in the morning. I've heard of late-night lock-ins, but this is ridiculous.'

Tom raised his glass towards the bar in a friendly

toast. The landlord grinned and set about pouring another whisky, which hadn't actually been Tom's intention.

'That's what comes of being chummy with the management,' he said, sighing again. 'I'm their best local.'

Vie glanced around in the gloom. The curtains were still drawn, and the wall-lights didn't seem to make much difference. 'Apart from Mr Pervert over there,' she mumbled.

'And I mustn't forget old Jim,' added Tom. 'Who used to be in the RAF, and the Navy, and the Home Guard, and practically everything by the sound of it. But he isn't usually around till gone lunch. Oh, and here's the delightful Mrs Mop. I'd better hide the fags or she'll have them.'

Vie and Scott looked round as the cleaner came in, wielding her accoutrements. She didn't even bat an eyelid in their direction.

'This place is totally bizarre,' concluded Vie, keeping her voice low.

The landlord trudged over and put the whisky down. 'All right, Tom?' he asked in a thick Norfolk accent. 'Can I get you anything else?' He looked at Vie and Scott, who both shook their heads.

'We're driving,' they said in unison.

Tom looked at them with gratitude, his eyes welling up. There they were, cold and tired, nursing their orange juices ('fertility's a tricky business'), having rushed over at his request after he'd woken them up on a Saturday morning, of all days. Damn, he was a sod. And they were absolute saints. He didn't deserve them.

'I don't deserve you,' he blurted out. 'Thank you. Thank you for—'

Vie flicked her hand at him dismissively: 'Don't. There's no need. We understand.'

'Kate was right though, you know,' Tom went on, hearing himself slur for the first time that day. 'What can I offer?'

'More than bloody most,' hissed Vie. 'You're a kind, sensitive man with far too big a conscience. And perhaps you've tried so hard to get close to *her*, you haven't let down your own defences enough. You haven't let her see what you're really like.'

Tapping his cigarette in the direction of an ashtray, Tom stared mournfully at the table. 'What *am* I like, though?'

'Well, for starters, you're not shallow. In fact, I might go as far as to say you're too deep for your own good. Look at the way you were brought up, you could have turned out like Scott here – no, don't look at me like that, darling, I love you really – but you,' Vie swivelled back to Tom, 'you've rejected all that. You've chosen your own path and turned your back on all the trappings. The road less travelled by, *et cetera*. You know what's important in life. OK, so your dad got you into cars, but you've turned your passion into a living. Like golf—'

'I'm writing a comedy drama, you know,' he burst out, feeling warm and groggy.

'A comedy drama?'

'Or izzit a dramatic comedy? Anyway, it's about this bloke who runs a vintage car hire firm.' Tom took another large swig of his drink. 'But s'not about me. I'm just using what I know best as my background.'

Scott looked interested. 'When did you start this?'

'I dunno exactly. A couple of weeks ago. It'll be a three-parter, about an hour each one. But I don't want it hammed up. That's why comedies are sometimes so crap these days.' He waggled his finger in the air. 'Actors dunno how to do ham properly. And the scripts!' he grunted derisively.

'I can't wait to read it.' Vie sounded sincere. 'But what about your Booker Prize winner?'

Tom pulled a face. 'Leave that to bloody sodding Aidan Patricks. I'm gonna do what I do best.'

'You always were an opinionated git,' chuckled Scott.

Tom's head sank lower, towards the table, exhaustion creeping up on him, which wasn't surprising. He hadn't had much sleep last night, keeping guard beside the sofa as if someone might have sneaked in and tried to steal Kate away. And his brain had been on overdrive. Round and round and round, dredging up remorse until even his thought processes had seemed to clog up.

'Looks like we ought to get you home,' he heard Vie say.

'I'll drive,' said Scott. 'You can sit with him in the back. If he throws up, make sure it's out of the window.'

'Is OK,' Tom muttered, wondering why his speech was going downhill so rapidly, 'I can walk. Is just half-a-mile. Dunnit loadsatimes.'

'No way.' Vie was already advancing round the table, Scott on the other flank. 'You might fall into a ditch or something. *I* could never live with myself, even if you could.'

23

Emmi peered around the bedroom door. Her mother was a shapeless mass beneath the duvet. Emmi took a few steps closer. The shapeless mass stirred, stretching out to become a body, with legs and arms and a head.

'Mummy . . .'

Now the duvet was slowly being moved aside. Her mother's face appeared, looking very white. 'Yes, darling?'

'Paloma said not to wake you up if you were asleep. But you're not asleep now, are you? So I haven't woken you up, have I?'

'Er . . . no.'

'Are you all right, Mummy?'

'I'm fine, darling.'

'Do you want some toast?'

'I'm not hungry at the moment. I'll have something later.'

'Are we still going to go to Great-Grampa's?'

Her mum looked at the alarm clock. 'I suppose we've got time before your dad gets here.'

'He's not coming today,' said Emmi, skipping to the window. 'Don't you remember? He said he had some business to take care of.'

276

'Oh, that's right. I'll ring your great-grandad then and see if it's OK for us to pop over.'

'I think it might snow today. If it does, I'd like to build a snowman.' Emmi turned away from the window. Her mum was struggling into her dressing gown and slippers. 'You look like you're still tired, Mummy. Did you have a bad dream? I think I heard you get up.'

'I only went to the toilet, darling. I needed a wee-wee.'

'Were you awake a long time? Did you toss and turn a lot?'

'No.' Her mum swayed towards the door. 'I slept like a log.'

'But logs don't sleep, do they? So why do people say that?'

'I don't really know. Maybe it's because logs are very still, so they *look* like they're asleep.'

Emmi thought about this. It made sense. She followed her mum out of the room. 'Mummy, why are you walking funny?'

'Just need to do another wee-wee, darling.' The bathroom door swung shut behind her. 'Won't be a minute, then I'll ring your great-grandad. Have you had breakfast yet?'

'Paloma made me Ready Brek. But she's in a hurry today. She's going out.'

'She's probably meeting her friend Lottie.'

'The other day she said Lottie was on holiday.'

'Well, maybe she's back now.'

'Maybe. But usually when I ask Paloma, she tells me where she's going. This time she won't, as if she doesn't know.'

'Perhaps it's a secret and she can't say.'

'But Christmas is over and it isn't my birthday for ages.'

'What do you mean, sweetheart?'

Emmi looked over the banisters. Paloma came into view down in the hall, fussing over her hair.

'Well,' said Emmi, from outside the bathroom door, 'people always have secrets around Christmas and my birthday, but they hardly ever have them the rest of the time.'

Kate ventured out of the cubicle, averting her gaze from the huge mirror directly opposite. She must look a fright. Keeping her head low, she washed her hands and turned ninety degrees to the hot-air dryer. It would be safe to look up now, just as long as she didn't look left. But her eyes seemed glued to her stomach anyway, to the tiny mound that always developed when her period was due. If she had X-ray vision, there wouldn't be any need to go to the chemist's at Liverpool Street on her way home from work.

Her period should have started three days ago. She'd always been fairly regular. Perhaps a day or so early, but never late. All the signs had built up towards it as usual, but then . . . nothing, and it wasn't as if she didn't go to the toilet often enough to check. This menstrual 'hiccup' was probably due to stress, though, nothing more. Surely the pressure she'd been under lately would be enough to affect her cycle? Besides, when she'd been pregnant with Emmi, her body had seemed to know something was up straight away, as if dozens of alarm bells had gone off inside her. She'd felt as if she was walking around on red alert, in a perpetual state of nausea.

Kate tore her eyes away from the bump beneath her skirt and turned to leave the Ladies'. Bugger, she'd forgotten about the long, narrow mirror on the back of the door. Immediately, her hands flew up to her head and started smoothing her hair back, but the strands clung to her clammy fingers until she looked worse than before. Wrenching out her clip, she rammed it in her jacket pocket. Her hair framed her face like a wide, frizzy curtain. Why did she bother to strive for neatness when it was obviously beyond her limited scope? Besides, if the bitter February wind was still gusting outside, nobody's coiffure stood a chance. Except perhaps Natalia's. Or anyone with a number one crop.

Talk of the devil . . . Kate had to reverse hastily as the door swung open and the receptionist entered. In Kate's opinion, it wasn't a terribly good advert for a design agency to hang a mirror where someone might get their nose broken, especially if the nose in question was your own.

'Hiya.' Natalia gave her a watery smile and proceeded to take out a comb, a tub of wax and a can of hairspray from her tote bag. She lined them up along the edge of the marble basin area.

With a faint 'Hiya' back, Kate hurried out and returned to her desk. Her in-tray and out-tray were both empty. At the adjacent desk, Steph was packing up for the day. Kate frowned, a familiar sense of failure stealing over her. It wasn't just that halving the workload meant they got more done; it was also the unequivocal fact that Steph was a born PA. She attacked every task with proficiency and speed, yet there was nothing sloppy about the finished product. At twenty-two, she exuded a confidence that Kate could only dream about, and possessed the enviable ability to fit in among any crowd. She got along with Natalia and co., and Dick, Charles and Henry, as easily as she did with Kate.

'Fancy a quick drink?' she asked now, sounding as brassy and cheerful as usual.

'I can't,' said Kate. 'I'd better get home.'

'In time for tea with Emmi?'

'If I hurry, and if her appetite can bear to wait for me. I don't know where she puts it all.'

'Well, go on then. Don't hang about. You can't keep a six-year-old waiting.'

And that was another thing, thought Kate, as she slipped on her coat. Steph was so nice. It ought to be a pleasure coming to work these days, but it had become more depressing than ever. Perhaps it was because she didn't feel needed any more. Like a spare tyre, when the others were all puncture-proof anyway. Kate knew she wasn't a bad secretary; no one had ever complained, and she always met her deadlines. But it was simply something she did, as opposed to something she wanted to do. Compared to Steph, she wasn't efficient.

She made her way to the lifts, apprehension seizing hold of her as her mind turned to other matters. Life was so unfair. Paloma didn't know which side her bread was buttered on. Kate remembered the single white rose that had been delivered that morning for 'Miss P. Reilly'.

The card attached hadn't said who it was from, and Paloma had acted so ungratefully, shoving it into a glass of water and moaning that she'd had it up to here with men. Kate hadn't dared ask why. Her nanny had been ratty lately, but then Kate could hardly talk. Oh, God. Buying a pregnancy test kit . . .

What sort of way was *this* to spend Valentine's Day?

'Now,' said Emmi, 'you sit here and watch what I do.'

Winnie the Pooh, in his classic red top, stared at her from the edge of the bath where he'd been propped up against the wall. His black eyes gleamed in the morning light spilling in under the blind. Emmi stood on tip-toe and looked out of the window. Her mother was hurrying down the front path, on her way to work. Emmi had already said goodbye to her, but now she felt a pang of sadness, as if she was missing her already. With a sigh, she picked up her toothbrush and showed it to Winnie.

'I should have told you this a long time ago, but honey is very, very bad for your teeth. I've just had some on my toast, so I've got to clean my teeth and gums extra carefully.' She smeared My First Colgate on to her brush. 'I'm telling you this because I know how much you like honey too.'

Winnie gazed up at her. In Emmi's imagination, he was taking it all in. When she finished brushing, she spat out and reached for a towel at the same time, sending Winnie flying. Wiping her mouth quickly, she saw that he'd landed in the waste bin. She bent down and retrieved him, catching hold of the edge of a tissue as she did so. It unravelled, and something fell out, back

281

into the bin. Emmi stared at it a moment, puzzled, then stooped to pick it up too.

'What's this?'

Paloma gave a start, scattering suds everywhere. 'What's what?'

Emmi had come up behind her, taking her by surprise. Paloma frowned and glanced away from the washing-up for a moment. She did a double-take. Emmi was brandishing a pregnancy test stick. Paloma tugged off her Marigolds and plopped down on to the nearest chair.

'Where did you find that?'

'In the waste bin in the bathroom, wrapped in a tissue. I was teaching Winnie how to brush his teeth and he fell in. I picked him up, and the tissue came too. That thing fell out. What is it?'

'It's a . . . thingamijig. It's mine. I use it for . . . *my* teeth,' Paloma improvised. 'The dentist gave me a whole pack. That was my last one.'

'I don't get anything like this when I go to the dentist,' complained Emmi.

'It's just for adults, that's why.'

'What's it for?'

'Er . . . it measures the acid levels in your gums. But you can only use it once, and then you have to throw it away. In fact, give it to me now and I'll get rid of it.'

Emmi did as she was told. 'Have you got a lot of acid in your gums?'

'Everyone has *some*. That's why it's important to brush after you eat.'

282

'I know,' nodded Emmi. 'That's exactly what I was telling Winnie. Do you think my mum uses those things, too?'

'Um, probably not. In fact, we'll keep it a secret between you and me for now, OK? I don't really like people knowing I've got trouble with my teeth.'

The little girl promised earnestly, as Paloma had hoped she would. Not that that necessarily meant anything, but it was worth a try.

'Now, munchkin, run along upstairs and get your bag, or you'll be late for school. And wash your hands, too. That acid test has a special sort of chemical on it. You shouldn't really have touched it.'

Her mind in a whirl, Paloma watched as Emmi ran out again. Later, when she returned from taking her to school, she would go upstairs, slip the disposable liner out of the waste bin, tie a knot in it, then chuck it straight into the wheely bin outside – exactly as Kate would expect her to, in readiness for the bin men to collect it. Paloma was conscious that she was getting better at this housekeeping lark, so it was hardly dubious behaviour.

Surely the pregnancy test had to be Kate's? The only other person it might belong to was Annabel, but Paloma doubted it. The result was showing positive, which, of course, didn't mean that Kate was definitely pregnant. Even with her limited experience, Paloma knew that some brands changed to positive within a few hours of doing the test. She racked her brains. Slotting the pieces together, though, a positive result *would* fit. Firstly, the opportunity was there, when Kate had stayed at Tom's. Secondly, Kate had looked exhausted lately. Paloma had put it down to stress, but there was another valid possibility.

On a guilty note, her gaze was drawn to the white rose on the windowsill. Lately she'd been spouting to herself that life was unfair, and now she felt that it was up to her to try to sort out this mess. As far as Paloma could see, there was only one way of going about it, even if it meant losing her job . . . and Kate's respect.

24

Like Incy Wincy, this spider was also in difficulty. Kate watched it skirt the plug-hole and attempt to climb up the side of the basin. There was no spout, or rain, but she was still reminded of Emmi's favourite song from when she'd been at nursery. This particular arachnid was dark brown and approximately half-an-inch in diameter. Any larger, and Kate wouldn't have been heroic enough to deal with it.

Dangling a scrap of loo roll into the dry basin, she followed the spider's progress as it paused in suspicion and then hesitantly crawled on to the paper. A moment later, it had been dispatched out of the window. Kate sighed, and was about to start using the toilet, which had been her original intention for going into the small downstairs' cloakroom, when there was a loud knock on the front door. Damn. Was Harry early again? Emmi was upstairs getting dressed and Paloma was taking a shower. Kate didn't feel she had much choice but to pull up her combat pants and go back out into the hall to answer it.

It wasn't Harry.

She froze in shock at the sight of Tom standing on her doorstep in his chauffeur's uniform.

Hesitantly, he removed his peaked cap. 'Can I . . . ?'

Kate galvanised herself into action, stepping back to let him through.

'There's a wedding going on across the road,' he explained. 'I'm driving the Bentley.'

'Right.'

'It's a bit cheeky of me to have slipped away, but they've got the ceremony to get through, and then the start of the photos. I don't think I'll be missed.'

'Right,' said Kate again, wondering where her ability to form intelligent speech had vanished to. She had been using it only this morning, on the phone to her sister. 'Tea?' she mumbled.

Tom shook his head. 'No thanks. I don't want anything. Well, actually I do. I want to speak to you.'

She was about to mumble, 'Right,' for a third time, but managed to change it to 'Really?' at the last moment. She gestured towards the lounge. 'Come through.' That was better, two words in succession. Things were looking up. 'Emmi's upstairs. And Paloma.'

'Right.' It was obviously Tom's turn to be unoriginal.

He sat down on the edge of the sofa, nervously swinging his cap in his hands. Kate settled opposite him in an armchair, panic setting in. Had he guessed that she was . . . ? How could he? No one knew. Or had he just come to make sure that it was definitely all-clear?

'The thing is,' he began, 'I've been vowing to myself to come and see you but I've been rushed off my feet lately.' He stopped and pulled a face, as if disgusted with himself. 'No, forget that. It's crap. I could have found time. But I was too . . . stubborn? I don't know. And then

286

today I was sitting in the car, staring across the road, and I knew that if I didn't do it now then in all probability I never would.'

'I see,' breathed Kate, making her decision.

Two days ago, she had found out that her world was about to be turned upside down again. Crazy, how a tiny blue line could herald something as mind-blowing and momentous as the dawn of a new life. Holding on to the mixer tap in the bathroom for support, she had stared down at the test stick as if she were nineteen again. Lightning couldn't strike twice – that had been the asinine argument she had used to reassure herself that the test would be negative. But the lightning still felt as if it were striking even as she sat here now, listening to Tom.

'It was something Vie said,' he was rambling on, 'about not letting down my defences enough. I was pissed at the time, so it's hazy, but it was something to the effect that I'd been so busy trying to get close to you, I hadn't actually let you get close to *me*. Do you understand?'

Kate nodded, then shook her head. 'Not really.'

'Well, as I see it, I owe you the truth about myself. After everything that's happened between us, I feel you ought to know who – what – I really am.'

In the movies, thought Kate dizzily, he would admit that he was royalty. Or a secret agent.

'I used to be a journalist,' he said matter-of-factly.

'I already know that,' she retorted, disappointed, before noticing that his gaze was firmly fixed on the floor but that his mind seemed to be focused elsewhere. She realised instinctively that what he was about to say next would cause him some degree of pain.

'Apart from writing my column,' he continued falteringly, 'I also wrote freelance pieces. Interviews and features, some of which you might call investigative.' His head bowed further, and Kate longed to stretch out and touch his soft, thick hair. He looked so virile in his dark grey uniform. The shiny brass buttons were just begging to be undone.

'I won't go into detail,' he ploughed on. 'Suffice it to say that there was a business scam, which I heard about by accident. I decided that uncovering it would make a good story. The problem is, we only see one set of victims: the people who've been cheated out of their savings or whatever else. We view it as black and white, and we don't acknowledge that a con merchant might be conning his own family. How can a wife and child be innocent when they're reaping the spoils of other people's misfortune? That's what we usually think. But in this particular case, they were. In their eyes they were just part of a normal, middle-class family. And it was only through me, through my "dazzling" exposé, that they found out the truth.'

'You thought you were doing the right thing,' Kate assuaged.

With an ironic laugh, he threw back his head and stared bleakly at the ceiling. 'I was a one-man crusade. A stupid, blind Clark Kent pretending to be Superman. And I couldn't cope with the result. In my opinion, I'd written my best piece ever – and for what? So that a fourteen-year-old girl could cut her wrists at the discovery that her precious father wasn't a respectable businessman but effectively a thief? Her world as she knew it was about to come crashing down, and her friends would never look at her in the same way again. I suppose she felt life wasn't worth the hassle.'

'Cut her wrists?' muttered Kate.

'Someone found her in time. It was only classed as attempted suicide. I was supposed to feel better about that.'

'How – How long ago was this?'

'She's seventeen now. The last I heard, she was studying for her A-Levels. Her mother's one of those strong, resilient, survivor types. They went up north to live with relatives. Start over again, that sort of thing.'

'And . . . ?'

'That's it,' he shrugged. 'The end. As I said, details aren't important. Everyone involved came out the other end, all with our own way of dealing with it.'

'Which in your case,' concluded Kate, 'was giving up writing altogether.'

He didn't reply for a moment. 'I couldn't carry on,' he frowned. 'I literally couldn't. Not at first. I didn't have it in me. The gift, the drive – whatever you want to call it – had gone. And then, when it started coming back, gradually, bit by bit, I refused to accept it. I didn't deserve it. And besides, in retrospect, there didn't seem to be anything worth writing about.'

There was another pause. Kate felt as if she would explode.

'I'm pregnant,' she said. It slipped through her lips as easily as that, carried along by a stream of emotion that refused to wait for a better time. She had made up her mind that she was going to tell him. He had a right to know, as much as Harry had had seven years ago.

At least he didn't look as if he was beating himself up over the past any more. Remorse had been replaced by sheer disbelief. 'Pregnant?' he repeated. 'You – You can't be.'

'I'd rather not broadcast it to Emmi or Paloma, so—'

'You *can't* be,' he said again.

'I wasn't on the pill, Tom. You jumped to conclusions, or maybe it was wishful thinking, and I went along with it because it seemed the easiest thing to do. Nothing might have come of it, and then it wouldn't have mattered.'

'Pregnant,' he said again, like an echo.

'About five weeks,' she continued. 'Medically, you start counting from your last period, not from when you actually . . . you know.'

'I see.' He rubbed a hand over his face.

'It's early days yet. Some women don't like to make it public until about twelve weeks. That's roughly when you go for the dating scan, too.'

'So . . . you're going to keep it?'

Kate had feared this moment, but now that it was here, she was surprisingly calm. 'I'm sorry if you'd prefer me to get rid of it.'

'Prefer?' His expression darkened.

It was impossible to know exactly what he was thinking. Naturally, he was stunned, as Kate had been. But she'd had time for it to sink in. Time to accept that, if the pregnancy progressed as normal, she would have another child to bring up at the end of it, another mouth to feed, another person to be responsible for. The rest of the family, including Emmi, didn't need to know yet. Kate had no idea how she was going to tell them, but she had a few weeks to work on it, provided no one guessed beforehand.

'So you're prepared to bring up the baby on your own?' Tom asked, almost challengingly.

She clasped her hands tightly in her lap. 'I'll do my best, like I have with Emmi. I'll take the minimum maternity leave I need, and when I go back to work, Paloma will be here to look after things at home. If you're worried I'll be chasing you up for maintenance, you needn't be. I can manage adequately on my own. I still have most of Emmi's things stored away.'

He was shaking his head, his expression darker than before, if that were possible. 'What about access rights?' he demanded.

She gathered her thoughts, then answered clinically, 'If you want to be involved, then I'm sure we can come to some arrangement.'

Tom was rising to his feet. 'Bloody hell, Kate—'

But he was interrupted. The door to the hall swung open and Emmi entered. 'Oh,' she said, her face lighting up. 'I thought you were my dad.' And she ran to him and flung her arms round his legs. 'I haven't seen you for ages and ages.'

Kate had to look away. There was something heart-wrenching about the scene. A small girl clinging to a grown-up man. And in a way, she was jealous. Envious of the ease with which Emmi could hold him when that was what she wanted most herself.

'How's Tina?' Emmi asked excitedly. 'And Ronan?'

'They're OK,' said Tom gruffly.

Just then came the knock on the front door that Kate had been dreading. She rose shakily to her feet. Ouch. It felt as if the baby – quite impossibly – was already using her bladder as a trampoline. Before Kate could even reach the hall, though, Paloma had clattered down the stairs and answered the door herself. Harry breezed in, coming to an abrupt halt at the sight of his daughter in the lounge hugging another man. Kate watched Tom extract himself gently and make a calculated bid for freedom. Harry seemed to put two and two together. He stepped casually into the escape route and stuck out his hand.

'You must be Tom,' he said smoothly.

'Er – yes.'

'I'm Harry Barrett.'

'I gathered.' Tom slapped on his cap. 'If you'll excuse me . . .'

'I assume that's your Bentley parked over the road? I prefer the 1931 model myself.'

The atmosphere was growing increasingly tense by the second.

Tom gestured through the open door. 'And I take it that's your Beamer. Very nice. Although I've heard the Three Series has more bite.'

Kate wanted to shout, stamp her foot, punch the wall, anything to release the misery and frustration building up inside her. If they hadn't been interupted, would Tom still have raced off? He was probably blaming her for the pregnancy and panicking that his life was over. Something pathetic along those lines.

Just as he was about to cross the threshold, he hesitated and looked back at her, his countenance indecipherable. 'Take care of yourself, Kate.'

She nodded desolately, and watched him stride away.

Emmi came to stand beside her. 'Mummy,' she whispered, sounding bewildered, 'why is he dressed like one of those Nasties in Great-Grampa's video *The Great Escape*?'

25

Nose screwed up slightly, Glynis Finlay regarded the unfamiliar surroundings with distaste.

Kate bit her lip to prevent a microscopic smile sneaking out. It was amazing how, even though she felt rotten, her sense of humour could get the better of her. Or was she just being callous? Kate glanced around the pub and decided she wasn't. The only thing preventing her mother from enjoying herself was plain old-fashioned snobbery.

It had all been Annabel's idea. 'We'll go for a few drinks to celebrate Dad's recovery,' she'd said happily. 'Nothing too arduous. The Willow Tree has a no-smoking section and a play area for the children. It'll be fun!' And so here they were, taking up two tables in the conservatory section of the large family pub on the outskirts of Addenham, the twins in traditional wooden highchairs, babbling and giggling while Emmi fed them rice cakes.

Kate felt a sudden rush of empathy with her mother, realising she wasn't the life and soul of the party, either. Sipping her non-alcoholic drink under the pretext of having to drive, she sat back in the high-winged chair and let her mind wander . . . Never out of her consciousness for long, the embryo inside her was around the size of a grain of rice, yet its heart was already beating. Kate had furtively rooted out the books she'd kept from the previous time, and had already made an appointment with the doctor for a check-up. She was taking folic acid, and remembering to avoid foods such as paté and liver. As if ticking off a list from an NHS booklet, the basics were all being dealt with, one by one. Yet since telling Tom that he was going to be a father, she hadn't heard a word from him. Admittedly, that had only been yesterday, but still . . .

'Something's on your mind, girl. What is it?'

She jerked her head up in military fashion, but her father was addressing Annabel, who, come to think of it, did look as if she was preoccupied about something. She was wriggling in her chair like an excited child, flicking at her newly highlighted hair and glancing at her husband as if they were co-conspirators.

'Actually,' she began, 'now that you mention it, I have got an announcement I'd like to make.'

Kate's sense of humour was now somewhere in the region of her feet. It was obvious – her sister was pregnant again. There would be a flurry of congratulations and she would have to go through the motions, too wary still to reveal her own, more staggering secret. Mainly in case her father had a relapse.

'I'm starting my own business,' said Annabel exultantly.

Kate blinked, allowing this information to penetrate. Her parents and grandfather looked as amazed as she was. But were they taken aback because it wasn't what they'd expected, or because it was Annabel saying it?

'What kind of business, dear?' asked Glynis, after clearing her throat.

'Interior design.'

Kate felt as if someone was squeezing her stomach in a vice. A second later, it was more akin to Noah's Ark opening its doors inside her. Dreams she'd locked away, ideas, hopes, ambitions, stampeded on to dry land, released from confinement and all the more rapacious because of it.

'It was my idea,' went on Annabel. 'But Oliver's behind me all the way. He's willing to back me financially, and also act as my accountant.' In a spontaneous display of affection and gratitude, she leaned towards him and pinched his cheek. He turned an unflattering shade of coral. 'It's not going to be a huge enterprise. I'm not the next Anita Roddick or Richard Branson. I'll only take on one job at a time, so I'll still be around for the twins whenever they need me. But I may as well take advantage of the fact that I've got a nanny.'

'Bella, have you thought this through properly?' asked her father.

She nodded. 'I've got a business plan and everything.'

Kate, who was conjuring up an image of her sister in designer overalls, wielding a paint roller and smearing more Lilac White on her face than on the walls, piped up, 'Er . . . are you intending to do all the work yourself?'

'Don't be silly, I'd be a painter and decorator then, wouldn't I? What do I know about that? I'll be sub-contracting, of course, and overseeing that everything's done properly. But, mainly, we'll be involved at the beginning and the end: the initial consultation and the overall design concept, then later adding all the little details and finishing touches. I can't wait!'

'There's only one snag,' said her grandfather. 'I didn't realise you knew enough about interior design to make it viable.'

'I don't,' smiled Annabel ingenuously. 'I'm far too OTT. I never know when to stop. I'd have chintz wallpaper if it was left up to me. No, I think I'll be best dealing with the less creative side of things. Drumming up business, liaising with clients, co-ordinating the subcontractors, that kind of thing.'

'So you're going to employ an actual designer?' asked her mother, looking confused.

'Not exactly. I'm calling the firm Rose Red Interiors. The "Red" bit comes from my surname Redwood, of course, and the "Rose" belongs to my partner. It's like the story, isn't it? *Snow White and Rose Red.*'

'Without the *Snow White* bit,' Kate couldn't help pointing out.

'I know,' shrugged Annabel. 'But they were sisters too, weren't they?'

'Oh, I see,' said their grandfather, his face flooding with comprehension.

'I wish I did,' Kate frowned.

As if their old roles had been reversed, it was Annabel's turn to sigh in exasperation. 'You! You're my partner, you numbskull. You've got more talent and flair for interior design than anyone else I know.'

'Me?' spluttered Kate.

Annabel looked at her seriously now. 'Without you on board, Katharine Rose Finlay, I can tell you now there won't be any business.'

It wasn't so much the sheer impracticality of it all that left Kate reeling, but the fact that it had been sprung on her without warning. Annabel had dreamed up the notion and gone ahead and announced it without even talking to her first.

Unable to believe her sister's gall, Kate stared into the grubby mirror in the Ladies' and shook her head. She'd had to escape, but even in here she felt trapped, as if Annabel had stalked her into a corner. It was a daft plan, though. Totally unworkable, despite the fact that Kate had contemplated something similar in the past, although her sister had never been part of it. Reality had thrust itself in the way, though, as always, and fantasy had been firmly pushed aside. If she hadn't dropped out of university, Kate might have gone on to study design of some sort. Maybe. But that hadn't been the case, and her responsibilities had multiplied since then.

She gave a slight start as the heavy wooden door creaked open and her mother entered. Oh sod it. This was all she needed.

'Still here, dear?' asked Glynis, looking around dubiously, as if even the germs were lower class.

'Looks like it, doesn't it?' The toilets were narrow, and her mother was blocking the way out.

'I get the impression,' continued Glynis, 'that you're not very keen on your sister's idea. I thought you liked making things look pretty?'

'It's not that easy, Mum. I've already got a full-time job. I can't spare the time.'

'Well, why don't you resign from Anthony & Whatsit then?'

Kate rolled her eyes. 'Because I haven't got a rich husband. Not like Annabel. I've got a fam— I've got Emmi to support. I can't afford to resign. Businesses need time to get off the ground. And if it went wrong, then I'd be stuffed.'

Glynis pursed her lips. 'You *could* have a husband who'd support you . . . if you wanted to.'

Kate took a deep breath. 'If you're trying to set me up with someone's son—'

'No, dear. I mean Harry. Who else? He's Emmi's father. If you married him, you wouldn't have to go up to London every day. Now before you fly off the handle, you ought to know that I had *my* doubts nearly thirty years ago about your father. And he wasn't half as good-looking as Harry Barrett. But as my mother, God rest her soul, kept reminding me, Stephen Finlay was destined for greater things. So I took my chance, and I haven't been too disappointed.'

'Mum, I know you think it's high time you organised another huge white wedding like Annabel and Oliver's, but I can tell you now, it isn't going to happen. Not with Harry. Not with anyone.'

'Of course not, dear. I don't think you'd qualify for white, especially if Emmi was a bridesmaid. Perhaps ivory or magnolia . . .'

In that instant, on a surge of defiance, Kate's secret almost came out. She was having great difficulty keeping it in – the bombshell that would undoubtedly bring a second dose of shame and scandal on the family. As if she was one of those women who appeared on TV talk shows lamenting the fact that she had five kids each by a different father. Her parents would love the new baby, of course, the way they loved Emmi. She could hardly accuse them of discriminating between their grandchildren. But they would still make Kate suffer for it, in their own unwitting way.

'Mum, please, I don't want to go into this now.'

'No, I understand. It's just that Harry is so—'

But Kate was saved, as the door swung open and another patron of the Willow Tree tried to squeeze into the Ladies'.

Kate sought sanctuary by the ball pit, supervising the children. The twins were squealing with delight in the shallow end, kept 'afloat' by Emmi, who had attempted to mount an inquisition into her aunt's new business, but by some miracle Kate had managed to divert her.

'I'm sorry,' came a voice from behind, disconcertingly penitent.

Kate didn't look round. She continued watching Sam and Suzy. Technically, they were a little young for this. She had visions of them sinking beneath the brightly coloured balls as if they'd crawled into quicksand.

'It's just,' said Annabel, coming up beside her, 'if I'd spoken to you about it beforehand, you would have said no without even taking the time to think it over.'

'That's an absurd excuse.'

'If I caught you by surprise—'

300

'However you caught me, I'd still have to say no. Thank you for asking, but sorry. I'm afraid I'm living in the real world.'

Annabel gave a contemptuous snort. 'The real world? That's a laugh! You're living in Kate's world, where you get to control the temperature to suit you and nobody else. The thermostat's been set to lukewarm for years now, because anything hotter means you might get burned.'

'Very profound,' said Kate, piqued.

'But you've become tepid yourself in the process,' Annabel continued obstinately. 'And you're planning to stay that way for the rest of your life, even if it means passing up one opportunity after another. First it was Tom, and now it's—'

'The fact that I won't be your business partner? Look, Annabel, if you want to do this, then I wish you luck. But I can't be part of it. And not because I'm "tepid", but because I've got Emmi to consider.'

Annabel folded her arms over her chest and looked petulant for a second before asking, almost defiantly, 'Did you think Oliver was fooling around with Jeanette?'

'Sorry?'

'It wouldn't shock me if that's what people think. Jeanette's so capable, after all, and I'm just Air-head Annabel. But it isn't like that. Oliver doesn't fancy her. At the beginning, when the twins were born, I couldn't cope very well. He took on Jeanette to help me. It wasn't her fault that I started to feel redundant. All my life, I've played a part. Perfect daughter, perfect wife. It's too much to live up to now. I just want to be myself.

Kate hesitated a moment, then admitted, 'I always thought you had it easy.'

'I did. Don't get me wrong. When I was a girl, it was brilliant. I didn't have to try at anything because no one seemed to expect it of me. You were the brains, and I found I got far more attention being the cute little kitten type. And I happily let myself get spoiled, because at the time, well, you don't realise or care. It's only when you have your own children that it makes you evaluate the way you were brought up yourself. I think,' Annabel floundered, 'that I first started feeling . . . unsettled, when you left home to go to university.'

'Me?'

'It made me wake up to the fact that I was never going to go myself. There was no way I'd ever catch up enough academically. And suddenly, it felt as if I were leaping off this cliff with my whole future ahead of me. But I had no idea what to do with it, I was just falling. So I turned to Oliver to catch me. He was my boyfriend at the time, it seemed logical. Mum and Dad liked him, even though he was already nearly thirty. I know what you're probably thinking.'

'Do you?' Kate seemed to be thinking so many things at once it was hard to distinguish one thought from another.

'That love shouldn't be logical. That by its very nature, it spurns logic.'

'Um . . .'

'But I think, in order for a relationship to work, there has to be some degree of common sense behind it. Getting together with Oliver was like that. And I did love him. I still do, even though we've had our rocky patches. But he treated me with kid gloves, you see. He continued spoiling me, like Mum and Dad did, even when I decided I didn't want to be. I know that was only because he loved me and wanted to protect me, but now we're both getting to know each other all over again as equals.'

'That's why he's helping you start the business?'

'It's very brave of him.' A wry smile crept on to Annabel's lips. 'I do enjoy being a mum, you know,' she added, as an afterthought, 'in case you were wondering. I made a conscious decision to act like one, take control, not leave it all to Jeanette. But I've got the chance to do something else now, too. Prove that I'm not an air-head.'

'You don't have to prove that to me,' said Kate gently, realising it was the truth. The maturity she'd seen in her sister lately was commendable.

'Maybe not. But I want to. You see, I was jealous of you when you went to university. Mum and Dad were so proud.'

Kate felt as if champagne corks were popping in her stomach. 'Were they?'

'They never stopped going on about it. So when Oliver and I got engaged, that brought the spotlight back on to me again.'

'But then I had Emmi,' deduced Kate.

'I was so jealous and broody. Oliver and I decided to start trying, but it didn't happen for ages. We had tests done, but there was nothing physically wrong. Anyway, eventually Sam and Suzy came along.' She gazed down at them indulgently. 'And I was crap at motherhood for a few months, as if I was being punished for acting like a selfish cow.'

'You're not selfish,' Kate assured her. 'And twins are hard work. I couldn't cope as well as you have. Look at me, I rely so much on Paloma.'

'And now I'm going to have to rely on you.' Annabel's large blue eyes were beseeching. 'Maybe if you start off just getting involved at weekends . . .'

'With Rose Red Interiors?' Kate shook her head, feeling lousy about it, yet justified in making a stand. 'I can't, Annabel. Weekends are for Emmi. I thought you'd understand. If you're really serious about this, you're going to have to find someone else.'

'And there's nothing I can say or do to persuade you?'

Kate swallowed hard and shook her head. 'No,' she said regretfully. 'Nothing.'

Slumped at her desk at Anthony & Gray, Kate unwrapped the ginger biscuit she'd rooted out of the communal 'Binge Bin'. She'd experienced her first twinge of nausea this morning, but how much of that was due to not eating breakfast?

It was a battle waking up in the mornings, as if she'd been heavily sedated. And once she *had* roused herself, she just wanted to bury her head under the pillow and go back to sleep again. Her only slim hope was that in the following few months she might feel better about herself and life in general. Despite all the niggly aches and pains of pregnancy, she had loved carrying Emmi. At first, the strange sensation of another life stirring inside her had made her squeamish, but within a short time she had come to love the intermittent prods and kicks and somersaults. As if she'd had a constant companion to ward off loneliness.

This time though, she was already beginning to suspect that loneliness was intent on sticking around. She hadn't missed Harry the way she missed Tom. The baby might only serve to remind her that once upon a time – although not in typical fairytale fashion – she had fallen in love with a tall, dark prince who preferred to live like a pauper. And what if the baby was a boy who looked exactly like his dad?

Feeling grottier than ever, Kate was about to sink her head into her hands when she noticed she had a new e-mail. From Dick. *'Heard from Laura yesterday. She wants to talk. Maybe things are looking up. But not just for me, I hope!?!'* She groaned and closed her eyes. If only he knew . . .

She hadn't even confided in him about the fact that she'd be needing maternity leave, let alone that she hadn't heard from the baby's father in the three days since she'd broken the news to him. Tom was clearly one of those men who couldn't cope with the notion of parenthood, and she wasn't going to pressure him into it. From a purely selfish point of view, it would be torture sustaining a harmonious, platonic relationship with a man she might never stop lusting after. This way, the baby might not have a father but at least he or she would have a sane, rational mother.

She heard Steph cough pointedly, and opened her eyes expecting to find Dick or Charles there. Instead, she sat bolt upright and almost yelped in astonishment at the sight of Tom in a trendy navy suit, dark shirt and contrasting red tie. He was carrying a McDonald's Happy Meal box and a vast cellophane-wrapped bouquet of exotic-looking flowers.

'Hello,' he said, wearing the look she loved best: rugged man and petrified boy rolled into one.

Kate wasn't sure if she could trust her knees not to buckle. She glanced at Steph, whose tongue was figuratively hanging out.

'Please,' Tom murmured. 'I need to talk to you in private.'

She stood up automatically and managed to remain upright. So far, so good. As she rounded the desk, Tom jiggled the box and the bouquet, freeing up one arm. He took her hand.

'I'm actually quite busy,' she said faintly.

'Dick gave me the all-clear to harass you. He's gone out to lunch, so we've got the run of his office.'

Oh cripes. People were staring. As they passed through reception, Natalia's eyes hurled daggers. Kate felt a frisson of smug satisfaction, quickly replaced by a hot flush as Tom opened Dick's door, steered her inside and shut it again behind them.

'I suppose you were beginning to doubt you'd ever see me again,' he said.

Kate didn't reply. She tugged nervously at the lapel of her blouse.

'Last Saturday, when you told me, it was a shock,' he went on. 'But now that I've had time to take it in . . .' He rested the bouquet on the edge of Dick's desk. 'I thought I'd break away from the more conventional red roses.'

'Thank you,' mumbled Kate, wondering why he hadn't actually handed them to her. She found out a moment later when he offered her the Happy Meal box.

'Go on,' he urged, 'open it.'

She didn't expect to find a hamburger and fries inside, but it was still jarring to discover a Beanie puppy.

'For Emmi,' Tom went on breathlessly. 'You get a toy free with the meal.'

'Yes, I know.' Kate rummaged further into the box and pulled out a baby's denim cap with a teddy bear motif on the front.

'And that's for . . .' He pointed sheepishly at her stomach. 'It's unisex, apparently. I was going to get some bootees, but I spotted the cap first. Mothercare was a different planet.'

Something was still rattling in the flimsy cardboard box. Kate reached in and fished out a much smaller, sturdier box, the sort found in jewellery shops, designed for rings. Her heart performed acrobatics. But when she pulled back the lid, there was nothing inside. Her heart froze in mid-leap. 'Oh,' she said.

'I walked up and down Hatton Garden for an hour,' Tom admitted. 'But there was too much choice. I knew I'd mess it up and get you something you'd hate. So I called Dick and asked him if he'd give you the afternoon off.'

'Oh,' she said a second time, her knees beginning to tremble again.

Tom seemed to be growing more flustered himself. 'So, er, if you like, we can go together after lunch and you can pick something out yourself.'

Kate rubbed her furrowed brow. 'Are you saying . . . ?'

'Well, technically I'm not "saying", I'm "asking". If you'll marry me, that is.' He rubbed at his own brow. 'So – how about it? Do you want to, or not?'

26

Tom knew, the instant he finished speaking, that it was the naffest proposal ever. But it was too late. He'd said it. There was no getting down on one knee now, the moment had passed. Kate had dropped into one of the visitors' chairs, still holding the little box he'd managed to charm off an assistant in one of the jewellery shops.

'Are you feeling OK?' Tom asked. 'Do you need a glass of water?'

Perhaps he'd been rash going about it like this, using the classic Hollywood routine of dressing up suavely, surprising her in public with flowers *et cetera*, and then metaphorically trying to sweep her off her feet in front of her colleagues. She was pregnant, for crying out loud. With his baby. What if the shock had harmed it? What if—

'I'm fine,' said Kate. 'It's just . . . I'm a little stunned.'

'I know, I'm sorry. But I was sitting in McDonald's yesterday, the one in Addenham retail park, and all these families were going in and out. So I sat and watched them, these kids clutching the Happy Meals their mums and dads had bought for them, and I felt so . . . alone.'

'You're saying you had some sort of life-transforming experience in McDonald's?'

'I had to have lunch somewhere. I was starving.' Agitated, Tom tugged at his tie. 'So that was when I finally decided how I was going to go about this. I went and bought that,' he pointed to the Happy Meal box with its colourful cartoon exterior, 'and then I went to Next and got the suit. Mothercare was just a few stores away so—'

'Convenient that you were at the retail park,' said Kate vacuously.

'The Golf Club's only a couple of miles down the road. I'd been there all morning. Anyway' – it was worrying him that she hadn't actually given her answer yet – 'I knew there was only one decent thing to do. The shock had worn off by then, and watching those families . . . it made me see sense.'

'Oh,' said Kate, blinking a lot, as if her eyes were hurting. 'There's no need for all this.'

'All what?'

'You don't have to do the decent thing. This is the twenty-first century, no one's expecting it of you.'

He frowned, bemused. 'What happened that night at my house . . . it was my fault. I took advantage.'

'*I* was the one throwing myself at you. I don't need you to act the big hero now and "save the day". We can be grown-ups about this, can't we?'

'I don't understand. You said you wanted a relationship with strings attached. You wanted commitment and security, and here I am offering you all that . . .' He suddenly remembered something else she'd said. 'You still think I'm not capable of it, don't you? You're convinced I'd walk out if things got stale or boring.'

She was shaking her head, tears visible on her lashes. 'I can't handle this, Tom. You were a writer, so maybe you're after a perfect ending to tie up all the loose ends. But it doesn't work like that. If it did, I would have married Harry seven years ago.'

'Do you have a problem with what I told you the other day, about that piece I wrote and what happened afterwards?'

She looked aggrieved. 'I'm glad you were honest. If anything, it helped me understand you better. But I still can't marry you. It's lunacy, and in the end the children will be the ones who'll suffer most. I won't put them through that. I can't.'

Desperate now, he pulled out a newspaper cutting from his pocket and thrust it at her.

'This is an advert for a car,' she frowned.

'But not a saloon or a hatchback. It's an estate.'

'And?'

'I'm buying one. Nought per cent finance. What do you think?'

'Um . . .'

'It's not what I ultimately visualised myself in, but it's the ideal size for a family. There's even room for Tina.'

'Tom . . .'

He'd beg if he had to. 'Please, Kate, I'm putting myself on the line here . . .'

'If you want to be a father,' she said, with an unmistakable wobble in her voice, 'then you can. I won't stand in your way. You can see your son or daughter whenever you want, within reason.'

Oh, help. The message still wasn't getting through. 'Do you know why none of my previous relationships worked?' he demanded, ignoring what she'd just said. 'Because I never wanted them too, I never made a conscious decision or effort. Until now, that is. And when it comes to being a family, well, we both grew up wishing our relationships with our parents could have been different, but we can turn that around for our kids. I could even adopt Emmi. There's no need for her to feel left out. She'd be a Llewellyn too.'

Kate groaned. 'We can't rewrite the past, Tom.'

Damn her. There was only so much a man could take. 'I'll never be good enough for you, will I? Not smooth like Harry or Dick. I'm just rough-around-the-edges Tom, who was different and fun for a while but not long-term material.'

From the look she was giving him, he'd hit the nail on the head. She was just the same as all the other women he'd known, although to give her credit she hadn't tried to change him.

The dour expression on his face seemed to have been chiselled in granite. He felt as if he'd never smile again.

'Have it your way, Kate. But, yes, I do want contact with my child. In spite of what you might have thought, getting rid of it never crossed my mind. I want to be there when you have your scan and when you give birth, and I'm going to be the best dad possible. If that means that you and I will have to learn to put all this behind us, then fair enough. As you said yourself, we can be grown-ups, can't we?'

She wasn't looking at him now, but just sitting there fingering the cap he'd bought for the baby, her hair partially hiding her face. There was no point waiting for a reply; on past experience it wouldn't be worth hearing. He opened the door and charged out of Dick's office as fast as he could without breaking into a run.

It wasn't until he was on the train home, his breath misting up the window as he leaned moodily against it, that he realised he hadn't actually told Kate Finlay that he loved her.

27

'I can't believe you did that,' bristled Kate, as she strapped herself into the passenger seat of Annabel's Renault Scenic. 'I ask Dick for the day off, at *your* suggestion. "Make the most of what's left of half-term," you said. "A good chance to spend more time with Emmi." And what do you go and do?'

'I just couldn't resist,' shrugged Annabel. 'I'm sorry. When Oliver told me someone he worked with had just had an extension built and his wife was looking for a design firm to maximise its potential, I knew it would be ideal for us. We need to start off small and acquire a reputation. I thought you did very well back there considering you were ad-libbing. As for taking the kids out, we've only lost an hour, and it wasn't as if they weren't being entertained. I knew Faye Kendall had children of her own, I would never have dreamed of it otherwise. It's hardly professional carting the twins around with me. But if I'd left them with Jeanette, you would have got suspicious.'

Kate groaned inwardly, and looked over her shoulder. Emmi was passing a small board book between the twins, pointing to objects on the pages and carefully enunciating, 'Apple', 'Ball', 'Clock'.

'Anyway,' Annabel was rabbiting on, 'I have to say, Faye liked most of your suggestions. If you can somehow put them down on paper . . .'

'I can't,' snapped Kate. 'How many times do I have to tell you?'

'This particular job wouldn't take long. You've done most of the work already. I could see it in your eyes – you were loving it.'

Kate frowned out of the window as the countryside rolled by. She could have murdered Annabel . . . And yet, if only for a short while, her spirit had been lifted out of the quagmire it had been rotting in lately. She had found herself gazing around the bare white space and becoming as excited over its hypothetical transformation as Professor Higgins over Eliza Doolittle. Even though she'd been dragged there under false pretences, and had had to bluff her way through the first few minutes, she had quickly got into it, spurred along by the animated look on Faye Kendall's face.

'Mummy,' asked Emmi, 'are we going to have lunch?'

Kate shook herself mentally and returned to the present. 'We're on our way to the café right now.'

'It wasn't as if Faye wanted something ultra-modern.' Annabel spoke up again. 'I know that isn't your thing. I suppose that's why you've never tried to get involved in any of the arty stuff at Anthony & Gray.' She took her eyes off the road for a moment and turned them full beam on Kate. 'You haven't, have you?'

How the hell did she know? 'I'm usually too busy,' Kate mumbled.

'That excuse again. You could have taken the risk, but

you're scared of being laughed at. All that contemporary nonsense isn't *you*. But look around us. There's a wealth of houses crying out for someone who won't paint purple splodges on every available wall space or remove the doors on a perfectly good, solid, antique wardrobe and replace them with chicken wire or some tacky bamboo shit.' Annabel glanced into the rear-view mirror at the children. 'Whoops, sorry. Must mind my English.'

Half-a-dozen negative emotions stewing inside her, Kate glowered out of the window again. She could have done without all this aggro. It had been embarrassing at work yesterday after the incident the day before with Tom. Steph, especially, couldn't seem to accept that Kate hadn't swooned at his feet. And Natalia had taken great pains to make sure everyone knew that Tom had fled through reception looking haggard and dejected; as if she'd sent round a general memorandum informing all co-workers that Kate Finlay was an ungrateful bitch. Even Dick had looked at her strangely. He'd had the tact not to bring it up, but he was probably saving his sermon until the gossip had died down.

Kate put a hand in front of her eyes, shielding herself from the low winter sun. The winding roads were making her queasy again. At her check-up, she'd been assured by her GP that her health in general was fine, and had been booked in for antenatal care with the midwife. Because of the problems she'd had with her blood pressure towards the end of her last pregnancy, she would require extra monitoring. 'Should all go well on that score this time,' the doctor had said in her soft, dulcet tones, 'have you and your partner discussed whether you want to try to deliver the baby normally, or whether you'd prefer to be booked in for another Caesarean?'

'Er . . . We – um – haven't talked about it yet.'

Kate wondered if civilities could be restored to that extent. It would be agonising, whatever. Meanwhile, there was her sister to contend with, and Rose Red Interiors. Which, she had to admit, for the sort of traditional design work Annabel would have them doing, was a particularly charming and appropriate name.

It was four o'clock by the time they drove into Beckton Lacey.

'A cup of tea would be nice,' hinted Annabel, as they approached the Old Parsonage.

Kate was worn out. It seemed as if they'd walked miles around the country park after lunch, pushing a twin each in state-of-the-art, all-terrain three-wheelers, with Emmi insisting on the occasional shove. Annabel seemed to own a small shop's worth of pushchairs, although the most practical one for the twins was the two-seater Maclaren. Kate wondered if there might be a buggy going spare by the time the baby arrived. It would be a tad more up-to-date than Emmi's old one.

'We won't stay long,' Annabel promised. 'It seems I'll have to park here, there's no room in front of the house.'

Kate looked, and saw that there wasn't. Not only was her car there, and Paloma's Beetle, but Harry's BMW as well. 'Bugger.'

'Were you expecting him?' Annabel frowned as she

slid the Renault Scenic into the nearest available space.

'No, but then he has this habit of just turning up when he feels like it.'

Kate climbed slowly out of the car and dragged her heels up the path. She opened the front door and pulled off her muddy boots, Annabel and the kids in her wake. Helping remove the twins' Baby Gap jackets, she took a deep breath, steeling herself.

'Mummy,' said Emmi, tugging off her own boots, 'can I play upstairs with Sam and Suzy?'

'I think we'll let them loose in the lounge where I can keep an eye on them,' Annabel interjected quickly.

'Emmi, you'd better go and say hello to your dad,' sighed Kate, who was delaying it herself. 'He must be in the kitchen.' She was surprised that Paloma hadn't called out to them yet, like she usually did.

The little girl took forever to shed her coat, scarf and gloves. Then she took just as long putting on her slippers. Annabel was already shepherding the twins away from the TV and video and mumbling to herself that they were due their teatime fromage frais. Taking another deep breath, Kate marched down the hall and opened the door to the kitchen.

The sight that met her eyes wasn't particularly scandalous, but she still sucked in her breath, as if she'd caught the man and woman *in flagrante delicto*, rather than just holding hands across the table. As she juddered to a stunned halt, Emmi crashed into her, then poked her head around to see what was wrong. Also at that moment, Annabel pushed open the door leading from the lounge and came sideways into the kitchen with a twin under each arm. Everyone seemed to freeze, except for Sam and Suzy, who were both squirming and grizzling.

'So,' said Harry, the first to break the semi-silence, 'here we are. The truth's out, at last.' He let go of Paloma's hand and stood up, facing Kate. 'It's about time we talked . . .'

'I'll make some tea,' said Paloma, scrambling hastily to her feet.

Kate felt herself open and close her mouth and wondered if she looked like a goldfish.

'Do you fancy each other?' Emmi piped up, looking at her dad, then at her nanny. She didn't sound upset; quite the opposite, in fact. 'That means you're not going to marry Mummy,' the little girl continued, blinking at Harry.

'No,' he said carefully, impervious to her relief, which perhaps, thought Kate, was only apparent to herself. 'I'm sorry if that's what you were hoping.'

'I wasn't,' said Emmi. 'I told Melanie that. After we had Music, the day I played the tambourine.'

'Oh.' Harry looked thrown.

Annabel roused herself to action. 'Emmi, sweetheart, could you root out a couple of Petits Filous from the fridge and bring them into the lounge? You can help me feed the twins. In fact, we could go up to your room. Wouldn't that be fun?'

'There's no need to go upstairs,' Kate assured her.

But, either way, Emmi didn't budge. Her gaze remained on her father. 'Are you and Paloma going to get married?' A frown suddenly wrinkled her brow. She turned worriedly to her nanny, who blanched. 'Paloma, will you stop looking after me now?'

'That . . . um . . . depends on your mum.'

Emmi swung round. 'Mummy . . .'

'Sweetheart,' Annabel's voice was gentle but firm, 'grab a couple of spoons and the Petits Filous and come into the lounge. Your mother and father and Paloma need to talk on their own.'

'But—'

'Emmi,' Kate finally felt composed enough to join in the conversation, 'do as your aunt tells you. Please, darling.'

'O-K.' The little girl collected the Petits Filous and the spoons and flounced out of the kitchen. 'But it's not as if I won't be able to leavesdrop!' she informed them petulantly over her shoulder.

'So,' sighed Kate, looking from Harry to Paloma, 'when did this start . . . ?'

'We couldn't help ourselves.' Harry fiddled with his watch. 'It just happened.'

'That wasn't what I asked. And you've got an annoying habit of sounding as if you're in a bad soap opera.'

Harry ignored that. 'I asked Paloma out on several occasions before she finally accepted, and her stalling didn't mean she wasn't interested. But she claimed that somehow it would be betraying you and Emmi.'

'I felt so guilty.' Paloma finally spoke up for herself, frowning down at the table. The kettle had boiled, but evidently she'd abandoned her idea of making tea. 'It felt

320

like an affair. Even though I knew you didn't love Harry. In fact, you probably resented him for ruining things with Tom.'

'I—' began Kate, then shut up, realising there was nothing to contradict.

'When I first returned to this country,' Harry admitted, 'I did half-expect to get back together with you, Kate. I was totally honest when I said there hadn't been anyone serious in my life since we broke up. But you didn't give me a chance, and the more you avoided me, the more time I found myself spending with Paloma.'

'You mean that I'm to blame for this?'

Harry shook his head. 'No one's to blame. This *isn't* an extra-marital affair. Paloma and I are both free agents.'

'Then why all the secrecy?'

'Because . . .' Paloma floundered, 'the situation was complicated enough already. I didn't know how you were going to react. Harry kept telling me I had nothing to feel bad about. But I was worried. I didn't know what impact it might have on Emmi. I didn't want to stop working for you, and I thought I'd have to. I assumed it would be too awkward for me to stay on here, living under the same roof.'

There was a convincing logic in Paloma's answer. Kate couldn't pick holes in it.

'What do you know about me, Kate?' Harry demanded suddenly. 'Have you ever taken the time to get to know me properly?'

'Sorry?'

'Maybe it's simply that I've let my guard down with Paloma, but that's only because she's the sort of woman who tries to get to know a man. She doesn't just skim over him and draw her own conclusions.'

'I – I don't understand.'

'When we were at university, you never questioned me much about my family, did you?'

'No,' said Kate cautiously, 'because you never wanted to talk about them.'

'But did you ever really ask me why that was?'

Harry sounded so accusing. She felt as if she were in a court of law, peering down over the edge of the dock. 'No,' she said, just as cautiously. 'I didn't feel you wanted to tell me.'

'Well, the fact that my father's been in a mental home since I was sixteen wasn't – isn't – something I particularly wanted to broadcast.' He shook his head. 'I don't even know what tense to phrase it in. He's got cancer now too; the prognosis isn't good. That's one of the reasons I came back home. That, and the fact that the work had dried up in South Africa.'

Kate chewed her lip, shame trickling through her. 'I'm sorry . . .'

He flapped his hand. 'The professional side of things doesn't matter. Business is slow at the moment, but it'll pick up. I don't regret starting up on my own. Anyway, I don't want to go into all that, it's too dull and nowhere near as important as what's going on right here, right now.'

'Is your father still in Leicester?'

Harry nodded. 'And my brother. I visited just before

Christmas, but I'm useless. Adam – well, he's always coped better than me, even though I'm the eldest. Since Mum died I've always been better at running away from my problems, one way or another. Which makes it that much harder every time I go back now.'

Paloma rested her hand on his shoulder. Harry covered it with his own. Kate felt a stab of jealousy, but it was the intimacy and devotion that she envied, the spontaneity of the gesture. After all, wasn't she single and pregnant and more in need of love and support than they were?

Oh, God. Just listen to herself. So conceited. The shock of finding out about Harry and Paloma had worn off and anger had taken its place. But now, for the sake of her integrity, which was possibly in tatters, Kate analysed the anger too and found that it wasn't justified. It all stemmed from wounded pride.

'Maybe I also let down my guard with Paloma because I felt she'd understand,' Harry sighed. 'She lost both her parents when she was fifteen. She's led a nomadic sort of lifestyle, as did I for a while. But the world has a funny way of bringing people like us together, and finally, *finally*, she agreed that we ought to come out in the open about it.'

'Why now?' asked Kate, looking directly at Paloma.

'Because' – the other woman frowned – 'I couldn't go on pretending any longer. It was all getting too much for me. I thought coming clean like this would be for the best.'

'Even if it meant that you'd have to leave here?' Kate narrowed her eyes, on tenterhooks for the reply.

'If I'm absolutely truthful,' said Paloma, meeting her gaze, 'I don't want to stop looking after Emmi, in whatever form that may take. I love childminding, whether the children in question are babies or school kids. But I never imagined myself *living here* until there wasn't any need for me any more. I suppose I thought that one day I'd meet someone and want a family of my own, but I didn't see that as a problem.' She shrugged, looking pale and strained. 'What happens now is really up to you – you're Emmi's mum. If you think my working here and going out with Harry is going to cause too much friction . . .'

Kate was in a quandary. If she let Paloma go, she knew that in the short-term her grandfather could step into the breach. Physically, he was recovered from his accident. But she couldn't rely on him once the baby came along, which meant that sooner rather than later she would have to start the painstaking search for another nanny. Paloma was to have played such an important role in the future, and establishing the same level of trust with anyone else seemed impossible right now.

'The best thing all round might be time and space,' Harry declared abruptly, smoothing down his shirt, which looked smooth and immaculate to start with. 'What if Paloma was to stay at my place this weekend, to give you a chance to think things through?' He addressed Kate, his blue eyes almost defiant.

Kate chewed her lip again. He'd been right when he'd said she hadn't made the effort to get to know him. It didn't mean that she would have felt differently about him if she had, but it might have made the path they'd trodden a little less bumpy.

'That's probably a good idea,' she said.

Paloma nodded. 'I'll throw a few things in a bag then . . .'

Kate found herself alone with Harry. The silence that followed seemed interminable.

'I want you to know,' he was the first to speak again, 'that whatever you may think, I did – I still do – want to be a good father to Emmi.'

Kate nodded, as graciously as possible. 'And whatever *you* may think, I'm not going to cut you out of her life because of all this. It's just,' she fidgeted with a coaster, 'this has all been sprung on me. There's a lot going on in my head at the moment.'

'I understand. We can discuss Paloma's position next week. She cares about Emmi. None of this has been easy for her. Even now, she's going through hell. The last thing she wanted to do was leave you in the lurch. We all know how much you rely on her.'

Kate's pride couldn't help rearing its head again. 'I'll be fine. You don't have to worry about me.'

'But I'm within my rights worrying about my daughter, aren't I?'

'I suppose so,' she muttered, not really wanting to concede that point.

'And whatever happens,' Harry said quietly, 'I've come to terms with the fact that, although she might call me Dad, she'll never truly mean it.'

Kate didn't know how to respond to that. It had taken her so long to understand that there was more than one bond linking a parent and child. Emmi would probably always be polite to Harry, and perhaps, when she was older, there might even be a spark of affection. But for now . . .

'You can allow me my jealousy, can't you?' Harry asked, his voice remaining low, so that no one could possibly eavesdrop unless they had their ear pressed to the door.

'*Your* jealousy?' she faltered.

'If she loves someone else as a father more than she loves me.'

'Oh,' sniffed Kate, as Tom filled her thoughts. She'd been trying to fend him off, but now she had to give in. He was too much a part of this.

'But, however I feel,' Harry concluded, 'it wouldn't be fair of me to begrudge you or Emmi your own opportunity of finding happiness.'

Fat chance of that, thought Kate glumly, following him into the hall as Paloma clattered down the stairs. Happiness seemed utterly lost in a maze that had no way in and no way out. She stared down at Paloma's overnight bag and felt inconceivably alone. Emmi ran out of the lounge and clung to her nanny's legs, aware that goodbyes were about to be said.

'Don't go!' she pleaded, tears springing on to her cheeks. She swung round to her mother. 'I don't want her to leave!'

'It's only for the weekend,' said Kate after a short pause, trying to sound reassuring as she bobbed down in front of Emmi and smudged away the tears with the pads of her thumbs. 'She'll be here to take you to school on Monday, the same as she always does.' And coming to the only decision that would save further heartache, Kate looked over her daughter's head at Paloma and nodded.

'Ooogee,' said Sam suddenly, pointing to his sister.

Annabel, as if to relieve whatever tension might still be hanging around waiting to be dispelled, scooped him into her arms and kissed him adoringly. 'He just said his sister's name!' she glowed. 'Didn't you all just hear him say her name? Go on, poppet, say it again. Suzy, Suzy . . .'

'Ooogee,' said Sam on cue, but this time pointing to the umbrella stand.

Just as the weather forecast had predicted, when the sun set that evening the temperature plummeted to below freezing. Kate sat on her bed, muffled in an old bobbly dressing gown, staring through the open curtains at the moon and stars. There wasn't even a wisp of cloud visible.

Part of her was still overwhelmed by what had happened, although, in retrospect, the signs had been there. She'd been so busy fretting over other things, though, it had been tantamount to wearing blinkers. The anger she'd felt earlier – unjustifiably – had all but dissipated, replaced by relief. Perversely, she couldn't wait to tell her mother. At least the pressure would be off her to settle down with Harry.

Who could blame the poor bastard? she mused now, drawing up her knees beneath the dressing gown and wrapping her arms around her legs. Who could blame him for choosing a beautiful, mercurial, free-spirited and affectionate woman over a cold, irascible, dreary sap like herself? Kate couldn't shrug off self-pity, she didn't have the energy. Much easier to let it gobble her up.

Moonlight filtered in through the lead-light window and cast criss-cross patterns on the ceiling. As the minutes strung themselves together to become an hour, she took off her dressing gown and snuggled under the duvet to try to get some sleep. But, as she'd been dreading, it evaded her.

In general, she realised, in a place like Beckton Lacey, her situation would be deemed nothing short of humiliating. The gossip was bound to have spread throughout the village by Monday morning. Sometimes Kate wondered if even the flies on the wall were spies working undercover for the ladies in the local shop. Perhaps it was already circulating that Katharine Finlay was 'with child' again. Groaning, she turned on to her front and buried her head in a pillow. A moment later, worrying that she might squash the baby, even though it was probably still in an unsquashable state, floating in its sac of amniotic fluid oblivious to the commotion going on around it, she curled up on her side.

Eventually, unable to tolerate her insomnia any longer, she sat up in bed, threw off the duvet and slipped on her dressing gown again. As she passed by Emmi's room on her way downstairs, she could hear the little girl snoring softly. A peaceful, innocent slumber, Kate hoped wistfully. In the kitchen, she made herself a camomile tea and then went into the lounge to switch on the TV. There would be nothing worth watching, but it was better than the oppressive silence of her bedroom. After finishing the tea, she must have finally dozed. It was five-thirty by the time she looked at the clock again. Her neck was stiff. She had a strong urge to sink into a warm bubble bath, but wasn't sure she could pull it off without waking Emmi, whose room was next to the bathroom. Still, she could try.

An hour later, after having managed it, she was drying herself off and dressing in her day clothes: a polo neck and her baggiest jeans, seeing that it was a Saturday. As she hovered on the landing, deliberating whether she should attempt to have some breakfast, she glanced up the second flight of stairs towards Paloma's attic bedroom.

Ironically, it was only this morning that she could appreciate how much of a friend Paloma had become to her. And it was also only now, strangely as a direct result of what had occurred yesterday, that she could see the full extent of the gap in her life. In fact, it was more than just a gap, it was a gaping void. A vast emptiness which effectively hadn't existed before she'd met Tom. Back then she had wanted someone, something, but at the same time she had also been, if not exactly happy, then definitely not *un*happy.

'Sod him,' she hissed, then repented and spread a hand over her belly. 'Oh, he's OK really,' she added gently. 'When you get to know him . . .'

In Emmi's dream, everything started to shake. Slowly, she found herself waking up, her mother's flushed face looming above her. At first, she couldn't work out what day of the week it was.

'Come on,' urged her mum. 'Get up, darling!'

'Huh?' Groggily, Emmi looked at the clock. 'But it's only seven.'

'I know. We're going out, it's a surprise. Here' – her mum pulled a fleecy jogging suit out of the wardrobe – 'put this on, then go use the bathroom. You only need to wash your face quickly, although I suppose you ought to brush your teeth, too.'

'But I always brush them after breakfast.'

'Er . . . well, we're going out for breakfast today. You haven't got ballet, have you?'

'No, Mummy, don't you remember? It's half-term. There's never ballet during the holidays.'

'Just checking. Now get ready. I'll meet you downstairs.'

Emmi used the loo first. Then she went back to her room and put on the jogging suit. Glancing at herself in the mirror, she decided that, for once, she would leave her hair loose like her mum's lately. As she hurried downstairs, she saw that the front door was open. It was snowing again!

'Mummy, look! Do you think it will stick to the ground this time?'

'It might. Here, put your coat on. And those boots, the ones over there.'

'Will I be able to build a snowman?'

'Maybe.'

'Where are we going?'

Grabbing the car keys from the key-box on the wall,

her mother answered breathlessly, 'You'll see – all in good time. Now hurry up, darling, but don't forget your gloves.'

Tom pulled back the curtains in the lounge and stared out grimly. Great. It was snowing. Practically a blizzard. The golf lessons would be cancelled and he'd have sod-all to do all day; although, on second thoughts, he ought to catch up on his accounts. He yawned and stretched and gave a tug on his prehistoric Aran jumper, his thumb slipping through a hole near the bottom and catching against a faulty rivet on his jeans. Ouch.

Well, if he wasn't going to the Golf Club, at least he didn't have to dress up. And he wouldn't have to bother shaving, or wrestling with the dials of the shower.

As he was trying to decide whether to have Shreddies or Cheerios – without milk, because he'd run out again – Tina started barking. There was an urgent rapping on the front door. Tom frowned. He wasn't in the mood for visitors, although it was only half-eight. Who . . . ?

He went into the hall. Tina was going mad. As Tom pulled the door open, a flurry of snow swept in, closely followed by two bedraggled creatures dusted with white and bundled up like Eskimos. The smaller of the creatures threw back her hood and started whooping with delight. The larger – although still diminutive by comparison to Tom – took longer over exposing herself. She unravelled her scarf and pulled back her own hood. Her hair gleamed gold, her grey eyes stared up at him. His stomach performed cartwheels.

'I couldn't wait,' she sniffed, scrabbling for a tissue in her pocket and wiping her nose, which was red from the cold. 'I really needed to see you.'

28

Having nestled up to the Rayburn for a while, Kate felt warm enough to risk removing her anorak. She draped it over the back of a chair. Her nose was still annoyingly runny. Perhaps she was coming down with something.

Tom returned to the kitchen, silent as a stealth bomber in his threadbare socks. 'Emmi's fine,' he smiled, answering Kate's unspoken question. 'Tina won't leave her alone, but she's managing to get through her cup-a-soup all right.'

'It was more like a bowl-a-soup,' Kate grunted. 'You were a little generous with the water, and your mugs are huge.'

'Well, here, have yours. I don't want you coming down with pneumonia. It was dangerous driving in this weather, let alone in that clapped-out car of yours. Is the heating still not working?'

Kate shook her head contritely. 'I was going to say the same about this house, but then I noticed that.' She pointed to a sheet of paper on the table.

'Oh, that. It's just an estimate. I haven't had any work done yet.'

'It's outrageous.'

'The most reasonable quote I had, actually. The whole house needs an overhaul. Regulation post-war plumbing, radiators in every room . . .'

'But—'

'It had to be done sooner or later, so it might as well be now. I wouldn't expect you to . . . Well, I wouldn't blame you if you refused to let me have the kid stay over with the place in this state.'

Kate stared down at her minestrone. An odd thing to be drinking at this time of the morning, but it hit the right note. Besides, she couldn't stand tea or coffee without milk. 'No,' she said. 'I suppose not.'

'While I'm at it, I'm going to have a new bathroom suite put in.'

Her eyebrows shot up. 'Where's all the money for this coming from?'

'The old bat,' chuckled Tom.

'Your mother? You haven't told her—'

'—that it looks as though she's going to be a grandma? I'm afraid I have. My brother and his wife know, too.'

Kate would have preferred it if he'd waited a few more weeks, but that side of things with his own family was up to him. 'How did they react?'

'Naturally they were surprised at first. Scott and Vie are trying for a baby themselves. They were very supportive. Mother took it in her stride and immediately said I had to finish renovating this place and that I wasn't to ask my father for any more hand-outs. She'd fork out whatever I needed.' He shrugged. 'I could have acted all proud, I suppose, and told her I'd fund it on my own, but it'd mean taking out a whopping great loan.'

'You could still pay her back, though, even if it took years.'

'If she'd let me.'

Kate munched on a crouton, growing increasingly sheepish at having charged round here the way she had. Because of the rapidly deteriorating weather it had been a nightmarish drive, taking her twice the time it would normally have. And now she was stranded. The radio playing quietly on top of the fridge-freezer was already warning people not to set out on any journeys that weren't absolutely necessary. She hadn't even told Tom about Paloma and Harry yet. The peculiar thing was, he didn't seem to find her uninvited presence too unusual. He hadn't actually asked her exactly why she was there.

'I'm glad,' she began tentatively, 'that we're not enemies. I couldn't bear it if you hated me.'

'Hated you?' There was a funny look on his face.

'After the other day . . . You were right to be angry, because what you did, what you said – it was sweet. The way I reacted was wrong. I was rude and ungrateful. A lot of men wouldn't be willing to go as far as you were to live up to their responsibilities. But we shouldn't . . . we shouldn't *rush* into making such a huge commitment merely for the sake of the baby.'

'I can see that now,' agreed Tom, staring at the floor. 'I assumed you'd want "rescuing" in some brash, heroic fashion, and I took that to the extreme. Marriage is always a gamble. It's never one hundred per cent guaranteed that it will work, but to get together for the wrong reasons from the outset . . . that can only spell trouble. We might end up resenting each other, and that wouldn't be fair to either of us, or the kids. I'll always be your friend, Kate. I've told you that before. I'll admit that it's helped to have a cooling off period after the other day. But now that I understand where you were coming from, it's easier to stomach.'

Kate nodded and drained what was left of the soup. All of a sudden, she felt as if she was going to cry. She blinked, keeping her head low.

'Can I ask you something?' said Tom.

'Hmm?'

'Are you still planning to go back to work after the baby's born?'

'I suppose so. I'll have to, really.'

'You could stop acting all proud yourself and ask me for help.'

She shrugged, veering off the subject slightly. 'Annabel's trying to persuade me to be her business partner. Some sort of interior design diva. She reckons I'd be good at it. Every time I think about it, I'm more and more tempted. But starting a business is a gamble too, and at the moment I can't afford to quit Anthony & Gray. Besides,' Kate realised she was wittering, but it seemed to be stemming the tears, 'I don't have any formal qualifications, and I can't spare the time to do any sort of college course.'

'You could always try out your different techniques on me, if you like.'

'Sorry?'

'This house – pretend it was a blank canvas. Go wild.'

'Oh. Right.' She felt extremely hot. 'But I'm not into purple splodges or Feng Shui.'

'I know you're not. I wouldn't have asked you otherwise.'

'Good.' Her lips cracked into a tiny smile, despite the fact that her heart seemed even heavier than when she had first arrived. Sighing, she said, 'I suppose I'd better check on Emmi.'

Tom was right behind her as she went across the hall and peered through the lounge door. Her daugher and Tina were both curled up on the large, red sofa, fast asleep.

'I should have put a guard in front of the fire, really,' said Tom softly. 'I'll have to before next winter.'

'Emmi's good about things like that. I can't believe she's asleep again.'

'Too much excitement for one day.'

'It's only quarter-past-nine.'

He led the way back to the kitchen. 'We might as well let them kip. That sofa has its uses.'

Kate felt herself blush. To make matters worse, Tom noticed it and grinned.

'Why are you embarrassed?' he asked calmly. 'You've come over all bashful.'

'No, I haven't,' she fibbed. 'It's just . . . that sofa . . . well, it's where we . . .'

'Made mad, torrid, passionate love? Are there any more adjectives you'd like to add?'

'Tom!' Kate broke out in a sweat. 'What happened, happened. You don't have to turn it into a joke. If we're going to be grown-up about this—'

'Not that again.' He lifted his eyebrows heavenwards. 'OK, if you insist.'

337

And before she knew what was happening, she was swaddled in his big, woolly arms, his mouth pressing against hers, softly, then fiercely, then softly again. The whole kitchen spun.

'There,' he said huskily, releasing her, 'was that adult enough for you?'

Kate stood reeling. 'Oh.' She put a hand to her lips. They seemed to be burning up.

He looked worried. 'Are you OK? The baby . . . ?'

'No,' she sniffed, fishing for a tissue again, 'I'm fine. The baby's fine. What – um – was that for?'

'Because there's something I forgot to tell you the other day. Something quite important. In fact, I ran it past Vie, to get a female perspective, and she told me it was crucial. The problem is, I've never said it before. I've never wanted to. So that's probably why I cocked it up. It isn't even that I'm rusty. I'm actually a complete novice.'

Dazed, Kate aimed her posterior for the nearest chair and sat down.

'And maybe I never would have said it,' Tom continued, 'because in my opinion, it's even harder than proposing. I felt as if I'd put myself on the line enough already. But then a lunatic woman turns up on my doorstep virtually at the crack of dawn, in a snowstorm. And I know. I just *know*.'

'Know what?' she frowned, starting to tremble.

'That she wouldn't have done that if she didn't feel exactly the same way. So, does that change things? About what I asked you the other day? Does it seem so crazy now? If you think about it, we haven't known each other that long; having a baby together could be classified as insane, but it's happening, we can't deny it. And if we didn't feel the way we do, then it probably *would* be crazy to get married and raise a family. But that isn't the case, so . . . ?' He dropped on to one knee, then winced and swapped it for the other one. 'Old cricket wound,' he explained incidentally. 'Used to play years ago.'

Kate knew that whether she thought about it for five seconds or five days, her answer would be the same. 'Tom—'

'The only problem,' he went on, 'is that I don't want anything elaborate. Do you? Want a big wedding?'

She wished he would just shut up and kiss her exactly like before. 'I wouldn't need a chauffeur, whatever I had.'

'In a roundabout way does that mean, yes?'

'It means—'

'Bollocks,' he said. 'I was almost forgetting again.'

'What?'

He pulled her close, his stubble scratchy against her cheek. 'To say, I love you,' he muttered. 'And sorry I haven't shaved.'